Jack M. Barrack Hebrew Academy

PRIVATEER

Jack M. Barrack Hebrew Academy Library
Love Where You Learn!

Dick Willett

Historical Fiction
set during
the Revolutionary War

Privateer

Privateering was the life Jonathan Weaver had come to love. It was an honorable profession, combining patriotism and profitability. Capturing cargo ships and vessels owned by the British, allowed the American citizens to continue the use and enjoyment of staples such as sugar, molasses, and coffee. But, capturing the ships and vessels was not without loss. The injuries from battle often left a man disabled and even a small infection could become deadly. But, to Jonathan Weaver it was worth the risk. After all, it was at the direction of British Tories that Indians in the Mohawk Valley were encouraged to brutally attack Jonathan Weavers family, killing his parents and scalping his sister.

Jack M. Barrack Hebrew Academy

Copyright © 1989 by Richard M. Willett
Revised Copyright © 2003 by Richard M. Willett

Privateer: a privately-owned ship authorized by a government (by means of a Letter of Marque) to conduct hostilities against an enemy. Privateering was a way of mobilizing armed ships and sailors without having to spend public money or commit naval officers. The cost was borne by investors hoping to profit from prize money earned from captured cargo and vessels. The proceeds would be distributed among the privateer's investors, officers, and crew. Privateering was considered an honorable profession, combining patriotism and profit, in contrast to unlicensed piracy, which was universally reviled. Also called a Private Man of War.

Sailing Terminology

ballast: Heavy material, such as sand, lead, and gravel, placed in the hull of a ship to improve the ship's stability and to counterbalance the pressure of the wind on the mast and the sails.

bending the sails: To make the sails fast to their proper yard or stay in preparation to sail.

boom: A long spar run out from different places in the ship to extend the foot of a particular sail.

bowsprit: A large spar running out from the bow of a vessel to which the foremast stays are fastened and from which some sails are rigged.

bosun: A warrant officer on a warship, or a petty officer on a merchant vessel, who controls the work of other seaman; in charge of rigging, anchors, cables, etc.

bulkhead: One of the upright, watertight partitions which form the cabins in a ship and divide the hold into distinct compartments for safety in case of damage to the hull.

bulwark: The wood trim running along the sides of a ship above the level of the water deck.

companion way: A ladder leading from the deck to cabins or quarters below.

crimping: Procuring seamen for a ship.

cutlass: A short, thick, curving sword with a single cutting edge, formerly used especially by sailors.

fid: A hard, tapering pin for separating strands of a rope when splicing. Also, a wooden or metal bar or pin used to support the weight of the topmast.

forecastle or fo'c'sle: A short raised deck at the fore end of a ship, originally for archers to shoot arrows into enemy vessels. Also an area below the front deck where the crew slept in hammocks.

foretop: The small platform near the top of the foremast.

gaff: A fore-and-aft sail mounted on an upper spar or gaff which extends aft from the mast.

gaskets: A light line for securing a furled sail to a yard, the horizontal spar from which a square sail is supported and extended.

grapnel: An iron bar with claws at one end which is attached to a line. As the overtaking ship closes in on an enemy ship, a sailor throws the grapnel at the enemy ship's railing to seize and hold the ship for boarding.

halyards: A rope or tackle for raising or lowering a sail, yard, or flag.

hard alee: A warning to the helmsman to tack, by turning the bow of the ship into the wind and on to the leeward side of the wind by using the tiller.

hawse-hole: Naval phrase when a person entered the service in the lowest grade; he rose from the ranks. The term also describes an opening in the bow of the ship through which the cable of the anchor runs.

jib: A triangular foresail which is forward of the mast and does not reach aft of the mast.

jolly-boat: A small ships' boat, used chiefly for work and usually hoisted at the stern of the ship.

keel: When building a ship, the keel is the first piece of lumber laid which forms the basis of the ship, running bow to stern. Ballast is added and ribs are attached to the keel.

larboard: The lefthand side of a ship when looking forward toward the bow. Today it is called port thus eliminating any confusion with the right side of a ship which is called starboard.

leeward: The downwind side of the ship, or in other words, the side sheltered from the wind.

longboat: A good size boat with high sides and fitted with a mast and sails. The boat was used for short trips to shore for supplies.

The boat was large enough to carry a cannon from the ship if needed.

mast: A single wooden pole, made from a fir tree, which supports the sail and rigging of a sailing vessel.

mizzen: The mast closest to the stern of the ship.

mizzenbooms: The booms on the aftermost mast.

powder magazine: A dry area below deck where gunpowder and ammunition was stored.

rake: To rake is to fire toward a ship at a ship's bow or stern, the weakest points of a ship. This type of shot wipes out men on deck, masts, and sails.

rake the mast: To lean the vessel's mast fore or aft to help increase the speed of the ship.

reef: To reef a sail is when part of the sail is rolled or folded up and secured with lines, attached in a line across the sail. This reduces the amount of sail exposed to the wind.

rudder: A broad, flat, moveable piece of wood hinged vertically at the stern of a ship, used for steering.

scuppers: An opening on a ship's side to allow water to run off of the deck.

ship chandlery: A provider of provisions or equipment to ships.

shrouds: Support ropes or wires for the mast that run from the mast to deck level on each side of the vessel to support the mast in its vertical position.

skiff: A small boat with one or two pairs of oars. Mainly used for trips in the harbor.

spar: A wooden pole used to support various pieces of rigging and sails.

stay: A strong support rope running from the masthead to the deck, either fore or aft.

sweeps: A sweep is a long, heavy oar which is used to move small sailing vessels or barges.

tack: To change the course of a ship by changing the side of the sails that the wind is blowing on, starboard or leeward.

taff rail: The rail around the stern of a ship, frequently decorated with wood carvings.

tiller: A horizontal wooden bar or pole, which is located on the stern deck, and is fitted to the rudder stock that controls the rudder and is used for steering.

yard: The horizontal spar from which a square sail is suspended.

yardarm: The very end of a yard.

Chapter One

Jonathan Weaver ran for his life, running harder than he had ever run before. His homespun shirt, torn by the dense brush and soaked with sweat, clung to his skin. Two Indians, their faces covered with bright red war paint chased him through the dense forest to the Mohawk Valley. He carried a long rifle loaded and primed, but even if he killed one Indian the other one would be on him before he could reload.

The Indians, confident that they would eventually run him down, ran swiftly and easily. One of them carried a pale blonde scalp, still dripping blood.

Tears blurred Jonathan's vision. He had seen his mother and sister killed and scalped. The scalp that the Indian carried had been his sister's. Jonathan had heard her screaming before one of the savages had crushed her skull with his war club. Pa would have never left the women alone, he would have fought as long as he lived. The boy knew that his father had been killed too.

The trees thinned, and he ran faster across a small clearing. As he entered the woods again, he looked back to see if his pursuers had come any closer. The two Indian braves broke out of the brush, running fast. Neither of them carried a musket, but they had tomahawks and knives. Jonathan felt himself tiring. He wouldn't be safe until he reached the fort, still miles away. If he threw the rifle away, he could run faster, but the Indians had not gained on him, and one shot might save his life. They must be tiring too, he thought. The raiding party had to have traveled twenty miles, during the night, to attack his family so early in the day.

Dense forest gave way to a small meadow with a stream flowing through it. High water from the early spring runoff made it wider than usual. He ran harder and jumped for the opposite bank. One foot landed on the grass above the water. The undercut bank gave way and he fell back, instinctively holding the rifle high to keep the powder dry. The two braves saw him fall and ran toward him with their tomahawks in their hands. Jonathan raised the rifle and fired. The closest brave fell and rolled over in pain. The second brave stopped on the opposite bank and raised his arm to throw his tomahawk. Jonathan swung the rifle by its barrel and threw it with all of his strength. As the Indian stepped away from the flying weapon, he threw his tomahawk. It missed and buried its head in the clay bank. The savage jumped into the water and waded through the waist-deep stream with a knife in his hand. He was only six feet away when Jonathan pulled the tomahawk out of the bank and threw it into the brave's face. Stunned by the blow, the Indian fell backward into the water. As the savage struggled to recover, Jonathan lunged at him and sank his knife into the red man's throat.

Without a second look, Jonathan scrambled up the bank and started to run again. There might be other Indians around, and he could not expect to be so lucky next time. He didn't attempt to recover the rifle, his family's most important possession. Without it he ran faster and with less effort. If the Indians didn't find it, he would come back for it later.

***

Thirty minutes more running brought him to the cleared area around the fort. Jonathan continued to run across the open space. The gate in the fort's wall swung open, and he ran through it to safety. Abner Fletcher greeted him with obvious relief.

"We been thinking they might have got all of you folks," Abner said.

Jonathan leaned against the rough log stockade gasping for breath. Tears burned in his eyes, and he turned away to hid them.

"It's alright Jonathan. Go ahead and cry. It'll make you feel better."

Abner beckoned to his wife. She put her arms around the boy. He buried his face in her shoulder, now sobbing helplessly.

"Abner's right, Jonathan," she said, holding him tightly and stroking his pale blonde hair. "It's all right to cry when you're only thirteen."

CHAPTERTWO

The Indian war party made a token attack on the fort and retreated from the region. The settlers returned to their farms and field work started again. Wherever they were, in their cabins, in the fields, or even when visiting the fort, they kept their rifles and muskets loaded and close at hand.

At the Fletcher homestead Mrs. Fletcher returned to her household routine, cooking, cleaning, washing clothes, feeding, and milking the remaining cow.

The black iron kettle that served as a laundry tub when not used for cooking hung over a small fire. When the water began to boil, she carved slivers from a lump of lye soap dropping them into the kettle, threw in the soiled clothing, and stirred the contents with a stout stick. While she worked, she listened to the sound of the axe that Jonathan wielded near the pile of newly cut wood. Abner Fletcher and Wesley Miller, a neighbor from across the valley, worked clearing the land that Abner hoped to plant in wheat next year. She could hear their distant voices as they worked. The sounds, so routine and normal, comforted her.

Jonathan worked near the cabin, cutting and splitting wood for winter fuel. A large wood pile was an important asset for a frontier family when the weather grew cold. Several cords might be burned during a cold winter.

The Fletchers had been happy to have Jonathan stay with them. Even though he ate a healthy amount of food, his labor more than made up for it. All frontier families needed cheap labor and having your own children or an orphan boy work with them, provided the ideal solution.

Jonathan had cheerfully done this same work for his own family, splitting wood and even helping clear the land, hard work for a young boy. Now it seemed like endless drudgery. His father had been cheerful and quick to lend a hand when Jonathan needed it. They had worked together, with easy conversation and laughter between them. But Abner Fletcher took life seriously. He seldom smiled and seemed to feel that laughter meant wasted time.

Mrs. Fletcher looked up from her chores, wiping the sweat from her forehead with the back of her hand, and examined Jonathan. He stood only a little less than six feet tall but thin as a rail, all bones and angles. He swung the axe with surprising strength and worked tirelessly for hours without complaint. He never smiled and seldom talked unless spoken to. Before his family had been killed, he had been a happy, friendly boy. She didn't know how to help him through his pain although her heart ached for him. In time he would forget the horror he had seen, but as the weeks passed she didn't see any change.

***

She watched the boy swing the axe and a block of wood split cleanly. He picked up one of the pieces and set it back on the chopping block, swung the axe again and the wood split into two smaller pieces. Stooping over to pick up the wood, he suddenly stopped, listening carefully to some foreign sounds. Still carrying the axe, he walked rapidly to the corner of the cabin. He looked around the corner and lowered the axe head to the ground. He turned to Mrs. Fletcher.

"There's a wagon comin' down the road from the west, Ma'am."

Mrs. Fletcher hurriedly lifted the pot away from the fire and ran to look. Visitors, few and far between in the valley, were a source of excitement for all frontier women.

The sun touched the horizon before the wagon reached the front door of the cabin. The wagon, pulled by a pair of oxen, carried all the possessions of a young couple that had come to the valley hoping to establish a home.

They asked if they could camp in the clearing near the cabin, and Mrs. Fletcher happily gave them permission and asked them to come for supper. The chance to talk to someone and perhaps hear news from other parts of the frontier excited her more than she would ever have imagined. Loneliness caused more problems for frontier women than Indians ever did.

After supper, the four adults lingered over the remains of their meal, talking about the problems of living in the Mohawk

Valley. The couple, Sam and Mary Pennyman, had dreamed of owning some of the cheap and fertile land in the Mohawk Valley, but they had no background or preparation for frontier life. The harsh living conditions had surprised them, and they had survived their first winter only with the help of neighbors. Frontier life had not met their expectations. Indians hadn't attacked them, but a neighbor's house had been burned to the ground. Both of them decided that Boston would be a better place to raise a family. Their conversation consisted of complaints and descriptions of their hardships, many of which would have been avoided by better planning.

Abner Fletcher listened politely, privately thinking that the new settlements along the Mohawk Valley would be better off for having these people leave. The frontier needed strong, self-reliant people, not city folk who didn't know how to care for themselves.

Jonathan, who had been sitting silently near the fireplace during the entire evening, now surprised them all by asking, "How far is it from Boston to Falmouth up in Maine territory?"

"Why I expect it's near a hundred miles," Sam replied. "I hear that it's an easy trail though. Do you know someone there?"

"My Ma's sister lives there."

"Oh, you have a sister in Falmouth?" Mary Pennyman asked Mrs. Fletcher.

"Oh no," Mrs. Fletcher replied. "Jonathan isn't our son. His family was all killed by . . . ."

Before she finished the sentence, Jonathan got to his feet and walked out of the cabin.

Mrs. Fletcher started to follow him. Abner raised his hand and she sat down again.

"Let the boy be by hisself," he said to his wife. "He's an orphan," he explained to the Pennymans. "His family was all killed by injuns a few weeks back."

The Pennymans sat in shocked silence for a moment.

"He's coming along," Abner said. "It takes time, but he'll be alright."

Outside the cabin Jonathan had heard the word "orphan" and gritted his teeth. He hated that word. He would always be an orphan unless he found some of his own family to take him in.

"How terrible," Mrs. Pennyman said. The others were silent.

When Mrs. Fletcher first called the Pennymans for breakfast, they hadn't finished loading their wagon. Another mark against them in Abner's opinion. They left long after Jonathan and Abner had finished eating and left the cabin.

All through the day Jonathan thought about traveling to Falmouth. By sunset he had convinced himself that his aunt and uncle would welcome him. It would be like having his own family again. The Fletchers never mistreated him, but he knew he would always be an outsider. He didn't have any claim on them and would always be the "orphan boy".

***

When the sun rose the next morning, Jonathan had already been traveling for two hours. He had been able to recover the family rifle and now carried it along with a powder horn and shot bag, as well as a small pouch filled with enough food for two days.

Abner Fletcher all but cried with frustration when he discovered that Jonathan had left during the night. Without Jonathan's help, he would have to take time from clearing land to do some of the other chores around home. He probably wouldn't have more than another two acres cleared and ready for next spring.

Abner picked up his musket and started for the door.

"Where are you going? You don't think you can catch him surely," his wife said.

"I can catch him alright" Abner said angrily.

"That boy can slip through the trees like an injun. Even if you did catch him how would you get him home? If he don't want to stay here, there ain't nuthin' can keep him now that he has the idea of going to Boston."

Abner pulled off his hat, threw it down on the floor and kicked it across the cabin. Mumbling to himself, he picked it up and started toward the fields.

***

On the afternoon of the third day, Jonathan saw the Pennyman's wagon, deeply mired in a muddy stream. Sam Pennyman stood beside the wagon shouting and beating the animals with a stout stick. The big beasts ignored him. After surprised greetings and explanations, Jonathan set to work helping them. With Mary Pennyman driving the oxen and Jonathan and Sam pushing, the wagon started moving again and reached the bank safely. Sam and Mary gladly accepted his offer to travel with them and help with the chores.

***

They reached Boston after an arduous but uneventful trip. The Pennymans supplied Jonathan with food, shot and powder, and a blanket. He set out to walk the more than one hundred miles to Falmouth.

He carried his rifle in the crook of his left arm, loaded and primed. He didn't expect trouble, but if trouble came an unloaded rifle would be useless. He rolled up the blanket and carried it slung across his shoulder. Ground corn and a small slab of bacon filled his pouch. Tucked in his belt he carried his knife and a small hatchet. Occasionally, the skinned and cleaned carcass of a rabbit or squirrel hung from his belt.

Jonathan walked during the daylight hours, resting only briefly at noon. At sunset he left the well-used trail and made camp back in the timber, out of sight from the road. He made a small fire, just large enough to cook his meal. Every night Jonathan drew the charge from his rifle and reloaded before he rolled himself into his blanket and slept.

Each day he awoke at sunrise out of long habit from his years of living on a frontier farm. He made a cold breakfast from the remnants of his evening meal and then started back on the trail to Falmouth.

Jonathan arrived in Falmouth in the early summer of 1775. At a creek outside of the town, he scrubbed himself as best as he could. He looked at his reflection in the still water and saw his long blond hair, snarled and tangled. He used his knife to cut it short and combed it with his fingers. After washing his shirt and trousers, he realized that his worn frontier clothing looked like the rags a beggar might wear. Even the clothing he carried in his pack looked shabby. He wanted to be clean and neat when he met his aunt and uncle, but he couldn't think of any way to improve his appearance.

When Jonathan knocked at the front door of the Morgan home, a pretty young girl with shiny black hair and pink, freshly scrubbed cheeks answered. She saw a ragged scarecrow of a boy carrying a long, heavy rifle. Jonathan smiled and started to speak. The girl interrupted him.

"I'm sorry, you will have to go around to the back door," she said firmly.

Jonathan's face grew red with anger.

"I'm Jonathan Weaver," he said firmly. "I've come all the way from . . . ."

The girl interrupted him by whispering, "I'm sorry. Mr. Morgan would punish me if I let you into the front room." Then she shut the door.

Jonathan choked back his anger. He realized that he looked too shabby to be anything but a homeless waif or a beggar. Still, he had expected a more considerate welcome. He bowed his head in shame and walked around to the back of the house.

"She don't know that the Morgans are my kinfolks," he told himself. "As soon as I tell them that, she'll treat me a lot better. My aunt and uncle will take me in, and it won't matter if I'm dirty and ragged right now. I've traveled a long way, and when folks know that, they'll understand why I look like this. When I meet my aunt, everything will be different."

Jonathan knocked at the back door. A large woman, apparently the cook, opened the door. Jonathan saw the same pretty young girl standing across the kitchen staring at him intently. He felt his face turning red again.

"What do you want young man?" The woman asked in a pleasant voice.

"My name is Jon Weaver, Ma'am. I came here to see Mrs. Morgan." He surprised himself by the choice of the name "Jon". It sounded more mature, and he didn't want to look like a child in front of the girl. The girl continued to stare at him for a few seconds and then left the kitchen.

"I'm Mrs. Morgan's nephew. I want to talk to her."

The woman's cheerful expression changed to one of concern.

"I'm Mrs. Sloan," she said. "I cook for Mr. Morgan." Then she called, "Faith," and the girl promptly walked back into the kitchen. Jon was certain she had been listening at the door.

"Faith, go up into the attic and open my chest. There are some of my boy's old clothes that will come close to fitting this lad. Now Jon, go out to the pump and wash yourself. Here's a towel and some soap."

Mrs. Sloan and her husband had raised a family of seven children. Four of the seven, all boys, had survived to adulthood and had moved west to the frontier. After her husband's death, she took the only job she could find, cooking for Mr. Morgan.

Mrs. Sloan didn't have any grandchildren, so the clothes she had saved when her own boys had outgrown them would serve Jon quite well.

The pump, Jon discovered, poured water into a washtub. He vigorously worked the handle and filled the tub. He saw that a large hedge concealed him from the house so he removed his tattered clothing and stepped into the icy cold water. The strong harsh lye soap and vigorous scrubbing made him feel clean again after weeks on the trail. As he dried himself he heard a soft rustle beyond the hedge and then a stifled laugh.

"Here are some clothes for you," Faith called out as she threw a fresh set of clothing over the hedge. He parted the hedge in time to see her running back to the house, giggling as she went.

When he returned from his bath, clean and wearing better clothing than he had worn at home, he saw Faith looking at him from behind a half-opened door with her hand over her mouth trying to hold back more laughter. Jonathan felt his face turning hot and red.

Mrs. Sloan looked at him and brushed his pale blond hair back from his face with her hand, ignoring his embarrassment.

"Now you look more presentable. Let me put that rifle in the storeroom for the time being. Faith, go and tell Mr. Morgan that his nephew is here."

Several minutes later Mr. Morgan entered the kitchen, wheezing from the exertion of walking through the house. Tall, obese, red faced, and scowling, he gave Jon no sign of welcome.

"Well," he said, "can you explain to me why you have

interrupted my work, Mrs. Sloan?"

"I'm Jon Weaver," Jon said quickly before Mrs. Sloan could answer. "I came all the way from the Mohawk Valley to see Mrs. Morgan. She's my aunt. Injuns killed my family. I'm the only one left."

The big man hesitated for a moment.

"How were you so lucky as to survive?" he asked, with some skepticism.

"I was away huntin' when they killed my family. When I came back to the cabin, they was all dead." His voice quavered as he spoke. "The injuns saw me in the brush and two of them chased me. I couldn't do nothin' to help." He ducked his head to hide the tears coming to his eyes.

"And how did such a young boy as you escape from those Indians?" Morgan asked. Clearly this boy thought he could get some special treatment with this tale.

"I killed 'em,'" Jon said.

The simple statement took all three of the listeners by surprise.

"My Ma used to talk about her sister in Falmouth," Jon continued, oblivious to the reaction to his statement. "So I decided to come here."

Mr. Morgan looked at Jon disapprovingly.

"Your aunt, if she was your aunt, passed away some six months ago."

He spoke without a trace of sorrow or regret.

Jon sagged, as if a heavy blow had hit his stomach.

After a moment Morgan continued, "I'm sure you don't expect me to take you, an orphan, into my family simply because I have been married to your aunt," Morgan continued.

Jon stood speechless. Mrs. Sloan and Faith shifted uneasily. The terrible lost and empty feeling filled his breast again. Mr. Morgan would never accept him as part of his family.

"However, I am a devout Christian. As such, I will allow you to sleep in the storeroom and eat in the kitchen. Temporarily! And I'll expect you to pay for your keep."

Mr. Morgan turned and walked from the room, smiling to himself. Providence had just presented him with a boy who could work for him at almost no cost.

Jon's despair turned to anger at the thoughtless, selfish man he had just met.

After an awkward silence, Mrs. Sloan spoke.

"Faith, show Jon where the storeroom is. Then serve Mr. Morgan his supper."

"Yes Ma'am," she replied.

"I'll have our dinner on the table in a few minutes."

***

The storeroom, a shed attached to the house, looked better to Jon than the loft in his home in the valley. He could make a sleeping platform and clean it up a bit. This shed would be as comfortable as the cabin his father had built.

Jon had been working for only a short time when the girl appeared at the door.

"I'm Faith Crawford," she said boldly and held out her

hand.

Jon took it cautiously. "I'm Jon Weaver."

His lingering anger disappeared as he talked to Faith. He had not known any young girls except his sister. The touch of Faith's hand pleased him, and he held it until she gently pulled it away.

"I'd best get to work on cleaning out this shed," he mumbled, his face red with embarrassment.

"Wait until after we eat and then I'll help you," Faith said. "It won't be near as much work if two of us do it together."

After supper, Jon and Faith began cleaning out the shed and arranging a bed for Jonathan.

"When I first saw you at the front door, I thought you might be my cousin," Jon said.

Faith said nothing for a few seconds. Then she said, "I wish I was. I'm indentured, Mr. Morgan owns my contract. It has four more years to run."

Her statement startled Jon. He remembered his father saying that being indentured amounted to the same thing as slavery.

"It ain't very nice 'cause I don't get a proper wage like Mrs. Sloan does," Faith continued. "But at least I've got a warm bed and plenty to eat. Not like back home in London."

Before she came to America, Faith told him, her family had lived in a London slum. Their home, one room in a rat-infested building, barely provided sleeping space for Faith, her mother and father, and her three younger sisters. Food was scarce and she couldn't remember any time when she wasn't hungry.

She dreamed of escaping from poverty by going to America. Several times she talked to the men who arranged passage for indentured servants, but they told her that they wanted strong young men suitable for work on farms and plantations, not young girls. The few women they recruited were skilled lady's maids.

Faith noticed that one of the recruiters stared at her every time he saw her. She became friendly with him. He was much older and married, but still a lonely man with no friends. She easily seduced him. Then when she threatened to expose their affair, the recruiter quickly arranged a favorable contract for her. Faith knew it was a sinful thing to do, but it had gotten her out of the London slum.

She had never revealed this part of her background to anyone. When asked she said that a distant relative had used his influence to help her.

When Faith reached America, Mr. Morgan saw a bargain and bought her contract at a considerable saving because of her youth and lack of training. Faith was happy to get any sort of work. Even though she had very little free time and even less money in her new life, she was far better off. She now had enough food and a secure place to live. Mr. Morgan would not pay for more domestic help, so Faith did the work of two servants, but she felt lucky to have a warm bed and plenty of food. Even if she did have a moment free, she didn't know anyone to visit. Church meetings and shopping with Mrs. Sloan were her only outings.

Mr. Morgan, a deacon of the church, expected regular attendance at the worship services from the two women, and now Jon attended too. However, the good church members tended to shun a lowly orphan and a servant girl. The two young people were drawn to each other.

Chapter Three

Less than a week had passed since Jon had arrived when a boy about Jon's age knocked at the kitchen door.

"I'm Todd Paget," he said when Faith opened the door. "Yes?" she replied, smiling sweetly. Jon stood a good four inches taller than this boy, but Todd, with his dark brown eyes and neatly combed black hair, looked just as handsome.

"Mr. Morgan asked me to come here and tell Jon to come down to the docks as soon as he can. I'll lead him to the right place."

"I'll fetch him for you," she said, and ran to find Jon.

***

Jon and Todd walked side by side toward the docks. At first the boys, both shy and quiet, hardly spoke to each other. They exchanged names and made a comment or two about the weather.

After a long silence, Jon said, "We used to have days like this in the Mohawk Valley. It was a might warmer though. It's really pretty there in the summer."

"Fall is the best time of year here," Todd said.

Another long pause and then Todd spoke again. "I heard you walked all the way from Boston. Is that a fact?"

"Pretty near," Jon replied.

"How come you wanted to leave home?"

"Don't have no home. Injuns wiped us out." After a short pause, he mumbled, "My whole family got killed by injuns."

Jon looked away with his head down while he struggled to keep tears from his eyes.

"Oh, I'm sorry I brought it up, Jon. I didn't know."

"It's all right. Ain't no way you could'a knowed about it."

They walked on in silence. Todd, too embarrassed to speak, and Jon trying to think of something to say to start the conversation again.

"It's a hard life out there," Jon finally said. "Besides the injuns, food is scarce sometimes, and the cabin loft I used to sleep in, it weren't no better than the shed I sleep in now."

They walked in silence for a time.

"I work for my father," Todd said. "He owns two ships and a ship chandlery. He keeps me busy running errands along the docks. I saw Mr. Morgan at the fishing dock, and he asked me to run and fetch you. I knew father would want me to be helpful."

"I think he has a job for you. Mr. Morgan I mean. Sailing on a fishing boat. I wish I could do that. Sailing all day in a boat. Sure would be more fun than running errands."

***

At the dock, Mr. Morgan introduced Jon to Danny Pound, a short, heavily muscled man with a permanent scowl on his weathered face.

"This is Mr. Pound. I have arranged for you to work for him," Mr. Morgan said. "You will sail with him and follow his orders. If you have no questions, I'll leave." Then he abruptly walked away, red faced and panting from the exertion.

"Well boy, we can't catch no fish just standin' here. Get into the boat, and I'll show you what to do."

Danny's directions came fast and to the point, punctuated by profanity that embarrassed Jon. The boat, a small cutter designed to be sailed by three men, sailed with only two. The skipper, Danny Pound, drove himself hard, and expected Jon to keep up with him. As a product of a frontier farm, Jon expected hard work. Danny Pound never let him know that life could be easier.

After sailing with Danny for a week, Jon had his first experience with heavy weather. They ran down wind, large rollers following them, and Jon feared for his life. As each wave approached, Jon knew beyond any doubt that the boat would be swamped and they would drown. But the cutter's stern always lifted at the last second, and the wave passed beneath them. He sat in the boat's cockpit staring at the following waves, his eyes large and filled with apprehension. He glanced at Danny and saw him smiling with a trace of sympathy.

"Nuthin' to worry about, boy," Danny shouted. "As long as we keep her stern to the waves, she'll keep us safe."

Danny's words were not convincing, but Jon slowly gained confidence in the boat and in himself and began to enjoy sailing. He mastered the basics of small boat handling well enough for Danny to trust him to take the tiller in all but the heaviest weather.

He would bring the cutter up to the dock with a gentle bump. Then, while Danny haggled over the price for the fish, Jon unloaded their catch, cleaned the boat, and stored all the gear. After he towed the cutter to its mooring buoy using the harbor master's dinghy, his work day ended.

As Jon's sailing skill increased and his fear lessened, the pain of the loss of his family began to fade. Jon had found a calling that he truly enjoyed. He liked to arrive at the pier early in the morning so there would be time to repair fishing gear or patch sails before Danny arrived. When they sailed out of the harbor, the feel of the boat responding to his touch on the tiller filled him with satisfaction. Running down wind with a following sea, feeling the stern lift to the waves, intoxicated him. Still, he knew that one minor error could capsize the boat and possibly cause the death of both of them, and he never took foolish chances. He had forgotten the terror of his first experience with heavy weather, but kept a great respect for the power of the wind and waves. Sailing, even on a small fishing boat, satisfied him more than anything he had ever done.

Other members of the fishing fleet respected him for his quick understanding of small boat sailing and his willingness to do the hard and sometimes distasteful work Danny required of him.

Todd Paget often arranged his errands to that he could meet

Jon at the dock in the evening. The two boys would walk back to the Morgan home, talking, laughing, and enjoying each other's company.

At times Jon would still be excited and full of adrenaline.

"Did you see us comin' across the bay, Todd?" Jon might say. "We was flyin'." Or he might carry on about other exciting events of the day. A good day of fishing or a new ship they had seen.

Twice Danny and Jon had seen British warships. One of them a frigate and the other a ship the British called a sloop. Jon told Todd that it looked more like a brig, but the British Navy has some strange names for ships.

They even sold some fish to the captain of the sloop. Danny charged them three times what the buyer paid at the dock, but the captain didn't haggle.

As Jon and Todd walked toward the Morgan home that evening, Jon said, "That British Captain asked Danny a bunch o' questions about ships sailin' out of Falmouth. Danny told him he didn't know much about that. He said he never paid no attention to ships, just fishin' boats. Course he knows every ship that ever touched at Falmouth, but he wasn't goin' to tell no Britisher about it," Jon explained.

They walked back to Mr. Morgan's home, talking and even laughed at times.

Faith arranged to be in the kitchen whenever the two boys arrived. Then the three young people sat at the kitchen table talking until Mr. Morgan came home from his bank.

On one of these evenings Todd brought up the subject of Jon's rifle.

"Faith told me that you have a big, long rifle," Todd said.

"My Pa's," Jon replies shortly. Memories of that terrible day flooded back into his mind. He had not told anyone in Falmouth the story of his family's death except to say that Indians had killed them. Now he had friends to confide in. The words came tumbling out in an unstoppable flow. He told how he had seen his sister and mother killed and scalped, how the Indians had chased him, and how he had killed both of them. Todd and Faith listened in awe.

When Jon's story ended, Todd and Faith sat in dumb silence. Neither of them knew what to say. Faith put her hand over Jon's clenched fists.

Finally Todd said, "I'll meet you at the dock again tomorrow," and left for home.

That night, at the Paget's dinner table, Todd told his father about Jon's tragic loss. Such a young quiet boy, Mr. Paget thought, yet he had not only survived, but had killed two Indians. He leaned back in his chair and began to reflect on his own life.

He had gone to sea as a cabin boy, thirteen years old. He made able seaman at fifteen, mate at seventeen, captain at twenty, and ship owner by age twenty-five. He had accumulated a considerable fortune over the years. Now a tall, elegantly dressed man, with soft hands from easy living, and a prominent place in Falmouth society, he usually felt content with his life. However, at times he envied the brave and competent men who stood on the quarterdecks of his ships.

This boy had to be tough and resilient, important virtues in Mr. Paget's view. He would keep Jon in mind.

Chapter Four

"Did you hear about what happened in Boston?" Todd asked Jon one evening as they started to walk back to the Morgan house. "They had a big battle." He went on before Jon could answer.

"A bunch of Militia held a hill against the British regulars for most a whole day. They ran out of powder and shot so they had to get out finally, but they sure surprised them lobster backs."

"What good did it do I wonder," Jon replied.

"Well it sure showed them that Americans can fight. They'll think twice before they try something like that again."

"What do you think they'll do now? They'll want to do something to get back at us for it." Jon said.

Jon soon forgot about the battle in Boston. His newfound love for sailing filled his mind and made the weeks pass by too quickly.

By the end of the summer he had grown taller and appeared

even thinner, particularly since he had outgrown Mrs. Sloan's stock of old clothing. Danny Pound, however, saw a boy with a large boned frame, who would grow in strength and size as he matured. He looked forward to years of help from Jon.

As the summer ended, the evening temperatures began to drop, and Jon suffered from the cold. He had no money to buy a coat, and Mrs. Sloan didn't have one for him in her chest in the attic.

"Why don't you buy yourself some warm clothes, Jon?" Danny asked him.

Jon, shivering slightly, replied, "Ain't got no money."

"I never seen you spend anything. You must be savin' it up," Danny replied.

"Mr. Morgan says all of the money you pay him goes for room and board. All I get is a place to sleep and two meals a day."

Danny shifted his gaze away from Jon and stared at the horizon, thoughtfully scratching his beard. He nodded his head as if he had discovered something and smiled to himself.

***

The following Monday, Danny had a new jacket and gave his old patched one to Jon, as well as an old set of oilskins. The coat sleeves didn't cover Jon's wrists, and the elbows had worn through, but Jon felt grateful for it.

Danny also bought some gear for his boat, gear he had said earlier that he couldn't afford.

***

Jon's job on Danny's boat ended abruptly on October 17,

1775, when a British flotilla of four ships anchored in the harbor. The British commander, Lieutenant Mowat, informed the town that a bombardment would begin the next day. The bombardment would be punishment for their rebel sympathies and their attacks on himself and others in his party the preceding March.

"Lord above," Danny said. "He ain't gonna bombard us. Our militia saved him from them hot heads from Brunswick. That damn fool Thompson took him captive, and our militia here in Falmouth got him free. I expect Lieutenant Mowat still remembers that."

"It wouldn't be a big job to move her, Danny," Jon said. "Then she would be safe even if they did fire at us."

"Don't you be tellin' me how to take care of my boat. That's my business, not yours."

Danny underestimated the British arrogance and disdain for the Colonists. British Vice Admiral Graves had ordered the bombardment and Lieutenant Mowat was happy to carry it out, at least in part because there were thirteen merchant ships anchored in the harbor which might be treated as prizes if captured. The prize money would be a considerable amount for the officers and crew of the British ships as well as for Admiral Graves.

Unlike Danny, the residents of Falmouth had realized their danger and set about evacuating the city. The militia moved their store of arms back into the surrounding forests, and the residents swarmed into the streets carrying their personal belongings beyond the edge of town.

Jon helped carry the belongings of Mr. Morgan, as well as

those of Faith and Mrs. Sloan, beyond the town limits. Fortunately, Mr. Morgan lived near the edge of town, and they could avoid the crowded streets and alleys.

***

When the sun rose the following morning, crowds of citizens, trying to save their belongings, still choked the narrow streets and alleys of Falmouth.

Although Danny Pound continued to scoff at the idea that the British would actually fire on Falmouth, owners of other small boats had rowed or towed their vessels into hiding behind the rocky islands and into the tiny inlets. Danny left his cutter in the harbor.

The morning mist still hung in the air the following day. Jon stood on the dock watching the British ships. The largest warship the <u>Canceaux</u>, carried eight guns. Now she lay anchored bow and stern close to the shore. As he gazed at the ship, she suddenly disappeared behind a huge cloud of smoke. An instant later he heard the roar of the British cannons and the shriek of the shells passing overhead. The other ships joined in the bombardment, firing cannon and mortar shells into the town.

Jon stood frozen in place, nearly panicked by the display of power.

"Lord help us," he heard as Danny Pound roughly grabbed his arm. "We got to hide her. Quick now, we can row her around the point. Their shells can't reach us there."

They hurriedly cast off the lines mooring the cutter to the dock and began rowing with all of their strength.

"Pull boy, pull," Danny shouted as they rowed the boat away from the dock.

A nearby rocky point would protect the boat's hull from the British guns if they could reach it in time.

"Get down," Danny screamed as a shell thundered past, leaving a shattered mast in its wake, and laying Danny's boat on her side.

Jon fell into the water. He swam to the shore, cursing Danny for his foolishness. As he climbed the rock bank, a second shell exploded and fragments screamed past him. Another shell struck Danny's boat sending splinters flying. Jon found himself lying on the rocks. As his head cleared he became aware of a searing pain in his leg. Blood soaked his trousers in a pulsing flow. He tore off his shirt and wrapped it tightly around his leg to stop the bleeding. Another shell thundered past, exploding more than one hundred feet beyond them. Still another exploded under water. Jon lay on the rocky ground, trembling with fear, waiting for another shell. None landed near them. The gunners had shifted their aim to more interesting targets. After a minute of silence, Jon realized that the danger had passed, but he could not stop shaking.

Danny had somehow reached the shore too. He lay half in and half out of the water.

"Danny," Jon shouted, his voice wavering with fear and pain. "I'm hurt. I need help."

Danny tried to crawl out of the water. He collapsed, coughing blood. Jon stared at him for a moment before he realized that Danny's wounds were far worse than his own. Gritting his teeth at the pain, he dragged himself along the rocky shore, one hand holding his shirt tight around his leg. Danny, alive but barely breathing, cried out as Jon pulled him out of the water and propped him up against a large rock. Danny coughed up more blood.

"You'll have to get help, Jon," Danny said in a weak and rasping voice. "I can't move myself." His face contorted with pain, he whispered, "Get help." Jon tried to make Danny more comfortable, but when he moved him, Danny groaned with pain. Jon staggered to his feet and slowly and painfully limped toward town.

He struggled through the hellish fire and explosions searching for help. A cannon ball passed by his head so close that it knocked him to the ground. A British marine saw Jon fall. The marine ran to him and thrust his bayonet into the ground by Jon's side, whispering, "Lay still now, you bloody fool."

A sergeant watched from half a block away.

"Good work. We ain't supposed to kill the bloody traitors," he shouted. "I say they deserve it. Now get on down the street."

Jon lay on the ground trying to understand what had just happened. Finally, the noise and shouting had moved away from him, and he painfully and slowly got to his feet. He would die if he couldn't find help and so would Danny. Blood still oozed from his wound, running down his leg and filling his shoe.

He limped along the back streets, gasping with pain.

At last he found one of the two doctors who practiced in Falmouth.

"I'll look for Danny after I take care of that leg of yours.

You'll bleed to death if I don't," the doctor said after Jon explained what had happened.

Jon sat on the ground with his back against the wall of a building. The doctor wiped blood away from the wound with his handkerchief and then rummaged through his instrument case until he found a curved needle and a length of what looked like ordinary thread. As he worked he dropped the needle to the ground, picked it up, wiped it against the leg of his trouser, and proceeded to stitch up the wound. He bound the leg tightly using Jon's shirt again, and the bleeding stopped.

"That should take care of it," the doctor said. "You're young and healthy, and there ain't any bad humors in your blood. You'll soon be good as new. Don't walk on it for a week at least. Now, where is Danny?"

Jon couldn't move for the pain, and the doctor didn't return to help. Loss of blood left him weak and thirsty. His dry throat became more painful than his leg. He had lapsed into unconsciousness when he dimly heard a faint voice that seemed to come from a distance.

"Jon! Jon wake up! It's me, Todd!"

Jon opened his eyes. He could make out a foggy outline of a familiar face.

"We've been looking for you Jon," Todd exclaimed. "We thought that you might be dead."

Todd pulled on Jon's arm, trying to get him to stand. Jon yelped in pain, but his head cleared.

"I can't walk Todd." Jon said in a hoarse whisper.

"Use this board for a crutch and put your other arm around my neck," Todd said.

They walked slowly to the Morgan home, where Mrs. Sloan and Faith helped Jon get out of his bloody clothes and onto a cot they set up in the kitchen. As they moved his leg, Jon sometimes gasped with pain, but bit his lip and didn't cry out.

Jon stayed in bed for five days while his wound grew steadily worse. The leg swelling, and the wound itself festering and oozing ugly yellow pus. On the fifth day, Faith found a bit of wood in the bandages when she changed them.

"It's probably a splinter from the boat," Mrs. Sloan said when Faith showed it to her. "His leg should heal better now." She knew more about cuts and other wounds than many doctors. She had raised a family of four boys with nothing but the knowledge passed on from her mother. Although no bones had been broken, the loss of blood made him too weak to walk without help for several days.

***

The bombardment had destroyed more than one hundred houses, as well as the courthouse and other buildings in the town. Of the thirteen merchant ships in the harbor, the British captured two, and destroyed the rest.

The doctor visited only once. He examined Jon's leg and felt his forehead.

"I need a large bowl now Mrs. Sloan."

"What ever for?" she asked.

"If you don't want blood on your floor, you had best get a

bowl. He needs bleeding."

"My husband and my four boys had plenty of bad hurts and they never needed bleeding."

"Don't question me about treating this boy. Just get the bowl."

He opened his bag and pulled out an instrument covered with dried blood.

"What is that dirty thing?" Mrs. Sloan asked.

"It's called a fleam, and it is used to open veins for bleeding," the doctor replied with some asperity.

Instead of a bowl, Mrs. Sloan picked up a large fire place poker.

"You'll not touch that boy with that filthy thing," she shouted, waving the poker at the doctor. "He's already lost too much blood. Get out of my kitchen."

The doctor left, fuming and sputtering, and never returned. Mrs. Sloan and Faith cared for Jon day and night. Mrs. Sloan washed him and changed the dressings on his wound. Faith spent all of her spare moments with him. She fed him and sat by his bed whenever she could take time from housework. Eventually, Jon's young and healthy body began to heal itself. Rest and food from Mrs. Sloan's kitchen helped him regain his strength. In two weeks he could walk with only a slight limp.

Danny Pound, less fortunate than Jon, contracted pneumonia. Although he survived, his health remained poor and he never sailed again.

Chapter Five

Mr. Morgan's home had suffered no damage other than broken glass, but his bank building had been destroyed. He moved his business into his home. His study became his office, and the hallway provided space for several clerks and served as a waiting area.

As soon as Jon's wound had healed well enough for him to walk, Mr. Morgan called him to his study. When the door closed, he began speaking.

"Jon, I have been generous to you. I took you in when you were a homeless orphan and provided for you."

The word "orphan" stung Jon. He had not heard it since he began working for Danny.

"And now you repay me by laying about the house without paying me so much as a penny for your keep," Morgan continued. "I know you have been hurt because of the irresponsible action of those rebel Militiamen, however, that is not my concern."

"Sir, I haven't even been able to walk for . . . ."

"I did not call you to my office to debate this problem." Morgan's voice rose in pitch and volume. "The only thing you have of any value is that rifle. I must sell it to pay for your room and board. You do not need it, and it will pay a small part of your debt to me. Now leave me to my work."

Jon opened his mouth to speak, but Mr. Morgan spoke first.

"I said leave," he shouted. "If you don't do so, I will have you thrown out."

As he walked out of the office, Jon saw Todd Paget sitting on one of the chairs looking at him with sympathy.

After Todd completed his father's business with Mr. Morgan, he hurried around the house to the kitchen door.

"Don't let him take your rifle away from you," he blurted when Jon answered his knock.

"He won't get my Pa's rifle. I can go back to the Mohawk Valley."

"What would you do there? You said yourself that you couldn't find any work. That's why you came here in the first place."

"I can't let him take Pa's rifle. It's all I got left of them."

After a long silence, Jon said, "I'll stow away on a ship."

"I know how they treat stowaways, Jon. You don't want to do that either."

Faith and Mrs. Sloan overheard them.

"I wish I could run away with you, Jon," Faith said, tears forming in her eyes.

"Todd," Mrs. Sloan said briskly, "one of your father's ships is back in port now. Go talk to him and tell him what happened. He can give Jon a berth on her can't he? I'm sure he will if you explain things to him."

Todd, taken aback by the suggestion that he should ask his father for such a favor, hesitated for a moment, then he agreed.

***

At the Paget home supper was served on a makeshift table in the parlor. The dining room had been severely damaged by the bombardment. Their home needed extensive repairs and the Paget ship chandlery would have to be completely rebuilt. Mr. Paget sat at the supper table silently eating his meal with a deep frown on his face.

Todd wondered if he should bring up the subject of Jon's problem at all. But it seemed like the only possible escape for Jon, and the ship would sail tomorrow on the evening tide.

Todd summoned enough courage to speak to his father just before his mother served dessert.

"Father," Todd began hesitantly. "Do you remember me telling you about Jon Weaver?"

"Yes. What about him?"

"Well he needs some help from us. I mean from you." Todd added hastily.

Mr. Paget looked up frowning.

"What sort of help does he need?" he asked.

"You know Mr. Pound got hurt during the bombardment."

Todd's father nodded.

"Well since Jon can't work for Mr. Pound, Mr. Morgan says he's going to take Jon's rifle away from him and sell it."

"Good Lord," Mr. Paget exclaimed. "That rifle is probably worth two years of room and board."

He threw his napkin down beside his plate.

"Father, please try to control your temper at the supper table," Mrs. Paget said.

Mr. Paget became silent. He concentrated on his food until his anger, now directed at Christian Morgan, cooled.

"Just how do you think I can help?"

"The Mary P. is ready to sail. You could give him a berth on her."

To Todd's surprise, his father readily agreed.

"Yes I could do that. It would be good for the ship too."

Mr. Paget sat back in his chair and savored the effect his action would have on Christian Morgan. He began to smile.

Chapter Six

Robin Clay, second mate of the topsail schooner <u>Mary P.</u>, stood on the quarterdeck watching a young boy walking along the pier. He appeared to be about fourteen or fifteen. Tall and large boned for his age, with a lot of filling out to do. The sleeves of the old coat that he wore hung two inches short of his wrists. His light blond hair needed cutting, but at least it had been washed recently. In one hand he carried a narrow bag almost five feet long, made of deer skin. In his other hand he carried the usual seaman's duffel. The <u>Mary P.</u> lay alongside the pier. The boy walked up her gangplank.

Robin Clay glared at him as he came aboard the ship.

"Are you Jon Weaver?" he snapped.

Jon looked at him and guessed that he must be one of the officers. The man wore rough seaman's clothing and stood three inches shorter than Jon. Muscular and stocky, he seemed to radiate an air of authority.

"Yes sir," he said, somewhat too loudly.

"What the devil are you bringing aboard there?" he asked, scowling and nodding at the long deerskin bag.

"It's my rifle, sir. Mister Paget said it would be all right if you was to lock it up in the arms chest."

Rob Clay's scowl deepened at the mention of the owner's name. Mate Clay had come up through the "hawse-hole" and had no respect for those who used their influence to get a berth. He wanted to throw the boy off the ship, but they would likely be sailing short-handed even with this new boy onboard. A green boy would be better than nothing.

"So you're a friend of Mr. Paget eh? Well don't expect any favors. You'll work just like anyone else on this ship."

"Bosun," he shouted, and a burly man with arms as thick as small kegs walked over to them.

"Yes sir, Mr. Clay," he said.

"Take charge of the deck while I see the Captain about this lubber's rifle."

He took Jon's rifle from him and walked aft toward the captain's cabin.

"Stow your dunnage for'rd in the fo'c's'l" the Bosun growled. "Then we'll see if you know how to work now that your Ma ain't here to wipe your nose!"

Jon knew that sailors would say "aye aye sir," but the words sounded strange and uncomfortable. Instead he mumbled, "Ain't got no Ma," and then walked toward the bow where he knew the "fo'c's'l" would be.

The bosun stared after him and shook his head. Here was another poor lad to make into a sailor.

Jon found a vacant bunk in the forecastle and threw his duffel onto it. The lingering smell of unwashed bodies and tobacco, overlaid by a strong odor of mold nearly made him gag. He closed his eyes and clenched his fists by his sides. This would be his home for months. Would it be any better than his life on shore? But there's no turning back now, he said to himself.

***

"Lay onto that line boy," the Bosun shouted when Jon came out of the forecastle.

He walked toward the group of men holding a line that went through a block on deck and another block high in the rigging.

"When I give you an order, damn your eyes, you run," the Bosun roared, and Jon ran.

"Now hoist away." The men began pulling and Jon pulled with them, swaying a load of timber aboard. They moved faster and broke into a run. Taken by surprise, Jon lost his balance and fell to the deck. A sailor tripped over him and another fell on them. The line ran free back through the block. Jon watched in horror as the timbers fell toward the deck. The line ran out faster and faster, then came taut, the timbers swaying a foot above the deck. A seaman had snubbed the line around a cleat. The ship became silent as the deck crew stopped work, looking at each other with expectant smiles.

"Get up, you damn miserable lubber," the Bosun snarled at

Jon. A string of profanity followed, worse than any Jon had ever heard, even around the fishing docks. When he ran out of breath, the Bosun paused and then said, "If we wasn't shorthanded, I'd throw you off the ship you worthless . . . ." Then he snarled at the rest of the crew, "Get back to work. You wasn't signed on to stand around watchin'."

The crew hurriedly went back to work bringing cargo aboard. Jon joined in, watching the other men carefully to see how they did each task and following their example, trying to avoid attracting the bosun's attention.

***

The schooner <u>Mary P.</u>, named after Mr. Paget's mother, had started her life smuggling cargo into Falmouth to avoid King George's taxes.

Her Captain, Elihu Hamm, an unimposing figure of medium height and a thin, emaciated appearance, ran the ship with a firm hand. He gave orders in a loud, booming voice when needed, but left the day-to-day operations to First Mate Aaron Blessing and Second Mate Rob Clay. Captain Hamm knew his officers and crew as neighbors as well as sailors. This close social relationship could not be tolerated in sailing ships in general, where men had to be ordered to perform dangerous tasks under extreme conditions. However, by far the largest part of the <u>Mary P.</u>'s crew had grown up along the coast and had sailed on fishing boats or came from families that lived by fishing. They all knew the dangers of the sea and had faced them more than once. Their lives depended on Captain Hamm's skill and judgment as well as their self-imposed discipline. They obeyed him without question.

For two years, Captain Hamm and mates Blessing and Clay had eluded British warships to carry cargos into Falmouth or to islands close by. From the islands, small boats moved the goods to the mainland to avoid the taxes imposed by the English.

They gained more knowledge about the shoal waters and channels along the New England coast than most men learned in a lifetime. Captain Hamm knew the rocks and shoals particularly well and had never even been chased by a British ship.

Now, although the Mary P. carried on the same trade, Americans called her a blockade runner instead of a smuggler, and they called her crew "Patriots".

As soon as the ship cleared the harbor, the officers divided the crew into watches. First Mate Aaron Blessing selected Jon for his watch.

Mate Blessing, a tall raw-boned man, owned a reputation for violence when provoked. He spoke no more than necessary, never using three words when two would do. The crew obeyed his orders without question. Most of the men feared him. While at sea he seldom drank anything stronger than coffee, but when on shore, ale and wine brought out his violent streak. Wise crewmen avoided him then.

Jon, young and strong, looked promising to Mr. Blessing. He knew that Jon had worked for Danny Pound for several months. Anyone who could satisfy Danny for that long had to be a good man. He selected Jon to be one of the topmen, the men who worked in the rigging setting and furling the topsails.

"It must be a beautiful sight from up there," Jon said to a seaman standing near him. He missed the quiet smile the man gave to the others.

When the order came to set the topsail, Jon tried to run up the shrouds as he had seen the others do. His foot missed a ratline and he found himself hanging on for his life. With the help of a kind hand, he recovered and continued his climb to the foretop, the platform near the top of the lower mast. The modest breeze felt cool and pleasant that morning, but the sea had begun to build. As the Mary P. rolled and pitched, the mast and yardarms moved with a sickening circular motion. Jon looked down and saw the sea below him. As the schooner rolled, the foretop swung out over the water, then back across the deck and over the water on the other side. He began to feel dizzy and nauseous.

"Let go of the mast and get out on them foot ropes," Mate Blessing bawled from the deck. He repeated his shout twice before Jon realized that the bellowing concerned him. Without knowing it, he had fastened his arms around the mast. He forced himself away from it and cautiously put one foot on the foot rope strung below the yard arm. Swallowing his fear, he slid one foot after the other out onto the starboard side foot rope. The man on his left, not much older than Jon, talked to him as he edged out along the yardarm.

"Put your belly against the yard," he shouted, "and don't look down. When we cast off the gaskets, the sail will fill and the ship will heel some more. Hang on then."

When they removed the gaskets, the sail bellied out and Jon

hung on grimly as the sail shook and trembled until it was sheeted home. The men outboard of Jon on the foot rope had to wait while he forced himself to relax his tight grip and start edging back toward the mast.

"You'll have to move faster, boy," the crewman outboard of him yelled in his ear. "We want to get down on deck before the watch changes." Then to Jon's amazement, the man climbed up onto the yardarm and ran along it back to the maintop.

"You did all right up there," the Bosun said when Jon reached the safety of the deck. "Except you hugged the mast hard enough to squeeze sawdust out of it."

The "traditional" hazing he endured, by far the worst part of his early days on the Mary P., continued long after he learned to perform the duties expected of him, including laying out on the yardarm, setting or furling the square topsails.

"Jon, grab that spar, we need some sawdust," would always bring laughter from the crew. His nickname became "Sawdust," and Jon hated it.

***

The Mary P. continued on her course through several near gales. Jon worked harder than he had for Danny Pound and slept in less comfort. Whenever a sudden squall hit them, Jon would be aloft, laying out over the yardarm, grappling with the stiff cold canvas. He had grown accustomed to the dangerous work and no longer felt the terror he had endured during his first time aloft, but his muscles ached and his hands were raw and bleeding. Tired, sometimes frightened, always uncomfortable, and worst of all, lonely, he missed his few friends in Falmouth. He thought about Todd Paget, his first friend when he arrived in Falmouth, and about Mrs. Sloan, who cared for him as she would have cared for her own son. Most of all he thought about Faith, the tears she shed and the hurried, impulsive kiss she had given him when he left.

As they sailed south the weather improved and now a moderate breeze had been blowing steadily for several days. The crew had time to spare from sail handling and trimming. Jon stood at the windward rail, gazing idly at the horizon and dreaming of Falmouth and Faith Crawford.

"Kind of peaceful ain't it," a voice said.

The voice startled Jon and he turned to find Scotty Lachlan, the man who had encouraged him that first time aloft, standing only a few feet from him.

"Are you gettin' used to shipboard life by now?"

"I guess so," Jon grunted. He didn't know how to react since not many of the crew had spoken to him except to belittle him.

"Don't let it get you down, Sawdust. I come aboard without never being on a ship before. It was kind of tough for a bit. I felt pretty lonely I remember."

"That so?" Jon had turned to face Scotty. "How long did it take to get to know everybody?"

"I don't rightly remember now. I think it took most of the first cruise. On the second cruise they acted like I was an old hand. The thing is, they had someone else to play their tricks on by then. Don't worry too much. You catch on fast."

Then the bosun shouted and both men scurried to do his bidding.

***

Memories of his home and family in the Mohawk Valley and of Faith and Mrs. Sloan began to fade. Scotty Lachlan spent much of his free time with Jon. Scotty, a tall, red-headed Scotsman, had grown up helping his father and younger brother run a small farm. The hard work made him strong and healthy, full of confidence, and firmly convinced that he didn't want to remain a farmer. Two years ago, he left the farm and traveled to Charles Towne. He saw the <u>Mary P.</u> in the harbor and signed on.

When Jon joined the ship, Scotty remembered his own experiences as the greenest crewman aboard and quietly gave Jon advice and a sympathetic ear. At times Jon thought he had acquired an older brother.

***

As a rule, seamen are good hearted souls. Jon's sailing experience with Danny, and his desire to do his share of the work gained him acceptance. He began to relax and enjoy their company, even if they did persist in calling him Sawdust.

"How did you decide to go to sea, Sawdust?" Scotty asked one day.

"It was about the only way out for me," Jon replied. He went on to explain how his family had been killed, and how his uncle had tried to take away his most precious possession, his father's long rifle. Jon surprised himself by talking about his life in so casual a manner.

"Sounds like a proper bastard," Scotty said, referring to Morgan.

After a slight pause, Jon nodded his head. "He is that."

***

As Jon became acquainted with the other crew members he found that one other man had seen his family die. Ryan Flynn, a short, dark Irishman, had suffered a similar tragedy. When cholera swept through the Dublin slum where his family lived, his mother, father, and three sisters died. He became a homeless waif. In desperation he stowed away on a British merchant ship. When the mate found him hidden away in the hold, the captain took pity and made him the cabin boy, and two years later made him an able seaman.

A British frigate had halted Ryan's ship and pressed several crewman, including Ryan, into the British Navy. Ryan served on the frigate for several years before the harsh discipline of a cruel and incompetent captain caused him to desert while in the Boston Harbor. He could not find work ashore, so he signed onto the <u>Mary P.</u> even though he knew he would be hanged if captured by the British.

In sharp contrast to Jon and Scotty, Ryan stood only a bit over five feet, with black hair and pale green eyes. His thin and wiry body possessed surprising strength and his hair-trigger temper resulted in some vigorous "discussions" at times.

***

The <u>Mary P.</u> approached the coast of Puerto Rico just at sunset one calm clear evening. All day long Captain Hamm had paced the quarter deck, restlessly watching the horizon. The watch aloft had been doubled early that morning, and either Mr. Blessing or Mr. Clay had been aloft watching the horizon for a possible sail.

"What are they looking for, Scotty," Jon asked in a quiet voice that no one else could hear. He didn't want to look foolish to the rest of the crew.

"The English keep a pretty tight blockade around here. San Juan is one of the ports that lets American ships trade with them and the British don't like it. We've got lumber aboard that they need on these islands, and they have all of the sugar and molasses we can take. You see, the British would like to starve us and make us give up the war. Think of all the people just in Falmouth that depend on buying and selling the cargoes we bring in. Besides that, them Tories would like to have our cargo for themselves, and when we leave San Juan, we'll have a cargo they want more than most anything . . . sugar. They want that in England so much it's like gold."

The sunlight faded and the wind dropped to a gentle breeze. As it grew darker, Captain Hamm visibly relaxed.

"Mr. Clay," Captain Hamm said, "have three red lanterns hung in the larboard shrouds."

"Aye sir," Mr. Clay responded, and soon the three lights had been lashed in place.

"Tack now, Mr. Clay. Let our friends on shore see our larboard side."

After a wait of several minutes, a red lantern flashed twice from the shore. A small boat sailed out of a hidden cove toward the schooner. Captain Hamm conversed with the boat crew for a few minutes and then handed down a small bag of coins. The boat pulled away with many a smile and wave from its crew.

The <u>Mary P.</u> sailed along the coast for five hours and entered the harbor of San Juan without even seeing the British frigate reported to be blockading the port.

After an afternoon of bargaining through Mr. Paget's agent, the crew began unloading their cargo of New England clear white pine. When the wood had been hauled away, wagon loads of molasses filled kegs appeared on the dock to be loaded into the <u>Mary P.</u>'s hold. Then kegs of sugar followed until a full cargo had been taken aboard.

Although ready to sail within a week, they remained at anchor in the harbor. The British frigate had returned to patrol along the coast.

Jon came on deck one morning and saw the three officers standing together on the quarterdeck alternately gazing at the sky and looking at the British blockade ship. The wind had begun blowing from the north, perhaps a little east of north. Captain Hamm made his decision.

"Mr. Clay, bring up the anchor. Set all fore-and-aft sails Mr. Blessing. It's time we went home."

The <u>Mary P.</u> cleared the harbor on larboard tack and sailed east, as close to the coast as they dared. The square-rigged British ship gave chase half heartedly. She couldn't come inshore after the <u>Mary P.</u> since the frigate could not sail as close to the wind as the American schooner and might well be blown onto the lee shore.

The <u>Mary P.</u> pulled away from the frigate and soon the British topsails dropped below the horizon.

"Bring her up a point Aaron," Captain Hamm commanded.

"Yes sir," the mate answered, and began bawling orders to the crew. The <u>Mary P.</u> now sailed east northeast.

"Will we turn north soon?" Rob Clay asked Captain Hamm.

"Not for a while, Rob. We'll see what the wind does."

As the day wore on, the wind changed direction, coming more from the northeast by east, forcing the schooner to sail a point south of east.

"We'll come about now Aaron. Make our course north by east" Captain Hamm said. "Hands to sheets," Mate Blessing roared. "Helm alee."

The ship turned through the wind and settled on her new course.

***

As the day wore on the wind swung farther east and freshened. Spray flew across the deck making rainbows in the bright sunshine. The schooner heeled in the freshening breeze and the leeward scuppers took water aboard. The <u>Mary P.</u> running on a reach now, "put her shoulder down" and flew for home.

CHAPTER SEVEN

As the schooner sailed into New England waters, Captain Hamm kept close to the shore, hugging the coast. He knew the area well from his smuggling days and sailed the <u>Mary P.</u> behind islands and through passages that few other captains would attempt, even if they knew about them.

The large number of small ports along the coast north of Boston stretched the British blockade to its limit and made it possible for merchant ships to reach port without any great risk if their officers knew the coast line well.

A small British frigate appeared out of the mist one morning, well off shore in deep water. Captain Hamm walked the quarterdeck as usual, showing no concern. The <u>Mary P.</u>, with her shallow draft sailed in water much too dangerous for the frigate. The British fired a cannon, but the ball fell well short.

"Do you recognize her, Aaron?" Captain Hamm asked the first mate.

"No sir. She must be new to this part of the coast."

"Won't be no trouble. As long as this onshore wind holds she won't come in too close."

Jon overheard the remark and asked, "Why won't they come in closer, Scotty."

"A square-rigged ship like that frigate can't sail as close to the wind as we can. If the wind shifts a bit or blows harder, we can sail clear of the shore. If that frigate came in closer, a wind shift would likely put her on the rocks. That's why that Frigate couldn't catch us when we left San Juan."

Jon nodded.

The frigate fired two more cannon shots that fell short.

The <u>Mary P.</u> approached a long narrow island, lying parallel to the coast. Captain Hamm sailed the ship between the island and the mainland shore as he had done many times.

***

Black granite boulders lined the sides of the narrow channel. The tall stately pine trees on both shores blocked the morning sun, leaving the ship in gloomy twilight. The <u>Mary P.</u> ghosted silently through the water, driven by the light breeze coming over the tree tops, so light it barely filled the topsails. Jon stood at his station near the shrouds with his arms folded across his chest, enjoying the peace and tranquility of the scene.

As they neared the end of the channel, a sudden shout rang out from the bow.

"Longboat comin' 'round the point!"

A boat carrying twenty or more men with a British officer

standing in the stern came toward them. The men pulling hard on their oars, and the officer shouting encouragement. A swivel gun mounted on the bow pointed at the Mary P.'s wheel. Captain Hamm gave no indication of excitement as he looked over the side, watching the boat as it grew nearer. If the British seamen could grapple the shrouds and climb aboard, the smaller crew of the Mary P. would not be able to fight them off.

"Mr. Blessing, pass out muskets and have the swivel guns brought up," Captain Hamm ordered.

They sailed on with no change of course as the British boat grew closer. Captain Hamm watched calmly until the British came within three boat lengths of the bow of his ship. Then he spoke in a conversational tone.

"Hard alee, Jeremy."

Jeremy Richer, the helmsman, put the helm over. The ship began to turn toward the British boat and would have hit it square on if the officer had not reacted quickly. The longboat met the ship with a glancing blow, the port side oars clattering against the Mary P. The oarsmen along that side tumbled backwards off their benches. Jon saw two of the oars floating in the water. Before the boat's crew could recover from the impact, the ship turned back on course again, and the stern swung to strike a harder blow. The British suffered no serious damage, but before they could recover, the ship moved past them.

Jon and the rest of the crew began cheering. They leaned over the rail to taunt their enemies. The British sailors sorted themselves out sooner than even Captain Hamm expected.

"Belay the shouting," Captain Hamm bellowed.

Jon realized that the danger had not ended. The boat would pursue them, and until they cleared the island to get the full force of the wind, the British might still take them. As if to emphasize the danger, the boat's swivel gun fired, and a hole appeared in the mainsail.

Three of the crew picked up muskets and began loading them. Jon knew that these old muskets would not be accurate at that distance. The British would stay out of range and pepper them with their swivel gun.

He darted down the companionway to the arms chest. Mr. Blessing struggled past him carrying one of the heavy swivel guns. Ryan followed behind carrying powder, shot, wadding, and a ramrod. Jon found the arms chest open and picked up his rifle, powder horn, and shot bag then ran back up to the quarterdeck.

At the taffrail he poured powder into the muzzle of his rifle, fumbled for a patch and ball in his shot bag, placed the patch over the muzzle and pressed the ball into the barrel. He pulled the wooden ram rod out from under the barrel and pushed the ball down against the powder charge.

A loud bang from the long boat and an instant later a small cannon ball struck the ship's hull below the rail.

Jon didn't flinch or pause. He withdrew the ram rod and held it and the rifle with his left hand. He primed and cocked the weapon. The English gunner rose to drop a ball down the muzzle of his swivel gun. Jon's rifle fired with its loud distinctive crack. When the smoke blew away, he saw the gunner lying in the bottom of the boat.

Before Jon finished reloading, the gunner had been lifted out of the way and another seaman replaced him. The swivel gun fired again. The ball went overhead, tearing another hole in the mainsail.

Mr. Blessing finished loading the <u>Mary P.</u>'s second swivel gun and aimed at the long boat. He stepped back and wiped the glowing linstock across the touch hole. The old untested swivel gun blew itself apart sending metal shards flying across the deck.

Mr. Blessing, blown across the quarterdeck, fell with blood gushing from his chest. Ryan lay under him, bloody but unhurt. Captain Hamm knelt on one knee, holding his bleeding scalp. Miraculously, the helmsman remained at the wheel, untouched. Jon calmly finished loading his rifle. He wiped his eyes, surprised that blood covered his hand. His rifle cracked again. One of the seamen fell over his oar, and the boat slued to larboard. The boat crew replaced the wounded man and continued the chase. Their swivel gun in the boat fired again, hitting the taffrail, sending splinters flying. Jon continued loading. He raised the rifle to his shoulder and aimed at the officer. For an instant, he saw the Tory who had led the Indians that terrible day, wearing his black coat and tricorn hat. He shook his head, steadied his aim and fired. The young officer fell backward over the stern of the boat. Alive, he floundered in the water. The boat crew backed their oars and one of them dove into the cold Atlantic to rescue their officer.

Jon wiped his eyes again and began to reload. Blood ran down his face and his hand slipped on the ram rod. His vision blurred and his eye stung as blood ran into it. Wiping his eye yet again, he continued loading.

Rob Clay came on deck with the second swivel gun and set it into its socket on the larboard rail.

Captain Hamm, stood by the wheel, looking at the long boat, one hand holding a bloody flap of skin away from his eyes so that he could see. Then he looked around the quarterdeck and saw the still body of the mate, with blood still oozing into the puddle around it. Glancing aloft at the sails, he judged their set and the wind direction.

"Belay that, Mr. Clay," the Captain shouted. "The wind is picking up. They won't get near us now. The other swivel gun did more harm to us than the British. Let's not risk another shot." He staggered and his body seemed to sag for a moment. Then he inhaled deeply and straightened his back.

"Get out your needles Rob. I need some stitching and so does the boy. I fear Mr. Blessing is beyond our care."

Jon wiped the blood off his hands onto his trousers and then, suddenly weary, leaned on his rifle. He stared blankly at the drops of crimson spattering on the deck. His bloody hands slipped down the barrel until he lay curled up on the deck, still clutching his father's long rifle.

CHAPTER EIGHT

The Mary P. glided sedately into Falmouth harbor on a crisp, clear December morning. She sailed under topsails only, both the main and foresails furled neatly. As the ship approached the pier, observers on the shore saw her topsails backed, and then they seemed to disappear as the crew hauled on clew lines and the topmen furled the sails. The ship lost way and came to a complete stop a few yards from her berth. The cold December breeze pushed the Mary P. sideways until she touched the pier.

Jon and Ryan stood in the foretop after the rest of the topmen had returned to the deck. They stood with their feet wide spread, arms folded across their chests, proud of their ship.

"Now that was as pretty a landing as I ever seen," observed Ryan. "But we'd best get back on deck. There's work to be done."

They raced each other down the shrouds, Ryan half a step ahead of Jon when they reached the deck.

Jon, happy and proud, both of his ship and himself, liked

working in the rigging, laying out over the yardarm, one of the most dangerous jobs on board. And he liked his shipmates, every one of them. Even the officers and the bosun, skillful sailors and firmly in command, but not harsh or cruel like some he heard of. For the first time in his life, he belonged to a group that respected his efforts and accepted him as an equal. Not truly a seasoned mariner, he knew that after another cruise or two he would be able to "hand, reef, and steer" as well as anyone. It seemed strange, even to Jon, that he took more pride in the skills he had acquired than in his action against the British long boat.

More than anything else, Jon treasured the moment when one of the crew had called him "Sawdust" and the bosun had snarled, "The man's name is Jon."

Before the Mary P. entered the harbor Captain Hamm had talked with a fishing boat whose owner swore that no British ships had been seen along the coast near Falmouth for the last week. When the ship had neared the dock, workmen appeared and the crew began removing hatch covers before the Mary P. had made fast to the pier. The cargo disappeared from the hold into secret places in the surrounding forest and even to the islands in Casco Bay. With the hold empty, no one could accuse them of failing to pay the tariff on the goods they brought into the port. After Mowart's attack on the town, none of the remaining Tory sympathizers would dare to report them, but if an unexpected British warship appeared there could be trouble.

***

Jon still wore a bandage but his wound showed no sign of

infection and had almost healed. When Rob Clay, now First Mate, had changed the bandage that morning he told Jon that he might be able to leave it uncovered in a day or two. Jon, Ryan and Scotty went ashore as soon as they completed their duties. Ryan and Scotty stopped at the first tavern they saw, but Jon walked on to the Morgan home. Mrs. Sloan answered when he knocked.

"Good heavens," she cried. "It's Jon. Come in and sit down. Oh, it's so good to see you."

"Jon," Faith cried out as she came into the kitchen. She ran to him and threw her arms around his neck, pressing herself against him. Then she withdrew suddenly, her face red with embarrassment.

"I hope I didn't hurt your head," she said, partly to cover her own confusion.

"No, you didn't hurt it. It's about healed in fact. Not much to it."

It pleased Jon that the wound had not healed too quickly. Without the bandage it didn't look as impressive.

"I heard you fought a whole boat full of Englishmen and saved the ship," Faith said. "You're so brave! It must have been so . . . glorious."

Jon stood silent for a moment, staring blankly at Faith.

"It wasn't like that at all," Jon said softly, thinking of Mr. Blessing lying on the deck in a pool of blood. Captain Hamm holding his torn scalp out of his eyes while he commanded the ship, and Ryan, lying unconscious under Mr. Blessing's body. He couldn't think of any words to tell how he felt, so he shook his head and looked at the floor.

Mrs. Sloan, more perceptive than Faith, broke the silence.

"Here, let me get you something to eat. Sailors are always hungry."

Jon, now hardened to shipboard food, had forgotten about Mrs. Sloan's cooking. As he wolfed down food better than any he had tasted in many weeks, his high spirits returned. Faith left the kitchen. Jon didn't notice her absence.

While relating a description of the sights of San Juan, he stopped in mid-sentence. Faith had returned to the kitchen wearing her best Sunday dress. Jon stared at her, open mouthed, and then tried to continue his conversation. He stumbled over his words, and, worst of all, he saw Mrs. Sloan watching him with a knowing smile on her face.

Faith had grown up during his absence.

Perhaps the changes had begun before Jon left and he hadn't noticed. No matter how or when, she had become a beautiful young woman.

Mrs. Sloan left the room, still smiling to herself. Jon tried not to stare at Faith. Her dress, in the fashion of the day, had a full, ankle length skirt and a snug fitting bodice. Jon remembered the dress. Now Faith filled it to overflowing. When she leaned over the table Jon stared at her breasts, pushing themselves over the top of her dress. She seemed to take no notice of Jon's awed silence and continued to work and talk. As she carried dishes to the cupboard, her hip brushed against him. While cleaning the table, she casually leaned against his arm and shoulder. Jon impulsively pulled her into his lap and kissed her fervently. Faith's arms went around his neck and they kissed again and again.

"Oh dear," they heard Mrs. Sloan exclaim from the parlor.

Faith leaped up from Jon's lap a moment before the door flew open and Mrs. Sloan rushed into the kitchen.

"Mr. Morgan just came in the front door. He hates you since you left with your rifle. He'll be so angry if he finds you here. We should have warned you earlier."

They pushed him out the back door and waited to see if Mr. Morgan called for anything.

***

Jon walked back toward the docks, confused, angry, and depressed. Mr. Morgan had driven him away from Faith simply by entering the front door of his home.

Jon went aboard the Mary P. and sat on a hatch cover, staring across the harbor, deep in thought. He began to realize that he had no control over his life. At sea he had to obey the captain's and mates' orders, even when they seemed pointless. Now on shore his friends ordered him away because of the fear of Morgan. He sat in the cold evening air, alone and unhappy, his earlier buoyant satisfaction forgotten.

***

When Scotty returned to the ship that evening, he found Jon lying on his bunk staring at the planking above his head.

"Did you see your friends?" Scotty asked.

"Yes," Jon mumbled, not looking away from the overhead.

Scotty sat on his own bunk, across the narrow aisle.

"Weren't they happy to see you?" he asked.

Jon didn't answer.

After a long silence, Scotty continued, "It happened to me when I went back to see my family once. My brother thought I wanted to take half of the farm away from him. He near ran me off." He laughed ruefully.

Jon raised his head to look at Scotty briefly.

"How did you feel about that?" he asked.

Scotty didn't answer.

After a long silence Jon said, "I guess you had it worse than I just did. Faith and Mrs. Sloan seemed glad to see me, but they ran me off when Morgan came home. Said he would be mad as hell if he saw me there."

Scotty stared back at the deck for a moment.

"A mug or two of ale might be what we need, Jon. It's the best thing in the world when you're feelin' low."

Scotty's understanding and companionship roused Jon from his indulgent self-pity.

"A mug of ale would taste good right now. Good company would be welcome too."

They left the ship and walked toward the tavern at the end of the pier.

***

In the failing daylight, neither of them saw the two men emerge from the shadows. Scotty heard their foot steps and half turned. He received a sharp blow to his knee from a wooden club. A blow to Jon's head by the second man left him lying stunned on the ground. Scotty regained his feet and, in spite of the terrible pain in his knee, charged at the two men. One of the attackers knocked him down with his club and kicked him when he tried to get up.

Jon groggily tried to get to his knees and they beat him down again. The attackers mercilessly beat them until they lost consciousness. The two men dragged the limp bodies into the shadows and roughly searched for any valuables, then threw them into a wheelbarrow and trundled them over the cobblestone streets to the jail.

Chapter Nine

Jon regained consciousness lying on the floor of a dirty cell. Scotty, awake and in pain, had tried to make Jon more comfortable and had retied the bandage on his head.

"Where are we?" Jon asked.

"We're in jail. They arrested us for some reason," Scotty replied.

Jon tried to sit up but collapsed with a groan. Bruises covered his aching body.

Scotty helped him as he raised himself to the bench along the wall.

Morning sunlight, shining through a small window high on the wall, provided feeble light. In the gloom, Jon saw that they shared the cell with two other men.

Neither of their cell mates had bathed for weeks, and the stench made Jon's eyes water. The two men sat staring at Jon and Scotty for several minutes. One of them, a large man with bulging muscular arms, wore an evil toothless grin. The other, a smaller, ferret-like man had a lopsided face caused by a scar running diagonally across his nose and one eye brow.

"Do you know why they arrested us?" Jon asked their cell mates. "Did anyone say anything when they brought us in?"

"Dragged you in you mean," the big man answered. Both of the strangers snickered.

Jon and Scotty sat on their bench trying to ignore the stares of their dirty, evil-looking cell mates. They talked enough to compare injuries. Both were sore and bruised but at least no bones had been broken.

The small man with the scarred face overheard their conversation. "Them Decker boys is too smart to break bones," he said. "They like to beat up on people, but they might get into trouble if anybody got hurt too bad. They're careful. That's why the Sheriff made 'em deputies."

***

Near noon, judging by the angle of the sunlight coming through the single window, a familiar voice roused Scotty and Jon from restless sleep. Captain Hamm, standing outside the bars berated their jailor in a loud voice. Beside him stood Ryan Flynn.

"Who ordered the arrest of my crewmen?" Captain Hamm thundered.

"They was arrested fer debt sir," the jailor answered hurriedly. "Mr. Morgan says Jon Weaver here owes him for room and board for near four months."

"That's nonsense. Why are both of them being held?"

"T'other one interfered with the arrest sir," the jailor said, whining now.

While Captain Hamm continued to browbeat the jailor, Ryan Flynn walked around to the side of the cell near the other two prisoners.

"Well, I'll be damned. It's Groot Hall. Looks like they caught up with you again."

"I ain't got nothin' to say to you Flynn."

Ryan's arm shot between the cell bars and roughly pulled the little man against them.

"Tell me about how those lads got so beat up," Ryan hissed into the man's face.

"I don't know nothin' about it," Groot quavered.

A knife with a long thin blade appeared in Ryan's hand, the tip touching Groot's throat.

"Witt and Paul Decker done it," Groot said quickly. Ryan's knife disappeared. "They like to beat up people, and the Sheriff lets 'em do it as long as nobody gets hurt too bad."

Ryan released him and nodded.

"What are you in here for? Did they get you for crimping that boy down in Boston?"

"Damn you Ryan, don't talk so loud. Nobody knows about that 'round here."

"You mean the lad's family don't know you sold him to that British frigate that used to . . . ."

"Ryan, I could get my neck stretched if the militia heard you," Groot whined.

"Oh don't worry Groot. I can keep a secret if I want to. By the way, these boys are good shipmates of mine. One of them saved my ship and my life on the last voyage. It would bother me a heap if they got treated bad in the jail here."

"Nothin' will happen to them here," Groot said hastily. "I'll see to it."

"Thanks for the help, Groot. Hope you get out of jail soon."

Captain Hamm had stopped browbeating the jailor and now spoke to his two crewmen.

"You both have a lot of bruises and scrapes on you. Were you in some sort of tavern brawl?"

"No sir," Scotty said in a loud clear voice. "We was just walkin' along the street when they jumped us. That's about all we know."

Captain Hamm looked at Jon and Scotty with flinty eyes.

"I believe what you said, but heaven help you if you're lyin' to me. We'll be back to get you out of here."

***

"I hate to leave two of our shipmates in that jail with those scum," said Captain Hamm as he and Ryan walked back to the <u>Mary P.</u>

"I know one of them," Ryan said. "He used to make a few dollars by crimping. He sold one young boy to a British frigate. Then he found out the boy came from a rich family in Boston. The family's been looking for the lad ever since. He doesn't want to risk me telling anyone about it. He'll see that nothing rough happens to Jon or Scotty."

They continued to walk along the pier.

"I'd sure like to get my hands on those deputies. They're mean bastards," Ryan commented.

"Yes they are," Captain Hamm agreed.

They walked a few more steps.

"I noticed the <u>Seraphim</u> anchored in the harbor," Captain Hamm commented for no apparent reason.

"Yes sir?"

"Her master is Captain Barr. Good seaman, but he has a hard time keeping a crew. Even uses the cat sometimes. They call her a hell ship. That's just talk around the waterfront you understand. It takes a real tough man to take that kind of treatment. I'd guess those deputies might think their pretty tough. I expect Captain Barr would like to have a couple of good men."

"If someone paid Groot Hall's fine, he might be persuaded to get back into crimping." Ryan said.

Captain Hamm handed Ryan a handful of coins.

Chapter Ten

The crew of a sailing ship make up a close knit community, closer than any small town. Jon's experience with Mr. Morgan had become common knowledge to everyone on board within a month after Jon joined the crew. Mate Clay was aware of the reputation of both Danny Pound and Christian Morgan and suspected that they had taken advantage of Jon's naivety. He began searching the water front for someone who knew the whereabouts of Danny Pound. He found him living with his sister in her home. Danny, sick and feeble, had never recovered from his wounds.

"Yes, I remember Jon," Danny wheezed in response to Rob Clay's question. "One of the best workers I ever had. I never paid him for any of the work he did. I give it all to Christian Morgan instead. Paid Morgan quite a bit over the months before my cutter got blown up. Claimed he took out room and board and give Jon the rest."

After a long pause, Rob started to speak, but Danny began

talking again.

"It bothers me, what I did. Jon's a good boy and a hard worker. I should'a treated him better."

"What did you do, Danny?"

"Well I guess it don't matter now. Back then I thought I needed more money than I was makin' fishin'. So when I found out how Morgan kept back all of the boy's wages, twice what room and board would'a cost in a good roomin' house, I made Morgan give some of it to me. Told him that I would spread the word around town if he didn't."

He chuckled softly, and then a fit of coughing racked his body. When he recovered, he wiped his mouth with a back of his hand and said in a hoarse whisper, "Think what his churchified friends would'a thought." He smiled to himself. "They never would'a had nothing to do with him if they knew about it, you see."

"Danny needs some rest now." His sister had entered the room. "He tires so easily," she said.

"I'll be back tomorrow morning to talk some more Danny."

Danny nodded with closed eyes.

***

Rob returned the next morning accompanied by a young man named Henry August. Henry August, tall, muscular and always well-dressed, had a reputation as a fiery patriot. To his great disappointment he could not serve in the continental army because of a deformed foot. He worked for the law firm of Cood, Hall, and Mitchel, the firm that did all of Mr. Paget's legal work.

When they arrived they found Danny sitting in a rocking

chair wrapped in a heavy quilt, even though the room seemed uncomfortably warm to his visitors.

Henry questioned him gently for an hour or more. Then he wrote out a formal statement and read it to Danny.

Danny nodded as he listened.

Henry wrote two copies of the statement and Danny signed them with a shaky scrawl. After the signing, he sat back in his rocking chair, closed his eyes, and fell asleep with a contented smile on his face.

***

Henry August knew of Christian Morgan's reputation. Morgan would not give in easily. No laws had been broken. However, the lawyer knew, as Danny had, the effect the statement would have on local society. Morgan hoped to remarry soon, and the prospective bride and her family, as well as all of Falmouth's quality people, would be shocked to learn of his treatment of a young orphan boy, a boy who now had the status of a local hero.

Rob and Captain Hamm presented a copy of Danny's statement to Mr. Morgan that same day.

Morgan read the document and looked at them with distaste.

"There is nothing illegal about this. . . ah . . . situation. I see no reason to waste more of my time. Good day," he said coldly.

"What would the good people of Falmouth think of you if they knew about this?" Captain Hamm asked.

"Are you threatening me?" Morgan's face turned red.

"Yes," Captain Hamm replied firmly.

Mr. Morgan sat back in his chair. Then he arranged his face in a simpering smile.

"Surely men of good will can reach a satisfactory agreement about this matter," Mr. Morgan oozed. "There is no need for this to go any further. The boy has no assets of any worth, so I'll withdraw the charges."

"And you will sign this paper saying that Jon owes you nothing." Captain Hamm said, laying another document on Mr. Morgan's desk.

Mr. Morgan's face turned a deep shade of red, but he signed.

The jailor released Jon within the hour. Scotty remained in jail another day, charged with resisting arrest. The jailor released him when the two deputies could not be found to testify.

***

The <u>Seraphim</u> sailed on the morning tide, her captain, Jericho Barr, well pleased with the addition of two strong healthy crewmen.

***

The weak rays of the setting sun did nothing to warm the two figures on the deck of the <u>Mary P.</u> Jon and Scotty stood leaning against the starboard rail staring across the bay, weary and bored, but reluctant to retire to the forecastle.

"Staying aboard again tonight lads?"

Rob Clay had just stepped aboard, returning from his own afternoon ashore.

"Yes sir," Jon replied, wincing as he pushed himself away from the rail. "We're both stove up a bit."

"I don't suppose you could see your friends anyway." Rob commented.

"No one from this ship can get near Morgan's house without being arrested for trespassing." Jon smiled. "He's mighty touchy. We're grateful to you and Captain Hamm for helping us, Mr. Clay."

"We're shipmates Jon. Of course we helped you. You saved our ship from the longboat, but we would have helped you anyway. We take care of our own."

Jon thought again about how his shipmates had worked to protect him from Mr. Morgan and exacted revenge on the two deputies who had attacked him and Scotty. He belonged to a ship and a crew. He wasn't alone anymore.

Chapter Eleven

Rob Clay had been promoted to First mate when the <u>Mary P.</u> sailed on the next voyage. The second mate berth was left open.

After the bombardment by the British ships and the incident with the English frigate Mr. Paget decided to move his shipping business to Boston. His chandlery in Falmouth had been destroyed, and furthermore, Boston had a better port for his business. His other ship, the <u>Princess</u>, sailed to Boston with the Paget family and the ship's stores that had been salvaged from the Paget warehouse. The voyages to San Juan became a steady pattern with only minor variations caused by weather and the British blockade.

When ashore in Boston, Jon frequently saw Todd Paget, either on the wharf or near the ship chandlery, but they seldom had any real conversations. Jon's experience as an able seaman made him seem older and more mature, and after a few minutes of conversation, both of them seemed to run out of things to say.

Between cruises, Jon spent his days ashore in Boston in the company of Scotty and Ryan. They made an odd trio. Scotty and Jon, young and carefree, were both tall and muscular in contrast with Ryan, physically smaller, much older, more thoughtful, and quiet. Ryan had never learned to read and write, but his common sense and maturity had steered the two younger men away from many potential troubles along the rough waterfronts of Boston and of the ports throughout the Caribbean. He berated his two friends if he found them drinking too much and tried to keep them away from the slatternly women Scotty sometimes sought, and who had become strangely interesting to Jon.

Ryan had no education other than that of an able seaman, but he recognized Jon's intelligence and abilities. Although he liked the life of a seaman for himself he didn't want his friend to waste his life as a common seaman "before the mast".

Ryan remembered that Jon sometimes watched Captain Hamm and Rob Clay using a quadrant and had asked both Ryan and Scotty about it.

"They's shootin' the sun," Ryan had told them.

"It has somethin' to do with navigatin'," Scotty had said.

Neither man knew or cared about navigation. However, Ryan saw that Jon wanted to learn more about all aspects of seamanship.

On their second day of their next voyage out of Boston, Ryan surprised Jon by pulling a book out of his ditty bag.

"What are you going to do with a book, Ryan? It ain't going to do you any good when the wind pipes up and you're laying out over a yard arm."

Ryan tossed the book to Jon who caught it easily.

"Read it. You might learn something, though it don't seem too likely."

Taken by surprise, Jon wondered what to do with the book. He couldn't disappoint Ryan, so he did begin to read in order to avoid appearing ungrateful. He found that the problems of navigation interested him more than he had expected. He began to realize that the earth was truly a globe and that the elevation of the sun above the horizon had great significance to a navigator. Jon enthusiastically shared his new knowledge with both Ryan and Scotty. The two men listened politely but could make neither heads nor tails of Jon's explanations.

Finding a ship's position on the trackless empty ocean proved to be a fascinating challenge to Jon. On the following voyage, he studied the book when his duties allowed. Ryan chuckled with pleasure when he saw how intently Jon read and reread the book. On some occasions Jon asked Mate Clay for help. Life aboard the schooner could be tedious after reaching the open sea. Helping Jon provided Rob with a welcome diversion.

Rob occasionally loaned Jon his quadrant and allowed him to "shoot the sun" to find their position. His first attempt showed that they had sailed into the mountains of Cuba. With practice and instruction from Rob, Jon's navigation improved. When the weather didn't allow sun sights, Rob taught Jon the basic methods of "dead reckoning". By the end of the voyage Jon had become competent in the use of the quadrant and with the calculations needed to find their position with reasonable accuracy.

***

Before they left for their next cruise, Mr. Paget bought four more swivel guns for the ship, more muskets, some cutlasses and a few pistols, and he doubled the size of the crew. Mr. Paget also gave Captain Hamm a document that pleased both of them. The Mary P. now sailed under a Letter of Marque signed by the governor of Massachusetts.

On impulse Jon climbed the ladder to the quarterdeck and eagerly asked Rob, "Does that mean we're goin' Privateerin'?"

"No Jon, it doesn't," Rob replied with a touch of exasperation. "It means we can take prizes if they fall into our laps, and if we defend ourselves against British ships we won't be called pirates. Privateers can make a lot of money, but they can lose a lot too. We still make our money by carrying cargo. Now get the hell off the quarterdeck."

Jon went down the ladder mumbling apologies. The answer disappointed him. He had heard many tales about privateers that had captured British merchant ships in the last few months.

Jon had hoped that he might have the opportunity to exact some revenge on the British. Memories of his family and their horrible deaths and the white man who led the Indians remained in his mind. In spite of all of his new found interests, his hatred for the English had not faded, and the thought of someday firing a swivel gun loaded with musket balls into a crowded quarterdeck of a British ship had become an enjoyable fantasy, second only to thoughts and dreams of Faith.

As they sailed east and south from Boston, Captain Hamm expended a considerable amount of expensive powder and shot training the crew in the use of the weapons. He named Jon as ship's gunner because of his proven skill with his rifle. Jon had never fired a swivel gun, so Ryan instructed the crew on loading and firing the swivels. Captain Hamm made Jon responsible for care of all the weapons, including the muskets and pistols.

Jon drilled the crew on loading and firing their weapons. Empty bottles or pieces of wood dropped over the side made excellent targets.

Captain Hamm watched Jon as he directed the crew in loading and firing pistols and muskets. Men over twice his age obeyed him without hesitation. Jon had potential.

***

On their return from the Caribbean, they sailed into the heavily traveled shipping lanes east of New York, hoping to take a prize.

The sun hadn't cleared the horizon one morning when the cry, "Sail ho!" roused Jon from his bunk. When he reached the deck, Jon found the crew in animated conversation looking toward a bit of white showing above the horizon.

"What can you see Ryan?" Captain Hamm called out.

Ryan, from his position in the maintop, shouted back, "She's a brig. Headed west. Not a navy ship by the looks of her rig."

"We'll close with her then. Mr. Clay, bring us up a point."

The distant spot of white grew larger as the day went on. It grew into a sail and the sail grew into a small ship, a brig as Ryan had said. The slow merchant ship could not hope to escape from the Mary P., and before mid-day they came within a half mile of her. The brig appeared to be unarmed, and flew an American flag. The Mary P., with her swivel guns loaded and manned, closed with her.

"This is the American ship Mary P. We sail with a Letter of Marque. Heave to so we can board you," Captain Hamm shouted through the speaking trumpet.

"We're an American ship too. There is no need for you to board us," came the reply.

"What port do you sail from?"

"We're out of Portland," came the reply.

"If that ship was from Portland I'd know her," Captain Hamm said. "Ryan, fire your gun across her bow."

The swivel gun barked, not much louder than a musket, but the brig hove to and the American flag came down.

"They knew we would get them sooner or later," Ryan said. "No sense in fighting and getting a lot of people hurt or killed."

Captain Hamm sent Rob and six men over to the British ship. Jon tried to go with them even though his name had not been called. Captain Hamm sternly told him to stay aboard the Mary P.

A few minutes after boarding the brig, Rob hailed the schooner.

"She's English all right Captain. The cargo is mostly muskets, powder, and shot. There are some swivel guns too, but the crew is so small that they couldn't have fought us."

"Do you have enough hands to take her into Boston?" Captain Hamm shouted back.

"Yes we do, but I'd feel better if you took the officers with you."

Captain Hamm ordered the officers of the prize transferred to the Mary P. Captain Hamm and Rob both knew that the officers of several prizes had led attempts to retake their ships.

The two ships sailed in consort into Boston Harbor.

A rough estimate of the value of the prize ship and her cargo led to a flurry of activity. Members of the Mary P.'s crew, including some who could scarcely sign their names, began calculating to the penny how much their share of the prize would be.

***

The disposal of the prize would take weeks, but Jon borrowed money from Mr. Paget against his share so that he could buy a few necessary items. New clothing, seaman's boots, a set of oilskins, and a new seaman's knife. He didn't need anything else. A sailor's life is a simple one.

The Mary P. would be ready to sail in four days. With extra money in his pocket, he decided to stay ashore at an inexpensive inn. After the first night ashore, he realized that his bunk on the Mary P. had apparently grown shorter over the months. Sleeping in a warm dry bed with his legs straight seemed shamefully luxurious.

***

Late the following afternoon Jon stepped out of the front door of the inn in time to catch sight of a shiny new open carriage. He paid no more attention to it until it had passed him. A man and woman rode in it. The man stared at him, his face contorted in hatred. With a start, Jon recognized Christian Morgan.

The woman sitting next to him wore a pretty dress similar to some that Jon had seen in shop windows. He knew that it must have cost a year's pay for a sailor. The woman looked at Jon with a start of recognition and quickly turned away. The carriage went around the corner and out of sight before Jon realized that he had seen Faith Crawford.

The sight of Faith disturbed Jon more than he would ever have expected. She hadn't nodded in his direction, though he knew she had seen him. He thought of their hurried kisses in the kitchen of Morgan's home and her "new" appearance. Most of all, he felt betrayed that she traveled in the company of Mr. Morgan. Jon walked the streets near the inn hoping for another glimpse of her. The carriage had evidently left the area. Jon didn't see it again.

Ryan and Scotty met Jon that night to investigate the delights of Boston once more. In his melancholy mood, Jon preferred to return to his room early. He studied his navigation textbook for a time, but he soon lost interest and went to bed, still pondering his strange emotions.

In two years of sailing on the Mary P. he had grown taller and stronger. Now considered an able bodied seaman, he expected to someday earn a berth as mate and later captain on a vessel similar to the Mary P. Now the prospect didn't seem as attractive as it had only yesterday.

When Indians murdered his family back in the Mohawk Valley, he swore that he would avenge them. So far he had done nothing but wound a British officer and learn the trade of a seaman. He had more money now than his father had ever had, but it didn't bring any satisfaction.

Jon had acquired the seaman's ability to fall asleep under the most adverse conditions, but tonight he tossed restlessly.

Perhaps if he joined one of the heavily armed Privateers that sailed out of Boston, he would feel better about himself. Taking prizes as they did caused great damage to Britain's commerce. The cargos they captured supplied General Washington's army and deprived the Red Coats of needed weapons and ammunition. He might even gain considerable wealth sailing on a privateer. Then he could go back to Falmouth and take Faith away with him. He closed his eyes, but the vision of Faith in the carriage with Morgan would not leave him, except to be replaced by the memory of her hastened kisses in the kitchen of Morgan's home. Her lips soft against his. Her body pressed against him.

Jon fell into a restless sleep. He did not hear the door open or the quiet footsteps crossing the room. He dreamed of Faith Crawford, her kisses and her warm soft body. In his dream, he put his arms around her. Slowly he became aware that the dream had become reality. Kneeling on the floor next to his bed, she held his head tenderly while she kissed him again.

"Oh Jon," she whispered. "I've missed you so much."

Jon pushed the blanket aside, pulled her into the bed and

kissed her passionately.

She pulled away slightly.

"We haven't much time Jon," she said.

She rose to her feet, opened her dress and slid her arms out of the sleeves. She dropped her garments to the floor and stood naked before him.

Jon lay in bed watching her, scarcely daring to breathe. Faith knelt on the bed and leaned over him moving her body so that her breasts brushed against his bare chest. She laughed when she heard Jon's gasp, then kissed him again and pressed her body against his. They held each other and Jon modestly pulled the blanket over them.

***

They lay in each other's arms, their passion finally exhausted. Faith idly ran her fingers through the hair on his chest.

"You have a lot more hair on your chest now," she said.

"How do you know that?" Jon asked, chuckling as he spoke.

Faith laughed softly.

"Once I watched you taking a bath. Mrs. Sloan caught me and gave me a real whippin'."

She laughed again.

"It was worth it though."

In spite of the experiences of the last hour, Jon felt his face growing red.

"Will you come back tomorrow?"

"No, I can't. We're going to a dinner and won't be home

until late."

She glanced quickly at Jon, hoping he didn't realize the implications of what she had said.

"Can't we see each other before I sail again?"

"No Jon. Mr. Morgan would be angry if he found out. He hates you. He thinks you got the best of him and then made him look like a fool when word of what he did to you got out. He wanted to marry again. The woman broke it off."

"I'll be back in Boston after our next cruise."

Faith laughed with delight.

"I'll see if I can get away from the house. We could sleep together again then."

Jon couldn't help but smile.

"We haven't done much sleepin' so far. I don't expect to do any more the next time."

Faith laughed too. She stood up beside the bed. Jon watched as she dressed herself.

"I'd better get back. If Mr. Morgan wakes up early, I want to be at work so he won't suspect anything."

She kissed him and went out into the darkened hallway.

Jon sat on the edge of the bed thinking about the evening. He heard a light carriage stop at the curb below his window. He looked out in time to see Faith open the door and enter it. She drew the curtains over the carriage windows.

Troubling questions lingered in the back of Jon's mind. How could she afford a hired carriage, and how did she pay for that expensive dress? Why would she ever be going to Portsmouth with Morgan? He could not bring himself to explore those questions too deeply.

Chapter Twelve

When the Mary P. sailed on her next voyage to the Carribean, she carried an even larger crew, and the muzzles of two four-pound cannons protruded through gun ports on each side. Mere four-pound "Pop guns" according to Ryan, but much more powerful than the swivel guns. The first day out of port they sighted two British Navy ships. With a favorable wind, the Mary P. easily outran them. Captain Hamm commanded Jon to start training the gun crews. Ryan had experience with guns on the British frigate he had been pressed into, and with his help, Jon began training the gunners.

"It's best to have the powder sewn into bags," Ryan explained. "Less chance of getting too much or too little powder into the gun."

Jon asked for and received permission to have it done.

The drills were a welcome diversion for the crew, but after a week at sea, the hands grew restless and bored. Heaving the heavy guns in and out soon lost its novelty. Their interest revived when the drills included loading powder and shot and firing at targets. Firing the guns, even mere four-pounders, was a wonderful diversion. A raft made of empty kegs lashed together served as a target. The Mary P. sailed by the raft, keeping it on her starboard side fifty yards away. The two starboard guns fired and spouts of water showed that the shots had missed. Then the schooner came about and ran past the target on the port side. The port side guns had no better luck than the starboard side. Ryan patiently coached the gun captains and then tried again. Finally, the target had been smashed into bits and the guns secured for the day.

The following day they fired at one hundred yards and tried to reload and fire a second time before the ship sailed too far past.

As the crew of the number one gun attempted to reload quickly, Enoch Pierce dropped the four-pound ball and watched as it rolled through the gun port into the sea.

"Yer supposed to shoot the damn thing, Enoch, not throw it," shouted William Jakes from the number three gun.

"Put a stopper on yer mouth er I'll throw one down yer gullet," Enoch replied.

Delighted laughter came from the number three gun crew as they fired, even though they missed the target by a good ten yards.

The daily drills continued until the speed and accuracy improved to the point that Ryan grudgingly allowed that they were better than most merchant ships.

The <u>Mary P.</u> could fight and beat an armed merchant ship, but in a fight with even a small navy sloop or cutter, their only chance of surviving would be their speed and sailing qualities.

***

The schooner returned to Boston Harbor with a cargo of coffee and sugar. Faith again came to Jon's room. Their love making, more passionate than the first night, left them both exhausted. When Faith began to dress, Jon felt empty and depressed.

"It would be nice if you could stay over night, Faith. I hate to see you leave."

"Yes, I'd like to stay here too. You know I can't. If Morgan ever found out about us, he might sell my contract to someone clear out in the frontier. Then we'd never see each other."

"I have a good bit of prize money yet," Jon said to Faith. "Maybe I could buy your indenture contract from Mr. Morgan."

Even as he said it he realized it would be impossible.

"Morgan would never sell my contract to you, Jon. You know that." She smiled sadly. "Let's enjoy ourselves as long as we can."

***

Falmouth had become less prosperous since the blockade had become tighter. The <u>Mary P.</u> had been able to sail in and out of the port only because of her speed and Captain Hamm's knowledge of the coast and the islands close by. But Boston had become the most important port in New England and shipping there had prospered.

Sailing into Boston on their return from the Caribbean was an interesting experience for Jon. He had seen the city only briefly when he passed through on his way to Falmouth years ago. The size of the port compared with Falmouth and the number of ships loading and unloading cargo amazed him. Scotty and Ryan laughed at his reaction.

The ship found a berth near a new warehouse with the name 'Paget' painted on a sign above the door.

When the three men went ashore they found many more interesting sights than Falmouth had to offer. Ryan and Scotty were happy and excited, but Jon knew that he might never see Faith again. He didn't share his friend's excitement.

Two days before they sailed Captain Hamm called Jon to his cabin.

"Jon," the Captain began, turning toward him without rising from his chair, "I've watched you for a long time now. You've learned more about seamanship and navigation in these two years than many men learn in a lifetime. You are young, but men are willing to take orders from you. They will follow when you lead. As of now, you are Second Mate of the Mary P."

He looked at Jon expectantly. Jon stood open mouthed, too surprised to respond. Captain Hamm waited a moment to reply.

"Well, you want it don't you?" he snapped.

"Yes sir," Jon said loudly.

"Then move your dunnage aft and see Rob about dividing the hands into watches."

***

They sailed the next morning, heading for the Caribbean again. Jon stood on the quarterdeck trying to look stern and competent. Ryan watched him with a proud, smug, smile on his face.

***

A British frigate spotted them on the third day out, and another on the fifth day. The schooner, sailing to windward, ran away from the square-rigged ships.

"They seem to be a bit more active than last year," Captain Hamm observed. "It might be interesting when we return."

***

The <u>Mary P.</u> sailed to the island of St. Eustatious, a longer and more dangerous voyage than the earlier ones. Gun drill every Monday and Thursday morning helped break the monotony of the long weeks at sea. At St. Eustatious they loaded a cargo of arms and ammunition, the life blood of the revolution. They waited in the harbor for four weeks until a tropical storm blew the blockading ships away from the harbor entrance. The <u>Mary P.</u> sailed before they could return.

***

"We'll tack now Mr. Weaver," said Captain Hamm.

"Hands to sheets," Jon shouted in his best quarterdeck voice, and Seamen ran to their stations. "Helm alee," he bawled and the <u>Mary P.</u> turned through the wind smoothly. Her sails filled and she heeled over on the opposite tack.

"That's the fourth time we tacked this morning," muttered Scotty to himself. "We're wasting time. If any ships was around, we would've seen them by now."

The <u>Mary P.</u> had been keeping station north and east of New York for the past three days in hopes of sighting a British merchant ship.

That afternoon the wind died away to light puffs. Just before the watch changes a fog settled on them, and after sunset, the visibility had been reduced to no more than one hundred feet. The fog muffled all sound. The crew worked quietly, intimidated by the silence. Captain Hamm ordered that there would be no conversation above a whisper. It wouldn't do to warn some British ship, either merchantman or warship, of their presence.

As the sun rose the next morning, the fog had become even thicker. Jon stood on the quarterdeck listening for any sound that might carry through the silent, wooly mass.

Out of nowhere, Ryan appeared at his side, pulling at his sleeve.

Jon started to curse him for leaving the maintop, but he saw Ryan put a finger to his lips.

"What is it?" he said in a low voice.

"There's a big merchant ship just to windward of us Jon. I saw her masts above the fog. They didn't see us. Nobody on watch. She can't be a navy ship."

Jon motioned for Ryan to follow him, and walked across the quarterdeck to Captain Hamm and Mate Clay. He explained Ryan's sighting, and, for a moment, they all stood staring and straining to hear any sound. If Ryan's judgment was sound, they might be able to take the ship by surprise and capture her. If Ryan had made a mistake, the <u>Mary P.</u> might be attacked at any moment. The tension on the quarterdeck passed throughout the ship. The entire crew became aware of the situation. They all stood stock still, staring to windward and listening. The watch changed, and even the men coming on deck kept silent. The dead silence continued for many minutes, and then the creaking of a block and a low harsh voice could be heard through the fog.

"Watch out damn you, you near knocked me over."

Sharp curses followed.

"Quiet, damn your eyes. If this was a proper King's Navy ship, you'd be flogged. Now be silent."

A merchantman all right, but how big and how well armed?

Captain Hamm whispered orders to Jon and Rob. They ran silently down to the deck and spoke to the gun crews, already at their stations. The guns were loaded and could be fired within seconds. The gunners quietly stood ready, blowing gently on the ends of their slowmatch. Jon and Rob silently passed out cutlasses.

Captain Hamm raised his speaking trumpet. "This is the United States Ship <u>Massachusetts</u>, twenty guns. Identify yourself before I open fire," roared Captain Hamm.

The gun ports flew open and the guns rumbled out on both sides. The guns on the leeward side ran back in and then out again until it sounded like triple their number.

After a moment of stunned silence from the other ship they heard a stream of curses.

"Strike your colors or I'll commence firing," Captain Hamm

shouted.

"Don't fire" a panicked voice cried. "I'll strike."

"Stand by for a prize crew to come aboard."

Jon, Scotty, and four men, armed with pistols and cutlasses, rowed across to the invisible ship. They hooked onto the main chains and climbed aboard. Jon walked briskly to the quarterdeck, pistol in one hand and a cutlass in the other. The English captain stared at him blankly.

"You're not an officer," he said. "I should at least be allowed to surrender to an officer of your navy."

Jon raised his pistol.

"You struck your colors. Order your men to lay down their arms."

Muttering to himself about the outrageous behavior of the colonials, the captain handed Jon his pistol. With the crew secured below deck, Jon sent the officers back to the Mary P.

The prize carried four six-pounders. She could have given the Mary P. a hot time if her captain had decided to fight.

"Ahoy Jon," Captain Hamm bellowed.

"Yes sir," Jon bellowed back.

The ships drifted closer together and became visible to each other.

"What ship?"

Jon looked at the ship's papers. "Dove, out of London."

"What condition is she in?"

"She's seaworthy. We can handle her."

"Take her into Boston then. Good luck."

"Thank you, Captain."

The wind began gusting and the ships separated. The mist closed in and the Mary P. became invisible.

***

The sun rose the next morning to a clear sky and a moderate breeze carrying the captured ship toward Boston. The Mary P., with her greater speed, had disappeared over the horizon.

The fear of recapture by the British crew caused Jon to order two six-pounders to be turned around to fire on the hatchway. He stationed men in the tops with muskets and then allowed the captives to come on deck in groups of four. When they saw the cannons and the men in the tops, they lost any enthusiasm they might have had for recapturing the ship.

***

Command of a ship gave Jon a heady feeling that surprised him and amused Scotty. He divided his men into gun crews and exercised them with live firing. He discovered that the Dove's captain had provided himself with a quadrant and a chronometer, an instrument Jon had read about but never seen before. After studying the books found in the captain's cabin, Jon "shot the sun" every day at noon and religiously calculated their position using the ship's chronometer and the former captain's books of tables.

"My first command," he said to himself. The full responsibility for the ship, its crew and the captives rested on his shoulders.

"This is what I want to do. It's what I'm meant for," he thought.

Chapter Thirteen

"Sail ho," the lookout called. Jon ran up to the poop deck expecting to see the <u>Mary P.</u> From the maintop, he saw a small white speck on the horizon, near dead ahead.

As the day wore on, the white speck grew to a sail, and then to a small ship.

"What do you make of her Scotty?" asked Jon. He passed the glass to him. "Here, take a look."

"There is something strange about her," Scotty said. He watched for a minute more.

"I think she's lost a mast. Could be she's sailing with a jury rig." He passed the glass back to Jon.

Jon looked at the ship for a long moment.

"I think you're right. At the speed she's making we'll catch her before the watch changes."

As they grew nearer they recognized her as a jury rigged sloop. She carried a clumsy square sail on the shattered remains of her single mast. No one appeared to be manning her two small cannons. The sloop's name, <u>Salem</u>, appeared in bright yellow paint across her stern.

A young boy wearing the uniform of a British Midshipman stood on the deck and answered their hail. He identified himself as Midshipman MacBurney, master of the prize crew put aboard the American sloop from His Majesty's frigate <u>Pinabel</u>.

"Strike your colors Mr. MacBurney. We have you out gunned and your ship can't sail well enough to make a fight."

"Aye, I know. We will strike."

The American sloop <u>Salem</u> had been taken by the British frigate <u>Pinabel</u>. The sloop, disabled by a shot from the frigate's bow chaser, had surrendered without a fight.

The frigate had suffered an outbreak of fever that left her undermanned. Earlier the captain had put prize crews aboard several captured vessels and could spare no more than two men and the Midshipman as a prize crew for the sloop. A day after her capture, a brief squall on a dark, overcast night caught the <u>Salem</u> unprepared and the already damaged mast went by the board. With little or no maneuverability and little armament, the young Midshipman wisely decided to surrender.

<u>Salem</u> carried a crew of eight men. With New York only two days away and a prize crew of only three men including himself, Midshipman MacBurney thought it safer to keep the captives in the hold. The British didn't even open the hatch to give their captives fresh air, water, or food for fear they would retake the ship. When the ship lost her mast in a sudden squall, they

sailed at a much slower speed. Instead of two days, the men had been held below in the unventilated hold for close to four days without food and only a little water. When Jon's men opened the hatches, the angry Americans had to be restrained from attacking the three English prisoners.

***

"Captain Reed," Jon said from his seat at the head of the table in the <u>Dove's</u> cabin. "Have another glass of wine. The captain of this ship must have been a wealthy man to stock wine such as this."

Jon, Captain Reed, and Midshipman MacBurney sat at a table in the captain's cabin. Jon knew little or nothing about wine, except that it loosened men's tongues. He had seen this particular wine in Boston and had decided then that it cost too much for his own tastes.

Captain Reed morosely shook his head. He sat staring at the bulkhead with a nearly empty glass in his hand. He didn't join in the conversation except for a "yes" or "no" reply to a direct question. His ship had been lost twice, first to the British and then to an American Letter of Marque. The British had held the vessel for more than three days, long enough for it to be treated as a British ship, and therefore, a legitimate prize for Jon and his crew.

"Mr. MacBurney, your glass is empty also."

Midshipman MacBurney, at least three years younger than Jon, refilled his glass and gulped the wine quickly, then filled his glass again. Exhausted from the strain of commanding the sloop, the boy could relax for the first time in four days.

"Do you think you can arrange for parole soon?" Jon asked the young man.

"Don't know, sir. None of <u>Pinabel's</u> crew have been captured and I have heard nothing about other ship's officers being paroled."

"I suppose she will put into New York for supplies and crew replacements. I would hate to serve on a ship that has had so many losses due to fever" Jon said. "Did you come down too?"

MacBurney sat heavily in his chair, his eyes dull and vacant. He slurred his speech when he spoke.

"Yes, I had a mild case," he said. "One of our officers died. Another near died before it ended. He is our Third Lieutenant. His arm had been amputated, and he wasn't fully recovered when the fever hit him. He had been wounded while attempting to capture a schooner using our longboat."

Jon choked on his sip of wine. He recovered quickly, hoping no one noticed.

"How do you English find our ships so easily?" Jon asked.

"We have friends on shore," the young man said, a smug smile on his face.

The wine had done its work. Jon nodded his head, but gave no other sign of interest.

***

The sloop sailed back to Boston with Jon trailing behind in the slow, clumsy merchant ship.

CHAPTER FOURTEEN

When the <u>Dove</u> entered Boston Harbor, Todd Paget greeted Jon as he stepped ashore.

Each time the two men saw each other after an absence of a few months, they saw changes that amazed them. Todd, no longer an adolescent boy, dressed and acted like a wealthy young business man, and Jon, tanned and strong, walked with an air of authority befitting a ship's officer.

"Join me for a cup of coffee," Todd said.

Jon readily agreed. He had first tasted coffee in San Juan and disliked its bitter taste. However, on board a ship that had not touched land for many weeks, the coffee tasted better than the fresh water they carried, and he acquired a liking for it.

They entered one of the many Inns along the streets near the waterfront. A waiter hurried to escort them to a table near a window. The deference shown to Todd made Jon chuckle.

"You've come up in the world since you ran errands for

your father back in Falmouth, Todd."

The waiter served their coffee and they sat comfortably sipping from their cups.

They talked of the good times they had before Jon went to sea in the Mary P. Then Todd said, "You've come up in the world too, Jon, from ordinary Seaman to Second Mate in only three years. How would you like to have command of a ship?"

At Jon's startled look he hurried on.

"I watched that little sloop sail into the harbor and I couldn't help think about fitting her out as a privateer. She looks fast and nimble and could carry four small guns."

"How could I do that? I don't have enough prize money to buy half of her, let alone pay for fitting out."

"I think my father will advance enough for that," Todd said. "Business has been good since we moved to Boston."

Mr. Paget's business had flourished, in large part due to the prize taken by the Mary P. and other armed merchant ships. Two of the British ships that had been captured proved to be fast with a shallow draft. Armed and provided with Letters of Marque, they had sailed carrying cargo, but prepared to take any careless British ships they might come across. Other prizes had been sold.

Todd leaned across the table.

"If you're willing, I'm sure my father will buy out that sloop. He'll pay for fitting it out as a privateer. We can get a privateer's commission for you and you will be the captain. It won't cost the company much, and it could bring big profits to all of us. I'm confident it will if you command it."

Jon sipped his coffee. "I'm pleased that you think so Todd, but I've never commanded a ship except for that prize. I've been in several fights with armed merchant ships, but never in command. Are you sure you can talk your father into it?"

"He won't be risking much. You might have to buy a quarter share of the sloop. That would make you a partner."

Jon stared into his coffee cup and nodded slowly. Then he looked up at Todd and smiled broadly.

"Lets talk to your father."

While most sailors spent their money wildly and sailed on the next cruise penniless, Jon had chosen to take his shares in goods, not money. The Continental dollar had begun to lose value as soon as the Government printed it. He stored his shares in the form of barrels of tar, bolts of fine cloth, rum, cordage and ship's stores. He stored all of it in Paget's warehouse. As the war went on, the value of his goods increased. He could buy one quarter share of the sloop, with money to spare. Outfitting and provisioning would require an advance from Mr. Paget.

Todd continued speaking as they walked toward the Paget ship chandlery.

"The sloop is a good ship, and she can out run anything you think is too big. She'll carry four guns, and we have four four-pounders stored away. They're small, but more than most merchant ships carry. And you said yourself she looks fast and handy."

"Why do you think you father would want me to captain a privateer. What about Rob or Captain Hamm? They've both had a lot more experience than I have."

"Father thinks highly of you Jon. You know that. And Captain Hamm would never leave the Mary P. he loves that ship. Rob Clay wants to stay with Captain Hamm. They've been together a long time and Rob looks up to him like a father."

"Todd, you sure make it hard to resist."

Jon had no intention of resisting. He dreamed of command of a ship, any ship, but he didn't want Todd to know how eagerly he looked forward to it.

"I'd want to have a free hand at picking my crew."

"Privateers can have a crew in less than a week, Jon. There are thousands of boys who want to go privateering. Pick any of them you want."

***

Refitting of the sloop had begun before Jon and Todd had finished talking. Mr. Paget had discussed giving Jon a command with Todd several days before. He knew Jon's character and assumed that he would accept the offer. Now Jon owned one fourth of the privateer, renamed Savage.

Jon insisted that both Ryan and Scotty be allowed to sign on if they wished to, even though the Mary P. might be left short handed.

Scotty smiled with delight when asked if he would join Jon's ship. "Sure I'll sail with you Jon," Scotty replied without hesitation. "There's no one I'd rather serve with. We'll have some excitement, and we might even get rich."

Ryan hesitated when Jon asked him to join the crew of the

Savage. He had grown more and more thoughtful about the punishment he could expect if captured by the British. Jon had saved the Mary P. from capture on his first voyage, and Ryan would certainly have been hanged if the Mary P. had not escaped. He owed his life to Jon. He agreed to one more voyage. With the green crew they would have, Jon would need all the help he could get.

Jon named Ryan first mate, because of his many years of experience, and Scotty second mate. Most of the boys who asked to join the ship had no experience at sea. Several of the Mary P.'s crew asked for berths, and Jon, both flattered and relieved, quickly agreed to sign them on. He took all of the experienced men he could get, but he still had too many green young farm boys in the crew for his liking.

***

The complexity of preparing a ship, even a small one, for a long voyage and possible combat overwhelmed Jon. The new mast had to be shaped and lowered into place. The boom and gaff cut and fitted. A sailmaker had to be found who would take time from other work to sew up two sets of sails, one for light airs and the other for heavy weather. Gun ports had to be cut into the sloop's sides.

Mr. Paget's chandlery supplied most of the ship's gear, but still Jon had to search the port for some scarce items. Guns came aboard followed by gunpowder and shot. Everything had to be checked and accounted for. Mr. Paget trusted Jon completely, but he also knew the business of shipping and sailing required careful record keeping.

Each night Jon fell exhausted into the bunk in his tiny cabin, too tired to go ashore to the inn.

When he declared the sloop ready to sail, Jon began a series of short excursions to test the sailing qualities of the sloop and to train the green crew.

"We'll rake the mast more, Ryan. She has too much weather helm. If that doesn't do it, we'll have the jib recut."

The next short excursion concentrated on training the crew.

"Next time, ease the staysail and jib sheets a bit as we start turning. Now once more. Ready to tack. Helm alee."

Scotty and Ryan watched and shouted instructions to the new men as the <u>Savage</u> began to turn. "Let go and haul," Ryan shouted. "You're hauling on the wrong damn line. Get hold of the loo'ard sheet," Ryan roared, followed by curses from Jon and quiet chuckling from Scotty who viewed it all as high comedy.

"Do you find something amusing Mr. Lachlan?" Jon asked coldly.

"No Jon, I mean, no sir," Scotty stammered.

"Your life might depend on these men. Don't take this drill lightly."

***

The preparations neared completion. As the pressure eased, Jon resumed his custom of sleeping ashore at night.

Overcome by fatigue and now able to relax, Jon lay on his bed, deep in dreamless sleep. The door opened silently and Faith entered his room. She quickly undressed and sat on the edge of

Jon's bed. She shook Jon's shoulder but he only mumbled and turned over. She shook the bed harder until Jon opened his eyes. Still half dreaming he mumbled, "Faith? How did you get here?"

Faith smiled, lifted the blanket and slipped into bed beside Jon.

"Mr. Morgan moved his bank to Boston. Business isn't so good in Falmouth anymore. Mrs. Sloan is here too."

They made love quickly and passionately. Afterward she lay in his arms and held her body against his, hoping to arouse him once more.

Jon began snoring gently.

Faith pulled her clothes back on and stomped out of the room, muttering to herself.

She slammed the door as hard as she could, but Jon didn't hear it.

***

The privateer sloop Savage cleared Boston Harbor on a clear summer morning with a brisk northwest wind driving her.

Jon's cares evaporated in the morning sun and wind. The Savage lifted on a wave and surged forward, as if eager to start a new adventure. Jon allowed himself a smile. Laughter would be unseemly for a ship's captain.

"She flies, Jon, she flies like a bird."

"She does Ryan," Jon replied. "Set the gaff topsail if you please."

Ryan began bawling orders. Men ran to the halyards and sheets, and the sail bloomed between the gaff and the mast. The

Savage heeled her lee rail under and flew faster.

***

A frigate sighted her within half a day out of Boston. The wind blew fair for the sloop and the frigate's sails disappeared below the horizon. The wind held fair for two more days, then deserted them to be replaced by a light variable breeze from the north-northeast. For five days they sailed without seeing another sail. At first light on the sixth morning, a cry, "Sail ho," came from the top.

"Where away?" Jon shouted.

"Port quarter Captain," came the reply.

Jon glanced at the top. He recognized Jeremy Ricker, who had left the Mary P. in order to sail with them.

"What do you make of her Jeremy?"

"All I can see is a scrap of sail. She appears to be square rigged though."

"We'll be safe from her if this wind holds."

All day the Savage sailed on. The wind picked up and the sea became rougher. The wind held strong and the sloop crashed through waves large enough to slow her. The heavier frigate plowed through them easily. Worse yet, the wind swung aft, favoring the frigate more than the sloop. By mid-afternoon the frigate's courses could be seen from the deck. The lookout identified her as the same ship that had sighted them as they left Boston.

The British ship held station farther off shore than the Savage and kept her bearing. The Savage could not change course to get the wind on her beam without sailing too close to the rocky shore or crossing close to the frigate's bow. The captain of the frigate knew his business and made no mistakes. Jon had no choice but to hold his course and hope for a favorable change in the wind.

Instead, the wind shifted more northerly, putting the wind farther aft of the sloop's beam, her slowest point of sailing, and the frigate's fastest.

***

The British ship drew nearer as the afternoon wore on. Through his glass Jon could see her clearly. An officer stood on the forecastle watching them.

At dusk, the wind fell to a breeze, and the sea flattened. The Savage's motion eased and she sailed faster. The frigate flew all of her sails but still lost ground to the sloop.

"By morning we'll be out of sight of her," Ryan said.

Scotty nodded his head in agreement.

"Perhaps," Jon said, grudgingly. A captain cannot indulge in too much optimism. He must expect the worst, and be prepared for it.

The wind continued to decrease until a dead calm settled over them.

"Have the sweeps manned. They'll have boats out towing her."

Sixteen men, two on each of the long oars, rowed all the night. Jon watched the British ship through his night glass and saw that she did have boats in the water towing her.

At first light, the frigate, no farther away than it had been at sunset, fired a ranging shot that fell short.

The north wind returned soon after sun up. The sloop moved briskly now, but the frigate continued to grow nearer. A shot from their bow chaser splashed into the water only one hundred yards astern. Jon saw the same officer still watching from the forecastle.

"It won't be long before they will be close enough," Scotty said.

"Rig tackle to jettison stores, Ryan," Jon shouted.

The Savage picked up speed after the stores had been dropped overboard. Shots from the frigate's guns fell farther astern.

"On deck," shouted the lookout

"What do you see?"

"They're pumping their water."

Jon looked at the frigate through his glass and saw the spray of water running through the scuppers. Lighter by several tons of fresh water, the frigate began to gain on Savage.

"They must have had poor luck taking prizes, or they wouldn't keep chasing us for so long." Ryan said. "We're just a little sloop, and they've taken their ship into shoal water trying to catch us. Now they've pumped their water and will have to put in somewhere to get refilled."

Jon had no time to consider an answer.

"Scotty, rig tackle and drop the guns overboard. All of the shot too. We'll get supplies in Charles Towne. Jettison everything except enough water and food to get us there."

Jon altered course to sail closer to the shore. With the ship lightened, the risk of sailing in shallow water decreased slightly. The frigate would not risk sailing so close to what might become a lee shore.

Jon watched her through his glass. The frigate changed course also.

"They're taking a big risk, sailing in so close. We ain't that much of a prize," Ryan said.

"Jeremy, have you ever seen that frigate before?" Jon shouted to the top.

"I don't know for sure. She might be the one that sent that long boat after us years ago."

Jon looked again at the British Officer in the bow of the warship. The man turned to give an order and Jon saw that he had only one arm.

The race went on for two more days. At times the wind favored the frigate, and at other times the sloop. Finally, a gale from the northeast blew in that forced the frigate to give up the chase. She sailed southeast to claw off of the lee shore. The Savage sailed due south, confident that the sloop's superior windward performance would allow them to sail off the lee shore any time they needed to. The frigate's topsails soon disappeared over the horizon.

"We've lost them, for now Jon. They might still be looking for us further south," Ryan said.

"Make our course for Charles Town Ryan," Jon said. "We

can get supplies there. We'll have to run through the blockade, but if we enter the port at night we'll have a good chance."

As night fell, the wind moderated. <u>Savage</u> sailed comfortably on a southerly course. A heavy overcast hid the stars.

Jon allowed the exhausted crew on watch to rest lying on the deck and sent the rest below. He went to his cabin to rest while Ryan stood watch.

In the dark moonless night no one saw a line of clouds in the distance. The wind began to build and in moments a squall that blew with fierce intensity struck them. A sudden and intense gust knocked the sloop down on her beam ends before Jon could get on deck. The inexperienced and exhausted crewmen panicked when the wind held the sails and mast in the water, and the sea poured down the companionway.

"Cut the weather shrouds," he heard Ryan shouting. "We have to get her up."

The green crewmen clung to the weather rail, too terrified to move. Jon saw Scotty running along the rail with an axe in his hand. He slashed at the shrouds until they parted. The mast went over the side with a sickening crack, and the sloop rolled back upright. Jon and Ryan cut the back stays and leeward shrouds, and the mast and sails floated away, held to the ship by the forestay. The wreckage dragging in the water acted as a sea anchor and held the sloop's head to the wind. She rode safely for the moment.

The squall subsided as abruptly as it had risen.

"Have the pump rigged," Jon ordered.

While Scotty organized a party to work at the pump, Ryan

surveyed the wrecked rigging and set to work on a jury rig.

***

Jeremy heard it before anyone else. The faint sound of surf breaking.

"Captain," he shouted. "I hear breakers."

Everyone stopped work to listen for the dreadful menacing sound.

"Ryan, get the anchor rigged. Quickly now. There's no time to lose."

"We lost the anchor, Jon. That squall tore it loose and it went over the side. We jettisoned the spare to lighten ship when that frigate got too close."

"Man the sweeps. We have to keep her off shore at least until daylight."

Of the eight sweeps, six had been lost during the squall and one broken.

"We'll have to get the boats in the water, Ryan. We can stand off shore until daylight. Then we'll land through the surf."

Ryan glanced at Scotty and then looked back at Jon.

"We only got one boat left," he said. "The other two got stove in when that squall knocked us down."

Jon said nothing. He walked to the rail and looked toward the sound of the surf.

"Get the boat over the side. Have Scotty help you. No panic. Arm yourself to keep control. Have Jeremy help too. He's a steady one. Ryan, take charge of the boat. Stand offshore until morning. Then try to land in the daylight. Scotty, have the rest of the crew rig some rafts. It might save a few," he said quietly.

The inexperienced crew panicked and loaded the boat to the gunwales in defiance of the officer's commands. Jon raised his pistol and commanded one of the men to come back aboard the Savage. The man refused. Threats of death meant nothing to him. All of Jon's pleading had no effect. The men, too afraid of the surf to think of the dangers of a small overloaded boat, simply refused to move.

"Ryan," Jon shouted. "You'll be lucky to stay afloat. You don't have to go with them."

"This bunch won't have a chance to survive if they don't have an officer with them. I'll stay in the boat and hope to see you alive tomorrow."

"They don't have much chance, but they are better off than we are I think," Scotty said, quietly to Jon, watching the boat pull away from the sloop.

***

The Savage struck stern first. A hard shock that knocked Jon to his knees. A wave lifted her and dropped her with a harder blow.

They launched the rafts after the second impact. The remaining crewmen scrambled onto them. The surf turned Savage beam on, and the waves beat against her, rolling her and breaking her ribs and beams. The first raft broke up when the wreck rolled against it. Everyone clinging to that raft disappeared into the sea. Jon, Scotty and seven seamen on the other raft reached the beach before the capsizing. The breaking surf pulled some of the men out to sea, and threw others higher up on the beach.

Chapter Fifteen

Jon and Scotty sat on the white sand, gazing at the remains of the sloop Savage. The heavy timbers that made up the keel and a few of the ribs could be seen on a sand bar two hundred yards beyond the shore.

"They killed my ship," Jon said in a calm and reflective voice. "And they killed Ryan and most of my crew."

"Yes they did, Jon," Scotty agreed quietly.

"And before that they killed my whole family," Jon continued.

He sat on the beach, sifting dry sand between his fingers as he spoke.

He suddenly threw the sand down and rose to his feet. He paced up and down in front of Scotty.

"Those bastards will pay for this Scotty." His voice low and filled with hatred. "They'll pay and pay, I swear it!"

Scotty looked at Jon, startled and somewhat frightened by

the outburst. He had never seen him in this state before. Scotty got to his feet and stood looking at Jon, wondering how to help him.

"We'll do it Jon. Together we'll do it. I lost my shipmates too."

Jon blinked as if startled. He relaxed a bit.

"Sorry Scotty. I know you feel it too . . . ."

He stared at the horizon and the booming surf, and then at the group of four crewmen who had also survived.

The four young men walked along the beach in hopes of finding some useful wreckage. Occasionally, they looked at Jon and Scotty and then conversed among themselves. They walked along the curving shore line until out of sight.

"Have you seen anything useful along the shore?" Jon asked.

"Very little. A keg of gun powder that's stove in so the powder's useless. A cask of hard tack and a few scraps of sail cloth. No water casks. No rum either."

"We can get by without the rum, and I suspect there's fresh water inland. The keg of hardtack will feed us for a time. We had better get off the beach. It is too easy to see tracks in the sand."

"You think there might be British troops around?"

"Maybe, but I think Loyalist's are more likely. They're worse than the British from what I hear."

"We're close to Charles Towne, ain't we Jon? Do you think the Loyalist would be this close to the city? Maybe we should take a chance on walking the beach for a way. It would be a lot easier."

"No," Jon said emphatically. "Injuns work with the Loyalists. I doubt they would take prisoners. We'll go through the woods."

The four crewmen came into sight as Jon finished speaking. Swenson carried Jon's rifle. Grinning, he handed it to Jon.

"We thought this might make you feel better, Captain. We found it pretty near buried in the sand. I hope it ain't hurt."

Jon held the rifle and ran his hand over the stock. The surf had packed the barrel full of sand, and the salt water had corroded the lock, but Jon, overcome with gratitude, could hardly speak.

"Thank you Swenson," he said softly. "And the rest of you too. I thought I'd never see it again."

He cradled the rifle in his arm for a moment and then abruptly changed the subject.

"We've got to get off this beach." he told them. "If injuns found our tracks, they would follow us and kill us all. British troops wouldn't patrol here, but their injuns and Loyalists would. Them Loyalist are as bad as injuns from what I hear. Our only hope is to get back into the woods. I know it will be hard goin', but it will be safer to walk through rough brush and swamp."

"If we go inland we can make our way to Charles Towne. Then maybe get passage on a blockade runner to get back to Maine Territory."

The men nodded in agreement, however, Jon knew they might change their minds when they found out how difficult it would be walking through mud and water in the dense timber.

At dawn they moved into the woods and stood waiting

while Jon tried to erase their tracks in the sand. He couldn't completely remove them, but at least it would be difficult for anyone to tell how many men had made the tracks.

They carried hardtack in crude pouches made of sail cloth they had found along the beach. From the beach, the land sloped upward through a series of small sand dunes. Then it dropped down into low swampy brush with rotting tree trunks lying half submerged. The treacherous footing made travel slow and difficult and caused a few falls. The six men, used to walking along the deck of a ship, quickly became tired and frustrated, and the resulting scrapes and bruises made their tempers rise. Furthermore, when Jon looked back over their trail he realized that any woodsman could find them.

At noon they stopped for rest and food. The four men, sullen and tired, sat by themselves. They talked in low voices, occasionally glancing at Jon and Scotty.

"We've rested long enough. It's a long way to Charles Towne," Jon said.

The four crewmen stood apart, and then one of them, Franklin Garret, approached Jon.

"Captain, we've been thinking things over. We don't see how we can get through this swamp. We want to go back to the beach. Walking along the beach to get to Charles Towne will be a lot easier than going through this swamp."

"If you go back to the beach, I doubt we'll ever see you again, at least not alive," said Jon. "Even if the injuns don't find you, you'll have to cross a lot of streams and rivers at their widest points, right where they meet the ocean. And remember, the Loyalist Militia don't like wading through swamps any more than you do, so they walk the beaches. You'll be safer here."

Garret looked at his companions. Then he shook his head.

"We'll never make it through this swamp, and we might meet injuns here too. We'll take our chances on the beach."

The four men began walking back toward the beach. Jon's rifle had been cleaned as well as possible, but there wasn't any shot or powder. Without weapons, Jon and Scotty couldn't stop them. The four men picked up their meager belongings and moved back toward the beach, retracing their trail. Jon and Scotty walked further inland. The afternoon sun had settled near the horizon when they heard the faint sound of a musket shot.

"Keep moving Scotty. There's nothing we can do for them. If injuns found them and not Loyalists, they'll start back tracking and find us. Try not to break branches and stay in the water. No muddy foot prints."

They moved on through the swamp, avoiding the occasional dry hummocks that would show their wet tracks.

A faint whoop carried through the still forest.

"They're getting closer and moving fast. We left a clear trail."

Scotty grunted in reply. He concentrated on moving carefully and leaving as little sign as possible.

The cries of the Indians grew louder. Jon pulled Scotty into a dense thicket. They laid flat in the shallow muddy water.

The sound of a man running through the brush and water

could be heard now. Garret ran past their hiding place, eyes wide in panic, straining to outrun his pursuers.

Scotty pushed himself to his knees and tried to call to the man. Jon's hand clapped over his mouth and pulled him to the ground.

An Indian appeared briefly, flitting through the forest. The two men heard a muffled scream and then silence. Another Indian appeared, running easily, following his companion.

Jon and Scotty waited silently, not daring to move. The Indians returned, talking excitedly. One of them carried a bloody scalp. They passed within a few strides of the two men but did not glance in their direction.

The Indians disappeared into the forest and Scotty began to stir. Jon gripped his arm and he remained still. They waited for what seemed like an hour to Scotty before Jon decided they could leave their hiding place.

They didn't stop to care for, or even look at, the body of their shipmate. Scotty protested that they should find him and give him a decent burial.

"We can't leave any sign that we are alive," Jon said. "If those red skins thought other rebels might be around here, they would look for our trail. Then we would be as good as dead."

"We haven't left any trail," said Scotty indignantly.

Jon snorted in disgust.

"An injun could find our sign easy. He could tell how much you weigh, how tall you are and maybe what you ate for dinner. No way we could get away if they came lookin' for us.

The only thing that kept us alive this far is that Garret came along the same path we took. That probably confused the trail."

Scotty said nothing after Jon's explanation and watched his steps more carefully.

At dusk they found a dry hummock of land and made camp. They ate some hardtack and tried to sleep, but mosquitoes swarmed around them and made sleep impossible. Slimy stinking mud smeared on their faces and arms helped, and at last they slept.

***

They walked in a westerly direction. Many streams and brooks, as well as patches of swamp, kept their clothing wet continuously. Their shoes, meant for walking on the deck of a ship, began falling apart. Their supply of hardtack ran out, and they existed on berries and a few snakes and frogs that Jon caught.

"Never thought I'd eat snake," Scotty muttered to himself. "Beats starving I guess."

As they neared Charles Towne the travel became easier. They found a road that led in the right general direction and followed it. Bridges over the streams allowed them to keep their feet dry and travel faster.

Late one afternoon the sound of horses and the jingle of harness behind them made them run for cover in the thick brush. They watched as a group of thirty riders trotted by, all wearing uniforms of the Loyalist forces. When the cavalry had passed, Scotty started to rise from their concealment.

"Best stay down boys," a quiet voice said from the scrub behind them.

Scotty dropped flat, and Jon rolled over on his back, pulling at his knife.

"Steady now. If I wanted to kill you, you'd be dead right now. Stay quiet. There's more of 'em comin'."

Soon they heard the jingle of harness again and another troop of cavalry trotted by.

"Get up now, but leave your rifle on the ground. Ian, watch them close."

"I will Adam," another voice replied from behind them.

The man referred to as Adam revealed himself to Jon and Scotty. He appeared to be a typical woodsman, tall and lean, his face darkened by constant exposure to the elements. His long fringed buckskin shirt reached to the knees of his breeches. He held a rifle in a casual manner, but it remained pointed toward the two sailors. His companion, Ian, a younger version of Adam, also carried a rifle that constantly pointed at them.

"I don't guess you're a God forsaken Tory, or you wouldn't a hid like you did. We like to know who folks are around here. Who are you and how'd you get here?" Adam asked.

Jon related their experiences including their ship wreck and the slaughter of the four seamen. When told of their plan to reach Charles Towne, Adam smiled briefly.

"Why're there so many Tories 'round here?" Scotty asked.

Adam smiled again.

"You boys've been at sea for awhile. The British took Charles Towne a little while back." Then he turned to Ian with raised eyebrows.

"What do you think, son?"

Ian looked at their two prisoners and nodded briefly.

"Foller me," Adam said and moved back onto the road.

Jon stooped to pick up his rifle. A foot stepped on the barrel. He looked up to see the muzzle of Ian's rifle in front of his face.

"I'll carry your rifle," Ian said.

Adam set a pace that Jon and Scotty could barely maintain. As they trotted along the road Adam said, "You was surely lucky. Them injuns is a bad bunch. I doubt any of your friends 're still alive." He nodded his head as if agreeing with himself. Jon could not spare the breath to reply. Adam continued, "So you're sailors. That explains why you near blundered out onto the road."

Twenty minutes later Jon and Scotty, staggering with fatigue, dropped to the ground when Adam called a halt.

"Well, you ain't Loyalists scouts, or you'd be able to keep up better, even at the easy pace I set. You talk like sailors I seen in Charles Town before it fell. I'm surprised you was able to get this far in these woods."

"Jon grew up in the Mohawk Valley," Scotty explained.

"A long time back," Jon added.

Adam rose to his feet, ready to start traveling again.

"Now you know all about us. What about you, Adam?" Jon asked.

"Just come with us, boys. We'll see if you're tellin' the truth."

They moved through the forest following game trails that

Jon and Scotty would never have found by themselves. They crossed a few shallow streams, but they never had to wade through swamps.

Just after sunset, they arrived at the edge of a clearing around a collection of three buildings. One of them appeared to be an inn. A road ran across the cleared area past the hitching rail near the door. Behind the inn stood a barn and a small building containing a large wood-burning cook stove. A black man, wearing a white apron, carried pots and dishes back and forth from the inn.

Adam stayed with Jon and Scotty while Ian walked across the clearing and into the cook house. A few minutes later the cook walked to the inn and returned with a man who appeared to be a waiter. He stood nearly six feet tall. He wore an apron tied around his ample waist. In spite of his bulk, he walked briskly with a rolling gate.

Jon and Scotty looked at each other and smiled slightly.

"He has a salty air about him," Jon said quietly.

"That he does," Scotty replied.

After the large man returned to the inn, Ian left the cook house and entered the barn. He reappeared soon and waved to them.

"We'll go to the barn now," Adam ordered. "Walk, don't run. Runnin' attracts attention," Adam told them.

***

They spent the night in the loft above the stalls. At first light the sound of cows being milked awakened them. A young boy turned the animals out to pasture and carried the milk to the inn. He returned and called to them.

"The inn's safe for you now. Come on in for some breakfast."

The waiter greeted them as he would any travelers who had come in off of the road. In spite of his bulk, he moved quickly and easily as he prepared their meal. Bald, with a fringe of red hair and a red stubble on his chin and cheeks, he called himself Jake.

With breakfast over, Jon and Scotty rested and dozed back in the barn. The rifle had not been returned to them, and either Adam or Ian had them within sight at all times. At midmorning, the waiter came out to the stable, pulled up the milking stool and sat down to chat. He questioned them about their homes, the ship they had sailed on, the British ships they had seen and been chased by, and their families. Then he began to ask detailed questions about their ship and their duties aboard her. One told him about the loss of their sloop, Savage, and how they had taken her as a prize when Jon commanded another prize. Scotty told how Jon had wounded a British officer with his rifle, and insisted that Jon show them the remnants of the scar he had gotten from the exploding swivel gun.

"I'm convinced," the big man said, nodding to Ian and Adam. The two woodsmen nodded back and picked up their small packs, rifles, powder horns, and shot bags.

"We'll be getting on then," Adam said. They walked across the clearing and disappeared into the woods.

Chapter Sixteen

"I'm Jake Archer," the large man said.

He extended his hand to shake with the two men.

"I used to sail out of Charles Towne before the British took it. I owned and commanded a sweet little brig, but they caught her at anchor in the harbor when Charles Towne surrendered. I went ashore a week before the damn Tories took her. When I heard what happened, I ran farther into the back country to keep from being thrown in prison."

Jake laughed ruefully.

"Quite a change from captain and ship owner to servant of all the customers at this inn."

"What happened to the rest of your crew?" Jon asked.

"Prisoners mostly. We had a Letter of Marque and four cannons on board. They pressed some of them into their own ships. Held the rest in a prison ship for a week, and then sent them to the prison hulks in New York. Most of them will probably die there." Jake sighed sadly. "Good men. Friends too."

Scotty interrupted Jake.

"There must be a way we can get out of here and back to Boston. Can we get some horses?" Scotty asked.

"It's possible, but I wouldn't want to try and ride all that way. 'Specially with my boy. Too many Loyalists around."

"If we had a boat like one of those we've seen on the rivers around here, we could sail along the coast," Jon suggested.

"They call them boats plantation barges, and they ain't meant for sailing off shore. The first bit of wind and they would capsize if they didn't break up first. Too risky by far."

Jake stared out of the door for a long minute.

"There is one possibility," he said slowly. "Maybe this is the time to bring it up."

He hesitated again, looking at Jon and Scotty, as if judging them.

"We can take a ship from Charles Towne harbor."

In the silence that followed, Jon and Scotty looked at each other, wondering if Jake might be insane. Seizing a ship at anchor could be done, but sailing out of the harbor under the mouths of dozens of cannons in forts, and hundreds of them on British ships, would be suicidal.

Jake saw their doubtful looks.

"I don't blame you for thinking it's crazy, but it can be done. There are hundreds of creeks that will float a small ship when the wind and tide are right. I've worked it out with a man who knows these waterways better than anyone else around."

"Why haven't you already done it? You've been ashore long enough," Scotty asked bluntly.

"I don't have a crew. The folks around here are good watermen, but they ain't seamen. They know these rivers and bayous like the back of their hand, but they wouldn't know how to sail a ship in a sea as calm as a mill pond. My boy Alex is a good seaman, though he is young and small. With the two of you, I think we could make it. A few of these watermen would go with us, and they would learn quick if someone showed them what to do."

"Just what do these watermen do here now?" Jon asked.

"Well, they sort of move cargo around." Jake waved his arms vaguely.

"Smugglers!" Scotty said bluntly.

"Well, yes. But we can trust them. You see, they can keep most of the cargo when we get the ship. We'll only take enough stores to get to Boston. Besides, the biggest smuggler around here is a cousin of mine."

Chapter Seventeen

A plantation barge moved silently over the water of the Ashley River propelled by six muffled oars. A thick cloud layer and drizzling rain blotted out the moon leaving the river and the barge in pitch blackness. A faint glimmer appeared downstream of the boat, and the rowing stopped. At a whispered command, they silently stowed the oars. The faint glimmer grew brighter and became the anchor light of a small ship. As they drifted toward the bow of the ship, one of the men passed a line around the anchor cable. The last of the ebbing tide swung them around. They let the line out until the boat touched the vessel. Jon, Scotty, and two others climbed the anchor cable and slide silently over the ship's side and onto her deck.

They found the deck deserted. A seaman should have been on watch, but as they expected the guard had gone below to stay warm and dry in the forecastle. In a safe mooring such as this, close to the Charles Towne waterfront, no one expected trouble.

They seldom came on deck and then only to check for mishaps such as a dragging anchor. The four men silently secured the companionway, trapping the men in the forecastle. At Jon's signal more men came aboard from the boat, armed with knives and cutlasses but no firearms. They allowed the two guards to come on deck and then tied and blindfolded them.

"We're at slack water now, Jon" Jake whispered. "Make the tow line fast. Then make ready to slip the anchor cable."

They had waited for weeks for the right combination of weather and tide for their attempt. Without the help of a flooding tide and a slight, favorable wind, it would have been impossible to move the ship up the river. When they had moved away from the anchorage, they set all sails. Jake insisted that they keep rowing. The farther they moved up the river before daylight, the safer they would be.

Every man took his turn at pulling the heavy oars. Alex, too small to be effective with the long oars, stayed at the ships wheel.

Jon pulled at his oar without complaint even though he found it to be the most frustrating work he had ever done. The tow line went slack after each stroke of the oars, and then as the next stroke took the slack out of the line, the slow moving ship jerked the plantation barge to a near stop. Still, they kept at it hour after hour. In the darkness, Jon couldn't see any progress.

The night dragged on with alternating periods of exhausted sleep on the deck of the ship and torturous rowing. His shoulders and arms began to ache, and after resting, the muscles were stiff and even more painful. Still he responded without hesitation when his crew went back into the boat. As the night went on, the pain grew more intense and muscles in his back began to knot up, yet he pulled with all of his strength during his turn at the oars.

The eastern sky had begun to grow lighter when they pulled into a sluggish stream that emptied into the Ashley River. Jon expected to see tall pine trees that would conceal the ship and her masts. Instead he saw a flat meadow with grass not more than two feet high. He groaned. Their work had been completely futile. Long boats full of English Marines would be here before midmorning, looking for the missing ship.

He knew that protests would be useless. Nothing could be done, and in his exhausted state he didn't care. He laid himself on the deck waiting for the inevitable.

***

"What took you so long?" A snarling voice roused Jon before sleep took him. "You was supposed to be here an hour ago."

"Stop talkin' and pass us a line. We'll be fine if you get to work."

Jon struggled to his knees and looked over the rail. A team of six draft horses stood patiently on the bank. A line had been passed from the ship to their harness. Jon watched long enough to see the horses lean into their harnesses and start moving the ship. Then he fell asleep.

"Jon, wake up lad. We need you." Jon opened his eyes to find Jake shaking him.

"What for?" Jon responded irritably.

"We need to send the topmasts down, else they might see 'em above the trees."

Jon looked up at the masts and at the trees along the shore.

They hadn't traveled far from the Ashley River, along a crooked winding stream. The ship, a brig and a small one at that, still had masts tall enough to be seen above the trees. Several skilled seamen could do the job easily, but only Jake, Jon and Scotty had even seen topmasts sent down except in a shipyard. Jake had grown too heavy and clumsy to climb the shrouds. The inexperienced landsmen would be useless.

Without good, experienced men, they could easily lose control of the topmast. If it fell, it might drive itself straight through the deck and the hull.

"We'll start by lowering the yard arms. When we have them on deck, we'll try to figure something." Jon said.

Jon, Scotty and Alex climbed the shrouds and began the work. Jake supervised the crew on deck. The yardarms came down without incident.

With the yards down on deck, the masts could be seen less easily, but a careful seaman with a good glass would find them.

"We have to get those masts down Jon. If we don't we'll be spotted for certain," Jake said.

"Those two prisoners might be able to help," Scotty said. "They claim to be Irish and say they hate the British as much as we do. If they're good seamen, we should let them help."

The prisoners, Colin O'Neil and his brother Dermot, had

signed on to the English ship because of the extreme harshness of their life in Ireland. With no families to support, the choice had been an easy one. Life on an English ship could be difficult for Irishmen, but they knew that those left behind in Ireland had even more difficult times. At least the two brothers didn't worry about starvation.

Jon, Scotty, and Jake talked to the two men. Although they could not be certain of the brother's loyalties, the need for good seamen overcame their doubts.

With Jon, Scotty and the two brothers working in the top, and Jake and Alex directing the watermen handling lines on deck, the topmasts came down smoothly. With a fresh team of draft horses harnessed to the tow line, they proceeded through the waterways of South Carolina, hidden from searchers by the tall pine and oak trees along the banks.

***

After several hours of travel, they moored to trees near the water. The smugglers had set up a crude crane using a large tree and a long timber. Jon and Scotty helped remove the hatch covers and watched as the smugglers lowered slings into the hold. The work went smoothly without lost motion or time. Jon wondered how many times a small ship had been unloaded by these men to avoid King George's taxes. When the cargo had been removed, the smugglers continued working until all of the ship's ballast had been put ashore.

By midday the ship's hold had been emptied. A fresh team of horses appeared and they resumed their journey.

Late in the day they moored to the bank at a point where the river widened and became shallow. The horses rested while Jake and one of the smugglers rowed a small boat ahead of the ship, sounding the depth with a long pole. At the same time, two teamsters harnessed a second team of six horses to a towline on the opposite bank. Jake returned to the ship and called Jon to the wheel.

"I'll be in the bow watching the bottom as best I can. You take the wheel and follow my directions. It's shallow here, but without any cargo and with two teams of horses we'll make it."

Both teams began pulling and Jon, following Jake's directions, kept the ship near the middle of the stream. Their speed increased until the horses began trotting. Then the water became more shallow and Jon felt the ship slow.

"The bottom's soft mud here," one of the watermen said. "Them horses can pull us through it."

The two teams of six horses each, strained to keep the ship moving. The keel began to drag on a harder surface, probably sand, and the vessel slowed even more. Jon heard several sharp reports, like gunshots as the teamsters cracked their whips above the horse's backs. The teams leaned into their harnesses. Then came a grinding noise as the keel hit some harder obstruction. Jon flinched and held the wheel tightly, expecting the ship to come to a halt. Suddenly, the bottom of the stream released them and they floated free. Gradually, their speed increased and soon the horses trotted easily, heads up, prancing, proud of their accomplishment. The drivers ran along beside their teams, grinning and talking to them with pride.

"We made it Jon, thanks to an empty hold and twelve good strong draft horses. I knew we could."

"Jake, if I didn't know better I might think you'd done this before."

"Good Lord Jon, what ever made you think that." Then he shook his head and chuckled to himself.

Chapter Eighteen

They cast off the starboard towline, and the team on the larboard side continued to tow them until after sunset. The stream widened into a deep still pond. The moon provided enough light for them to see a short pier. They moored beside it.

A few of the men found comfortable spots on the deck and soon began snoring. No watch had been set. Was it confidence or sloth Jon wondered.

Smoke began rising from the small galley as the black man that Jon and Scotty had seen at Jake's inn began preparing their first meal of the long day. Jon thought himself too tired to be interested in food, but after his first bite, he couldn't stop eating until his stomach could hold no more. The rest of the crew ate well too, some of them after being roused out of their sleep by the smell of fried pork and beans.

"I don't know your name," Scotty said to the cook, "but you can cook for me any time."

The cook smiled. "Folks call me Jubal, sir. And I expect to be cookin' for y'all for some time."

The day had been exhausting, but the meal revived him. He stayed on deck for a few minutes, leaning against the rail staring at the water and thinking of their plans for the ship. The cool damp air seemed to settle on his shoulders like a cape. He shivered slightly. A loon called from the darkness. In the stillness, a fish jumped among the reeds near shore, the splash sounded oddly out of place. Jon inhaled the scent of the lake, not at all like the salty smell of the sea. The surface of the water held a silvery reflection of the moon, so clear that the "man in the moon" shown clearly in the water. Jon sighed, both from weariness and the restful beauty of the scene.

"I like this time of day better than most any other," a voice said.

He turned and saw Alex standing near him at the rail.

"Yes, it's surely a peaceful time," he replied. "Until these damn mosquitoes find you."

Jon waved his arms around his head and slapped the back of his neck. He sucked in his breath at the sudden pain. In the swamp, he and Scotty had been wet continuously for hours and their hands had softened. Pulling at the oars had blistered his hands, and while working aloft that day he had carelessly gotten a rope burn.

"Let me take a look at it Jon. I can patch up some hurts pretty good."

Alex ran below and returned with bandages and ointment.

With surprising skill and care, he bandaged Jon's hand.

***

Jon awoke the next morning at dawn to the noise of cargo being loaded. The sun rising over the quiet pond revealed a group of wagons and men along the banks. They loaded the ballast back into the hull, and to Jon's surprise, they loaded a considerable part of the cargo also. When the cargo had been stowed, the man who had directed the work came aboard.

"Are we square now Jake?" he asked.

"We are if you're satisfied Martin. It looks like we struck a good bargain."

A brief handshake ended the conversation, and the man named Martin left the ship. The wagons pulled away on the rough road through the forest. Five of the smugglers stayed behind. They had chosen to sail with the ship, looking for wealth and adventure.

***

Jon and Jake agreed to change the brig into a schooner. She could be sailed with a smaller crew, and with her fine bow, she would be nimble and fast to windward.

With the work well underway, Jake gradually gave Jon more and more authority. He watched carefully, but allowed Jon to make his own mistakes. He spoke out only if he saw a serious error that Jon failed to correct promptly. He put more and more responsibility on Jon's shoulders.

Privately, Jon thought that Jake's age had begun to show as he became less helpful every day, spending more time in his cabin or sitting on an upturned keg observing the work. Scotty, although skillful and hard working, preferred to let others make decisions unless he knew exactly how to proceed. Most of the responsibility fell on Jon, not Scotty or Jake.

As days passed, it became apparent that Jake preferred to let Jon take charge of the entire operation, and the crew accepted him as their leader.

This change in leadership disturbed Alex more than it did anyone else. Not because Jon had weakened his father's authority, but because his father accepted the new status so readily. Jake had always been an energetic, decisive man except for the times the fever had hit him.

Alex's worry about his father made the boy edgy and defiant, and he became another source of frustration for Jon. While Alex liked working in the rigging and would go aloft whenever he could find any excuse, Jon sometimes preferred to have one of the watermen do the work, if only to gain experience.

"Damn you Alex, I told you to let one of the new hands do that. Now get down here on deck," Jon shouted one day.

"What for? There's work to be done here," Alex shouted back as he reluctantly started down the shrouds.

When Alex reached the deck, Jon took him by his ear and led him to Jake's cabin.

"Jake, our boy seems to think that he doesn't have to follow my orders. What do you say?"

Jake's face grew redder than usual and his breathing became hoarse and raspy.

"Leave us for a minute, Jon."

When Jon left, he saw Alex looking apprehensively at his father. Jake closed the cabin door behind him.

Five minutes later Alex appeared on deck, much subdued. He approached Jon politely. Jon kept his eyes on the work aloft, ignoring the boy.

"Captain Weaver sir," Alex began. Jon glared at the boy, still angry.

"I'm sorry if I acted poorly. I know a seaman can't talk to his captain like I did. I won't do it again."

Jon felt a surge of satisfaction that Jake had supported him.

Only later did he realize that Alex had addressed him as Captain. Now he wasn't sure just what his position might be. Did Jake want him to take command, or did he say that just to impress Alex?

The relationship between Jon and Alex improved, but on occasion Alex still defied Jon on small matters. As one of the most able topmen in the crew, he knew that Jon needed his skill. The suggestion that they might have to talk to Jake again usually kept the boy under control.

Added to the pressure and frustrations of his work, Jon found that he could seldom sleep through the night. He could not avoid thinking about Faith and their nights together. He would toss and turn in his bunk and sometimes leave his cabin and pace the decks. Alex sometimes appeared on deck at night also, complaining that Jake's snoring kept him awake. They talked casually about the ship and the work yet to be done. Alex liked to listen to Jon's sea stories, and Jon found that he enjoyed the boy's company.

A pause in the work developed after the rigging neared completion. Only the task of swaying up the yardarms and bending on the sails remained.

The ship carried a light cargo, but they could not get through the passage to the Atlantic without the help of a high tide. The spring tide would come in two weeks.

With time to spare, Jon unpacked his rifle, now cleaned and repaired, and decided to hunt for some game to vary their diet. To make amends for their disagreements, he asked Alex if he would like to go with him. Jon half expected the boy to refuse. Instead he accepted with surprising eagerness.

They spent the day away from the ship walking through the woods watching for game. Jon saw game trails that he pointed out to Alex, but they didn't find any fresh signs. He decided that some target practice would help entertain the boy. Although Alex had never fired a rifle before, he proved to be an adequate marksman. The long, heavy barrel weighed more than he could comfortably hold, but when resting it on a tree limb, he became as accurate as Jon.

Jon showed him how to load and fire quickly.

"Put one or two balls in your mouth to start. Then pour powder down the barrel, spit a ball into the barrel without a patch, bang the stock on the ground to settle the ball onto the powder, cock, prime and fire," he explained.

"It don't shoot as straight without a patch, but sometimes

it's better to shoot fast when injuns are close by."

"Did you ever kill an injun, Jon?"

"Yes I did," Jon replied quietly. "It ain't something I like to talk about."

"It must have been exciting to grow up like you did. Did you have a lot of fun?"

"No," Jon said shortly, and started back to the ship.

***

The new rigging had turned the ship into a beautiful topsail schooner. Jon stood on the bank of the lake admiring her appearance. She lay next to the pier, waiting for the right tide.

"If the work is really finished, maybe we could go huntin' again Jon." The eagerness in Alex's voice surprised Jon.

"The tide won't be right for near a week, Alex. We might as well have some fun."

The boy liked guns and hunting and always paid careful attention to Jon's instructions. He proved to be an eager student. He fired at targets until his shoulder became too bruised to continue. Then the next day, he would go into the woods with Jon and fire at targets again.

The noise of the target practice, as well as the work on the ship, had made game scarce. One lucky day they saw fresh tracks of a good sized deer. Jon began tracking it, Alex watching and following in his foot steps, carrying the rifle. They found the deer standing alone in a clearing. Jon motioned to Alex to shoot. He made a clean kill. With Alex's help, Jon skinned and cut up the deer. The meat provided a welcome change in diet for the crew, and Alex felt as proud as any boy could.

***

The final work on the schooner had been completed. Jake expected the spring tide within two days. While swaying the topsail yardarm aloft, a line jammed in the block at the top of the mast. Alex picked up a large fid and ran up the shrouds to take care of the problem. He reached the block and began prying at the line. It had jammed tightly, and he leaned out away from the mast to get a better purchase. The line came free without warning.

Jon watched in horror as Alex fell from the rigging, his body twisting in the air. He hit the shrouds, bounced away from the ship and splashed into the water. The crew ran to the rail waiting to see him rise to the surface. After a few seconds, Jon jumped up on the rail and dove cleanly into the pond. Through the clear water, Jon saw Alex's body lying on the bottom nearly invisible in a cloud of sediment. He swam to him and seized the collar of his shirt. He kicked powerfully toward the surface. His head broke the water and he took a deep breath. Alex's shirt tore suddenly, and Jon held only a scrap of cloth. He dove again, found the boy, and pulled him to the surface by his hair. He swam to the bank and carried Alex ashore, face down over his shoulder. The boy coughed, vomited, and began gasping for air. Jon laid him on the ground as Jake ran toward them.

"He's alright Jake," Jon shouted. "Just a bit water logged."

He looked back at Alex.

"Mother of God," he gasped.

Alex's shirt, torn open to the waist, did not reveal the body of a young man but of a developing young woman.

Chapter Nineteen

She had been named Alexis after her mother, who had sailed with Jake from the day they married. Alexis had been born at sea. A tomboy as a small child, the crew of her father's ship treated her as they would a young boy. After her mother died, Jake insisted she dress and be treated like a boy, at least when aboard ship. He feared that some of the rough men they would have to deal with might take advantage of her. Alexis didn't object to the idea. When ashore in Charles Towne, she sometimes stayed with an aunt who cared for her and tolerated her outbreaks of independent thought. No matter how hard she tried Aunt Margaret could not make her behave like a girl. Alexis had seen some of the older girls simpering and primping and decided she wanted no part of their dull useless lives. The excitement of sailing a ship in a stiff breeze could not be equaled by any of the shore side activities. Besides, with the vocabulary she had picked up at sea, some considered her to be socially unacceptable.

The present crew, though amazed by the discovery of her sex, accepted her and, much to Alexis' disgust, became overly protective.

Jon had more difficulty adjusting. It disturbed him when he saw her slim young body running up the shrouds at the slightest excuse.

In his frustration, Jon shouted at her, "Dammit Alex, stay on deck."

She would laugh and then do as she pleased.

"Don't worry so much Jon. She's the same person as when you thought she was a boy," Scotty told him. Fortunately for him, Jon didn't see the knowing smile on his face. Jon still frequently paced the deck at night when sleep would not come. On some occasions Alexis also came on deck.

They stood side by side staring at the reflection of the rising moon on the rippled water of the lake.

"It looks like a silver path leading to the moon," Alexis said.

"I remember the last time I stood here thinking about that pretty moon. I tried to swat a mosquito with my sore hand."

He chuckled, pleased to hear her laugh too.

"Do you remember wrapping my hand?"

"Yes I do. Does it give you any pain now?"

"Not now. My hands are hard as leather."

"I think mine are too," she said, turning her hands palm upward for his inspection.

Jon took her hand in his and ran his fingers over the

calloused palm. Her hand, seemed so tiny and fragile compared to his own. Without any conscious thought, he lowered his head and kissed the palm. His arm moved around her waist of its own volition and drew her to him, her slender, hard muscled body held against his own. The stark contrast to Faith's soft yielding flesh surprised him and aroused him more than Faith ever had. He stepped quickly away from her, still holding her hand and staring into her eyes, surprised and shocked by the intensity of his emotions. She pulled her hand away and touched it to her cheek for a moment. Then walked rapidly to the companionway, glancing back as she went below.

***

The ship, her new rigging completed, was moved through narrow bayous and streams to a nameless river that emptied into the Atlantic Ocean. Jon, Scotty and Jake rowed out of the river mouth to locate an anchor said to lie on the bottom.

"Pull ahead another ten yards Scotty," Jake wheezed. He leaned over the side of the skiff peering into the clear water. Scotty pulled on the oars at Jake's command.

They rowed the skiff back and forth near the mouth of the small river, many miles south of Charles Towne. The low tide and the clear water made it possible for them to see the bottom clearly. They expected to find an abandoned anchor. "A great huge anchor," according to Jake.

"Swing to larboard," Jake grunted.

Jon, sitting in the bow, watched Jake apprehensively. Jake sat leaning over the side, tired and breathing heavily for no apparent reason.

"There it is," Jake gasped hoarsely. He sat up and breathed deeply. "Now you must go over the side." He paused to breath again. "Carry the line down."

Jon dove into the water carrying the end of a one-inch line. The anchor lay in fifteen feet of clear water, and Jon reached it easily. He passed the line through the shackle at the end of the anchor shaft and swam to the surface.

With the line fast to the stern of the skiff, they began to row back toward the ship. The schooner, now named Retribution, swung at anchor in the river. A shallow bar at the river's mouth kept her from sailing out into the Atlantic.

They were using the same method that a generation of smugglers had used. At high tide and with the help of the "great huge anchor" so conveniently placed, they could pull the Retribution across the bar.

Jon and Scotty rowed the skiff back to the ship pulling the messenger cable. The crew on the schooner's deck took a turn around the windlass drum and began heaving the heavy anchor cable out to the anchor. When the end of the cable reached the anchor, Jon again dove into the water to pass the cable through the shackle and bring the end of it to the surface. With the cable made fast to the anchor, the three men returned to the schooner.

"Now we wait a few hours for the tide to make," Jake said. Then he made good use of the time by going to his cabin for rest.

"Jon," Scotty said, somewhat pensively. "I don't mean to fault Jake, but I wonder if he is as strong as he likes us to think.

He spends more time in his cabin than a healthy man should."

"The heaviest work is past. Maybe he'll get over whatever ails him on the way to Boston." Jon said carelessly, his mind occupied by a hundred other matters. "A sea voyage is supposed to be good for you."

As the tide rose, Jon ordered the crew to start heaving on the windlass. The cable came aboard until the ship cleared the mouth of the river. Then she grounded fast and refused to move. With the rising tide, she stirred restlessly after a few minutes. Then the heaving at the windlass would begin again, and continue until she grounded again.

"A bit too eager, Jon," said Jake who had come on deck when he heard the windlass. He observed the operation from his vantage point at the ship's rail. "We'll make it fine, but if you had started later we wouldn't have to sit here in plain sight for so long."

"I know, Jake. I would have appreciated your wisdom more if it had come sooner." Jon had the same concern about being seen by a British or Tory ship. His remark sounded more harsh than he had intended.

The sarcasm seemed lost on Jake, but not on Alexis, who glared at Jon.

As the tide continued to rise, the <u>Retribution</u> moved farther across the bar. When Jon judged that the tide had reached its highest point, the crew heaved continuously on the winch bars and dragged the ship's keel across the bar until she floated free. Then, with all fore and aft sails set, Jon set a course to the southeast to clear the coast line.

"Scotty, have Alex cast the log. Then give me a reading."

"Yes sir," Scotty responded. The roles of captain and mate had been assumed again.

"Alex, bring the log line and glass aft here."

Alexis brought the log line on its large reel and the small 'hour' glass aft to the quarterdeck. Dermot held the reel and Alexis stood by to drop the wooden drag over the stern. Scotty held the glass until the sand had completely run through it, then nodded his head to Alexis. She cast the drag over the stern. The line ran off the reel through her hands.

"Turn," she shouted when the first knot ran through her hands.

Scotty turned the glass over.

When the last grain of sand had run through the glass Scotty shouted, "Pull."

Alexis pulled sharply on the line to trip the drag, and then began pulling it in hand over hand.

"Five knots and a quarter fathom," she called.

"Set the gaff topsails," Jon shouted.

The new crewmen ran up the shrouds and topsails bloomed above the main and foresails. Set and trimmed without any further orders. The watermen might make blue water sailors quicker than Jon expected.

"Scotty, cast the log."

They cast the log, turned the glass, and measured their speed again.

"Five knots, and a half fathom," Alexis called.

"Good turn of speed for this wind, Scotty."

"Yes it is. She's faster than the <u>Mary P.</u>"

The <u>Mary P.</u> remained their reference for performance of all ships.

The <u>Retribution</u>, without armament of any kind, would need all of the speed she could produce to avoid capture.

"What do you think of her, Jake?" Jon asked.

"She ain't got even half a cargo. I'd expect her to be fast," Jake said in a flat tone of voice, indifferent to the ship's performance. He stood leaning against the taff rail for a few more moments, and then went below to his cabin. Alexis followed him.

***

"He's asleep again," Alexis said when she came back on deck.

Jake had become less active with each passing day. He rejected offers of assistance and didn't ask for help or special favors, but he had grown weaker and more irritable.

As captain, Jon knew he should be able to offer advice on any and all subjects, including sickness.

"I can't tell what's wrong. I thought he might just be tired. Now I believe it's more serious. He's so weak he can't walk more than a few steps at a time," Jon said.

"He looked hale and hearty when we first met him," Scotty observed. "It must be some sort of sickness."

"With this fair wind, we'll be in Boston in two weeks. We can't do much except keep him resting until then. Alex, keep him in his bunk as much as you can."

***

The wind didn't stay fair. It began blowing out of the northeast, and the <u>Retribution,</u> on larboard tack made heavy going into rising rollers. Her sharp bow sliced into the waves, throwing spray across the deck. Double reefed main and foresail drove her lee rail into the sea as the wind increased.

After Jake fell from his bunk for the second time, Alexis came on deck.

"Jake can't take much more of this. He's so weak he can't hold himself in his bunk." She had to shout to make herself heard. "I rigged some netting to keep him in, but he's still being thrown around a lot."

"We don't have much sea room so I can't heave to. We might have to run south if this keeps up."

The wind shifted to the west of north as the day wore on. Now the velocity increased, and the waves grew into huge rolling hills.

"Scotty," Jon called. "We have to put her before the wind. Get the main and foresails off, and put double lashings on them. Set the storm jib."

"Aye sir," Scotty replied. "Hands to sheets and halyards. Snub them when the gaff gets close to the boom so we don't smash anything. Then get them gaskets around them sails so they don't blow out when the wind comes aft."

At Jon's command, the schooner luffed into the wind. The sails came down in a rush, halyards snubbed enough to keep the gaffs from damaging the sails and booms. The storm jib went up and three lands men sheeted it in.

Jon watched the waves and waited for the right moment.

"Hard a weather," he shouted, and Colin O'Neil spun the wheel. The <u>Retribution</u> turned in response to the rudder and the pressure of the wind on the storm jib. The ship now ran due south.

As the day wore on, the wind increased, and the waves became larger and larger. Both Colin and Dermot O'Neil, the most experienced helmsmen, stood at the wheel. The rising wind and larger waves required the strength of both of them to control the ship. When one of the huge rollers lifted her stern, the <u>Retribution</u>'s bowsprit just skimmed the water in the bottom of the trough and green water surged waist deep along her deck. Between the waves, the ship lay becalmed, sheltered by the following wall of water. As the waves grew higher still it became more and more difficult to hold <u>Retribution</u>'s stern to the waves while in the troughs. The storm jib had lost its effectiveness. If they lost control and broached to, the following wave would hit them broadside and she would roll over. No one would survive. The ship pitched and rolled violently. Spray flew with stinging force. Water ran over the deck, tearing at the crew like some living thing trying to pull them overboard. The crew of green landsmen stood clinging to the rail and the shrouds, wide eyed with fear.

"Set the fore topsail. Double reefed," Jon shouted.

The square topsail on the foremast would be high enough to catch the wind in the troughs between the waves and hold her stern to the wind.

"Get aloft you topmen," Scotty shouted.

The five men didn't move. Some stood with their backs to him, heads bowed and shoulders hunched. Others stared at him, amazed that he expected them to climb the shrouds in such conditions. He raised a knotted piece of rope to drive them up, but he knew they wouldn't respond.

Before he could strike a blow, a small figure elbowed its way through the men standing by the shrouds and ran up to the fore top.

"Get moving you yellow bastards," Scotty shouted. "You'll rot in hell if you let a slip of a girl work alone up there."

The man nearest the shrouds stood gaping in surprise at Alexis as she began moving out on the starboard foot rope. A heavy arm brushed him aside and Scotty saw three men racing up the shrouds. Then the last two followed.

With the double reef topsail set, the ship became more manageable. Jon walked the deck, watching the foremast. The groaning of the shrouds and stays sounded ominous to him. He laid his hand on the foremast shrouds, iron hard from the tension in them.

"Rig heavier stays on the foremast," Jon shouted.

Once again men ran up the shrouds in response to Scotty's bellowed orders, carrying gear and lines for the added stays. Alexis stayed on deck, her arm firmly held by Scotty.

"Alex, if you ever do that again, I'll swat you so hard you won't be able to sit down for a month," Scotty said. Then, under his breath, "Even if you did save the ship."

Giddy with her success, she laughed.

"Do you think the captain would let you do that?"

"If you had seen his face, you'd know he would, and then he'd shoot me for not stopping you. Now get below and put something on your hand. It looks like you tore out a finger nail."

Alexis, still high on adrenaline, looked at her hand in surprise. She bit the remains of her nail off and spat to leeward. Then she went below as ordered.

***

The <u>Retribution</u> sailed south for two days until the storm blew itself out. Then the weather became too calm. The wind blew in gentle puffs, if it blew at all, and the clear blue sky didn't give any sign of more wind. Jon set a course for the nearest port open to American shipping.

Scotty began whistling to call up a breeze. The superstitious crewmen muttered among themselves, knowing that whistling would likely call up another storm worse than the one they had survived. But Jake had grown weaker still, and he would surely die if they didn't get to a port where a doctor could care for him.

***

Jon entered Jake's cabin in response to his summons. The smell of death hung in the air, and he knew that Jake wouldn't last another day. Jake could not talk above a whisper and clearly suffered great pain.

"I need your help," Jake whispered, "I won't live much longer and I want to say a few things."

"Sure, Jake, but hang on. We'll get you to a doctor soon."

Jake closed his eyes and shook his head.

"The ship is yours, Jon. Yours and Alex's. Equal shares. I won't never need it. If you take it, you got to promise me." He closed his eyes again and groaned through clenched teeth.

Jon leaned closer to Jake as his voice grew weaker. "I want your word that Alex will be taken care of. She's too young to be alone in this world." Jake's voice became even weaker as he spoke. "That's all I ask Jon."

"I'll be proud to do that Jake, but we'll be in port soon. We can get a doctor to fix you up."

"I've been sick a long time Jon. I hid it from Alex for as long as I could. That's why I decided to take a chance on you and Scotty. She needs someone to take care of her after I'm dead. Both of you lads are good people. I'll rest easier now."

"Hang on Jake. We'll be in port in a day or two. We'll get you fixed up."

"I don't think I'll last through the night."

Jon sat watching helplessly as Jake's breathing became slower. He called Alexis to the cabin. She sat crying and holding Jake's hand until he died.

***

Jon read the burial service over Jake's body at noon the next day. The body, sewn in sail cloth and weighted with stone from the ship's ballast, sank out of sight.

Chapter Twenty

"Scotty," Jon called, "Set a course southeast by south."

Scotty didn't allow his surprise to show, and shouted the orders to sail trimmers and helmsman.

"We'll make port in San Juan. We need some repairs and more crewmen. If we're lucky, we might get more cargo to carry back to Boston."

After years on a merchant vessel, the idea of taking a cargo back to Boston seemed only natural. He hoped to make arrangements through Mr. Paget's agent in San Juan. If the agent would advance him the cost, he would return to Boston with a valuable commodity that would pay for some of the losses.

As they entered the harbor at San Juan, Jon and Scotty immediately saw a familiar ship. To their amazement and good fortune, the Mary P. swung at anchor dead ahead of them.

***

When they were safely anchored Jon called for the ship's jolly boat and had himself and Scotty rowed to the Mary P. As the boat approached the schooner, Jon saw Rob Clay give them a cursory glance and then star at them in amazement. Rob waved at the boat and then sent a man below to fetch Captain Hamm.

"My god, it's good to see you two," Rob shouted. "We thought you had been lost with your sloop."

They climbed aboard and Rob eagerly shook hands with them.

Captain Hamm walked hurriedly toward them and took Jon's hand in both of his, an unusually broad smile on his face. For a moment, Jon thought the Captain would embrace him like a Frenchman might do and embarrass both of them in front of the crew.

Captain Hamm recovered his composure and released Jon's hand and took Scotty's.

"Happy to see the two of you. We'd heard you went down with your sloop."

"Well Captain, it was a near thing. Scotty and I survived. The ship went aground on the Carolina coast and broke up in the surf in just a few minutes. Of the six of us that reached shore, injuns killed four. Ryan, and everyone else, drowned. Just Scotty 'n me lived."

Rob and Captain Hamm nodded in sympathy. The loss of friends at sea occurred too often among seafaring men for prolonged public grieving.

When Jon explained that he hoped to get a cargo to take back to Boston, Captain Hamm wasted no time in taking Jon ashore and introducing him to Mr. Paget's agent, Jose Rodriguez. The agent not only found enough sugar and molasses for a cargo, but helped Jon dicker about the prices. While gangs of slaves loaded the cargo, Jon and Captain Hamm searched the water front for experienced sailors. They found that merchant ships didn't attract crewmen. The available seamen preferred Privateers.

Jon made it clear that he intended to convert the <u>Retribution</u> to a Privateer as soon as they reached Boston, but most seamen still preferred to stay in the Caribbean. Ten men volunteered, all able seamen hoping to make their fortune as Privateers. Five of them black, two Spanish, and three white men, deserters from a British merchant ship.

"Will the rest of your crew accept these men?" Captain Hamm asked.

"We have some people who ain't real seamen yet, and they may try to cause trouble. If they do, they can damn well swim," Jon replied.

The <u>Mary P.</u> and the <u>Retribution</u> sailed together for Boston.

Many ships, particularly in the Caribbean, had black crewmen. In some cases black men made up the entire crew, the officers and the owner. But slavery still flourished in America and the North Carolinians didn't know that color lines didn't exist on sailing vessels. On the second day out, all five of the watermen approached the quarterdeck. A man named Barlow led them.

"We don't like it much, you makin' us and them sleep

together in the same fo'c's'l. It just ain't right."

Jon's face turned white with fury.

"I'll explain this to you once, Barlow. Then if I hear anymore from anyone, he'll regret it the rest of his days. Do you all understand?"

Blank stares came from the seamen.

"Do you all understand me?" Jon said in a loud voice.

"Aye, sir," several of the seamen grudgingly mumbled.

"If there are any incidents that effect the efficiency of the ship, I'll have the trouble makers in irons within minutes. Now, get back to your duties."

The Carolinians heard the anger in Jon's voice, and returned to their work.

Barlow muttered, "How am I ever going to tell my Ma I slept with a bunch of damn . . . ."

"Mr. Lachlan," Jon's voice rang out. "Put that man in irons." Jon stood on the quarterdeck, white lipped and trembling as Scotty and two others took the man below.

Jubal watched from his galley, his face entirely blank.

"Might be I'll like this here ship." he mumbled to himself.

***

The wind remained fair and the sky cloudless. The two schooners made good time toward Boston. The new crewmen showed their superior skill and knowledge, and in a short time had raised the competence of the landsmen. Before long, the Carolinians realized that at sea everyone depends on everyone else, and competence and courage are the only measure of a blue water seaman.

"I think we are out of trouble for awhile," Scotty observed to Jon.

"There are more ways to get into trouble than you or I know Scotty. We might still have some excitement."

***

Three days out of Boston Jon's pessimism seemed justified when the lookout saw a strange sail. The two ships changed course to avoid the stranger. The stranger followed them. The Mary P. armed with four, four-pounders dropped astern of the unarmed Retribution. Through his glass, Jon saw a large schooner flying the red and white striped American flag. With a sigh of relief, he watched as she approached the Mary P. Then the American flag disappeared and British ensign rose in its place. A sharp pang of fear pierced Jon's chest. As Jon watched, the Mary P.'s starboard four-pounders fired in unison, with no apparent effect. The large schooner, a British privateer, continued toward Captain Hamm's ship. As they ranged up along side, six cannons fired in rapid succession. Grapnels flew over the Mary P.'s rail. Sailors aloft in the British ship tied the yard arms of the two ships fast and they lay side by side. Boarders streamed onto the deck of the Mary P.

With no cannons on his ship, Jon knew he should crowd on all sail and run as fast as his ship possibly could. He looked at Scotty standing nearby, watching the fight. Scotty appeared calm and confident, ready to follow any order that Jon might give.

Even without guns Jon knew that he couldn't abandon his

friends on the Mary P. He took a deep breath and bellowed, "Hands to sheets. Ready to gybe."

The experienced hands reacted instantly and without confusion to Jon's orders.

"Helm aweather," he shouted. The ship turned downwind, crossing well ahead of the Mary P.'s bow. The main and mizzen booms crashed across the deck, snubbed smoothly and the sails filled. As the Retribution ran down the length of the two ships, Jon bellowed, "We'll board her over our larboard bow. Arm yourselves and follow Mr. Lachlan."

Jon brought his ship around quickly, close hauled on larboard tack.

"We'll run across their stern, Ciro," Jon called to the Spaniard at the helm. "Trim as we point up," he shouted to the sail trimmers.

"If only we had cannons," Jon muttered as they passed the sterns of both ships.

"Ready to come about. Hard alee." The Retribution spun around. The maneuver put them on the same tack and closing with the British schooner, heading directly toward her foremast.

Scotty ran to the bow shouting, "Boarders. Boarders to the bow."

The men followed without question or confusion.

At the last second, Jon shouted, "Hard alee."

The schooner turned sharply. The bowsprit missed the British ship's foremast shrouds and drove through the fore stay sail catching the privateer's forestay and the two ship lay side by side, locked together.

<u>Retribution</u>'s crew swarmed over the bow onto the deserted deck of the British ship.

The landsmen from South Carolina pushed to the front of the boarding party, trying to prove their merit. They leaped, screaming, up onto the privateer's deck. Before Jon could run from the quarterdeck to the bow, a dozen men had crossed the privateer's deck and joined the fight on the <u>Mary P.</u> Others followed as closely as they could in the mad dash. Armed with belaying pins, boat hooks, windlass bars, and their sailor's knives, they attacked the rear of the British boarding party. Jon ran forward to the bow, leaped aboard the British ship and then onto the deck of the <u>Mary P.</u> He found a cutlass lying on the deck where a dying sailor had dropped it. He engaged a young ship's officer, also armed with a cutlass. The officer parried Jon's clumsy slashing, and smiled as he drew back for a killing thrust. A cutlass slashed down on the officer's shoulder. Blood gushed from the deep wound. The officer tried to raise his cutlass and seemed surprised and confused that his arm wouldn't respond. He fell to the deck and never moved again. Booker Waite, one of the black crewmen, rushed by Jon, pulling his cutlass free from the body. Jon followed and engaged another sailor, slashing and beating him down. Jon's men drove the British back toward Captain Hamm's crew on the quarterdeck.

The British privateers found themselves between two groups of screaming men who seemed to relish the fight. Another of their officers fell, and they began to lose their spirit. A few threw down their arms and asked for quarter.

Jon jumped back onto the British ship and ran aft. The British captain had left the ship deserted except for two men on the quarterdeck. When they saw Jon running toward them, they raised their cutlasses and stepped toward the top of the ladder. A rifle cracked and one of the men staggered back. Jon stepped away from the awkward slash of the second crewman, then brought his own cutlass down with all of his strength. The British sailor dropped to the deck with blood pouring from his wound. The man who had been shot tried to regain his feet. Jon hit him with the hilt of his cutlass, knocking him unconscious. He ran to the stern and slashed at the flag halyard.

As the flag fluttered into the water he shouted, "She struck, she struck." The British seamen demoralized by the attack from the rear, saw that their colors had been cut down and that two of their officers had fallen and lost heart for the fight. They threw down their weapons and asked for quarter.

Captain Hamm came aboard the captured ship as soon as the prisoners had been secured and the wounded taken below.

With typical understatement, he said, "Much obliged to you Jon."

"You're welcome," Jon replied, hoping his voice sounded natural. He leaned back against the rail, trying to conceal the tremor in his knees. His heart still pounded so hard that he thought Captain Hamm might see his shirt move with the beating.

Rob Clay joined them on the prize's quarterdeck, showing no more excitement than he would when stowing cargo at dockside in Boston.

"They must have figured you'd keep running. Else they would have kept more men on their own deck," he said. "A prisoner told that a lot of their men had been put aboard prizes, so the crew was smaller than usual."

Jon nodded in agreement. "I expect they wanted to finish you off in a hurry. Then they would have chased and likely caught us. I figure we had nothing to lose when we came back to help you."

He spoke in what he hoped sounded like a calm and steady voice.

"Aye, that's true," said Captain Hamm, nodding in agreement.

"Give my thanks to your man with the rifle, Captain," Jon said. "I think I might have had a hard time with those two on the quarterdeck."

"Don't have no rifle on board since you left the Mary P. Jon."

***

The weather stayed fair, and the three ships sailed on toward Boston. On a clear bright day Jon stood on the quarterdeck, "shooting the sun," using a quadrant he had found in the former captain's cabin.

He held his quadrant to his eye and adjusted the elevation until the image of the sun touched the horizon.

"Mark," he called out to Alexis who noted the time using Jake's old pocket watch. She wrote the time in Jon's rough-copy log book and when Jon read out the elevation of the sun, she copied that down also. They repeated the process several times, and then Jon retreated to his cabin. He could calculate latitude with fair accuracy, but longitude depended on the accuracy of Jake's old watch and was only a little better than a guess, even though they had set it to Captain Hamm's chronometer only a few days ago.

A few minutes later Alexis heard Jon call out, "Send Miss Archer to my cabin."

She entered the cabin expecting a question about the sun sights.

Instead Jon asked, "Did you clean my rifle before you put it back in the arms chest?"

"Yes I did," she said, then realized her mistake and stammered, "I mean the last time we went hunting."

"Don't lie and make it worse," Jon snapped. "Where did you shoot from?"

"From our quarterdeck. I had those two Britishers in my sights before you got back on their deck. It's a good thing for you I did."

"Dammit, they had men in the tops. One of them could have shot you."

"They spent all their time looking at the Mary P. They didn't know where I was even after I shot that one."

"I don't want you to get hurt," Jon shouted without thinking. "I mean . . . well I promised Jake I'd look after you."

They glared at each other for a moment.

"If we see any other hostile ships, I expect you to stay below."

"You can't tell me what to do. I'm half owner you know."

"And I'm the Captain. You'll do as I tell you."

Alexis laughed scornfully. "How would you take care of me if I'd let them men kill you?"

She slammed the door as she left.

Jon sat in silence for a moment, staring at the door. Alexis had become a better sailor than many of the crew. Still, it infuriated him to see her take the same risks that seamen took as a matter of course.

Jon opened the cabin door.

"Send Booker Waite to my cabin," he called.

Soon a short stocky black man with his right arm neatly bound in bandages from finger tips to shoulder, knocked and entered at Jon's call.

Jon stared at the bandage for a moment.

"Who bandaged you arm like that?"

"It was Barlow, Captain. Done a good job too. Claims it will heal up good as new if I don't use it too much."

Barlow had been held in irons for the first week out of San Juan and Jon expected him to be bitter toward the blacks.

Jon made no further comment. Apparently, Barlow had realized that on board a ship at sea, shipmates came in all shapes and colors.

"Booker, I want you to look after Miss Alexis. If we get into another fight, I want you to keep her below decks. Do you understand?"

"Yes sir, I understand. But I ain't sure I can. When she makes up her mind, there ain't nothin' can change it."

"Do your best and make sure it's good enough. Tie her to something if you have to."

Chapter Twenty-One

The Mary P., the Retribution, and the captured British privateer sailed into Boston Harbor on a clear spring morning. They anchored in the harbor, and the captains went ashore to settle their business with the owner. The sick and wounded were carried ashore, and the more fortunate crew members went ashore to celebrate. They had their pay and the prospect of prize money once the captive ship had been disposed of. The bars along the waterfront opened early and stayed open late.

Captain Hamm and Jon reported to Mr. Paget without so much as stopping for one mug of ale.

Mr. Paget, having seen the three ships from his office window, had assumed that the Mary P. had captured them both.

The sight of Jon walking into his office stunned him. He stood staring at him, open mouthed.

"I thought you had been lost with your sloop, Jon. Now

you have reappeared along with two more ships. Can one of you please explain all of this?"

"I'm responsible for the loss of the sloop, Mr. Paget. I'll make it up to you as soon as I can."

Mr. Paget stared at Jon for a moment. He looked at Captain Hamm who smiled with amusement. Jon seemed to be apologizing for leaving Boston with a sloop and returning with a schooner and a captured privateer.

As Captain Hamm related the story of the capture of the privateer, Mr. Paget smiled proudly. He had given Jon his first opportunity as an ordinary seaman on the Mary P. His act of compassion had repaid him many times over, just in the satisfaction of seeing Jon do so well.

"So, Jon, you risked your ship to save the Mary P. even though completely unarmed. A risky, not to say brash, act."

He stared at Jon for a moment. Jon braced himself for the inevitable angry outburst.

"Well done, Jon. Well done indeed. Allow me to shake your hand." Mr. Paget walked around from behind his desk and took Jon's hand in both of his own.

"There is a gap in your story though. How did you get that schooner after your sloop went down?"

"Well, sir," Jon said, "A frigate forced our sloop close inshore and a squall dismasted us. We grounded on a bar off the South Carolina shore, and she broke up. Scotty and I were the only survivors. We met up with some rebels, and they took us to a man named Jake Archer."

"He owned the schooner you brought back?" Mr. Paget asked.

"Not exactly. Scotty and I helped him steal her. She was rigged as a brig then. We took her from the harbor at Charles Towne."

Mr. Paget leaned back in his chair, chuckling with delight.

"We hid her in the backwaters and changed her rig. Then we sailed for home."

"And what about the young lady you brought back."

"She's Jake's daughter and now an orphan. I mean her father died." Jon hated that word, orphan. "Jake died at sea. Before he died, he told us that Alexis and I owned the schooner, half each."

The words were said bluntly and unemotionally, but Mr. Paget heard a trace of a tremor in Jon's voice.

A long silence followed, then Mr. Paget spoke briskly.

"Well Jon, let's count up what you owe me," he said. "You left here with a small sloop. You returned in a schooner loaded with cargo. On the way you saved the Mary P. and captured the British Privateer that had attacked her. Now you want to repay me?" Mr. Paget shook his head and smiled. Then he continued.

"Jon, we both took financial risks with that sloop. Remember, you owned part of her. Her loss is just part of the cost of doing business. In fact, you have brought in a ship at least four times the value of the sloop, helped capture a privateer, for which you are owed prize money, and brought in a valuable cargo from San Juan."

"Jon, I think we will have a happy and profitable relationship for many years."

***

The maritime Court assessed the captured English privateer at a disappointingly low value. She did not carry a cargo and her ship's stores had been depleted. No one in the two ship's crews became rich, but all had enough for a few days of carefree living.

After the cargo of the <u>Retribution</u> had been sold, Jon and Alexis shared a sizeable sum as owners of the ship.

***

The captured privateer, refitted, provisioned, and renamed <u>Gypsy</u>, sailed within two weeks. Owned by Paget and Son, with Captain Rob Clay commanding. The fight with the privateer had convinced Rob that he should be sailing on a fighting ship, and he reluctantly left the <u>Mary P.</u> Only armed privateers could cut off supplies to the British army and protect American merchant ships. The American Navy, hamstrung by the political bickering in Congress couldn't stop British shipping from supplying their army. Privateers made up the only effective American maritime force.

***

The English blockade had tightened all along the coast. Many owners did not want to risk their ships to the British Navy. As a result seamen could be easily found. Within a week, Jon had a full crew for <u>Retribution</u>. Good experienced men, who knew the dangers of privateering and would willingly face them.

The <u>Retribution</u> needed more than an experienced crew. Her size justified more complete fitting out than had the sloop whose timbers lay rotting on the Carolina shore. She needed to be reworked from stem to stern to operate at her full capability as a fighting ship. Below deck Jon had partitions removed so that hammocks could be strung for a large crew. A well armed privateer required a powder magazine, a difficult and expensive modification. Five gun ports cut through the bulwarks on each side gave her the appearance of a fighting ship. The deck and hull had to be reinforced to take the weight of the guns and the jarring force of them firing. Jon calculated that she could carry ten six-pounders, more than most merchant ships and many of the small navy ships carried.

***

Alexis, in spite of all Jon could do, insisted on being on board and helping with the refit.

"Don't fight her about it Jon," Scotty told him. "We need all the help we can get. She's a good topman."

"She ain't a 'man' dammit. She should stay off the ship," Jon growled helplessly.

Alexis dressed in the same sort of rough boy's clothing that she had worn in South Carolina. Just as in South Carolina she found herself under the protection of all the men aboard the ship. Anyone who took the wrong attitude toward her would have his error forcefully explained.

The Bosun objected to her presence when she first appeared on board. He could hardly communicate with the crew in language suitable for a young lady. He accepted her after he heard her conversation with a careless seaman who dropped a fid from the main top that hit the deck near her. After all, she had grown up on board ship, and she had all of the skills, verbal as well as physical, expected of an experienced topman.

***

The Retribution's size allowed room for a reasonably comfortable captain's cabin. Jon had his bunk modified to suit his long legs and muscular frame and slept aboard in relative luxury while the refitting took place.

He found a respectable rooming house for Alexis, but after only two days the landlady, a stout, sour-faced woman, came aboard the Retribution. She marched straight up to Jon on the quarterdeck.

"I run a respectable room house Captain Weaver, and I want that girl out of it. I told her she would have to stop wearing those dirty men's clothes, and she called me a fat old biddy. When the hired man tried to quiet her, she hit him with a chair."

Jon struggled to keep from smiling.

"I'm sorry Ma'am. I'll see that she is moved out as soon as possible."

Salvation for Alexis came that same day when Jon stopped to chat with Mrs. Sloan on the street.

"Here now Mrs. Sloan, let me carry that load for you," Jon said.

"Oh, thank you, Jon. It's hard sometimes to get it all back to the house."

"Why don't you have Faith help you?"

Mrs. Sloan looked away and said nothing.

"Is something wrong with her?"

"She's healthy and strong as an ox, but lazy as sin if you want to know. I know you're sweet on her, but . . . ."

She stopped suddenly. "I shouldn't have told you that, Jon. Please try to forget I said it."

Jon couldn't leave it at that. "Do you have to do all of her work too?"

"Yes," she said crossly. "And I ain't sure I can keep it up."

Jon walked with her for a few steps thinking about her problems.

"Would you leave them if you could get a new and better job?"

"Now how could I get a better job? Mr. Morgan would never give me a recommendation."

"Would you work for me? Cooking and keeping house for a young girl?"

"Who is she?"

"Her name is Alexis and she doesn't have any family. She owns half of my ship."

Jon suddenly realized that Alexis could be called an orphan just like himself. The thought brought a sudden flow of sympathy.

"Where is she staying now?"

"Aboard the ship for now, but I'll find a decent place for the two of you if you'll take the job."

"I think I'd like that, Jon."

"I'll not try to mislead you. She's pretty headstrong. She might be hard to handle."

Mrs. Sloan laughed. "I'm pretty headstrong too."

"Here son, help Mrs. Sloan with her packages," Jon called to a young boy who had been standing idly beside a shop window looking at the candy display.

"I'll give you a penny to carry her packages to the Morgan house."

That same day Jon found a small house on the hill about a mile from the waterfront. To the owner Jon looked like a naive young seaman and doubled the asking price. Jon offered half of that figure. To his surprise the owner argued only a short while before he accepted the offer.

The former owners had even left their furniture. To Jon, after years aboard ship it looked perfectly satisfactory. Somewhat shabby but certainly usable.

As Jon should have expected, Alexis didn't like the house when she first saw it.

"It's dirty and ragged. I'll stay on the ship."

Before Jon could object, Mrs. Sloan appeared at the door, carrying a small chest. "It certainly is dirty, child. There's a wagon outside. Help me unload it, and we'll get to work cleaning this place up."

Jon winced in expectation of an outburst from Alexis.

Mrs. Sloan smiled at the young lady. "Jon didn't tell how pretty you are. Didn't he buy you any nice clothes?"

"No ma'am, these are all I've got."

Jon's face reddened with frustration as he recalled the times he had urged her to wear women's clothing. She had plenty of prize money to buy whatever she wanted.

"Just like a man," said Mrs. Sloan. "Well let's get to work. We'll get this place cleaned up and then see about getting you something to wear."

Alexis meekly followed Mrs. Sloan. As she went through the doorway she turned and gave Jon a smug smile.

***

For the next week, Jon devoted his full attention to preparing his ship. His only relaxation came when he visited Alexis and Mrs. Sloan. He ate supper with them as often as he could get an invitation. Partly because of Mrs. Sloan's cooking. Mostly because, in spite of himself, he liked Alexis' company.

One evening after an excellent meal of roast pork and potatoes, Jon and Alexis carried three chairs out on the lawn so they could all sit watching the ships in the harbor. Mrs. Sloan complained that the damp evening air bothered her and went back into the house.

Jon and Alexis talked idly about the cargoes the ships might carry, the reputations of their officers, their sailing qualities and appearance. Both of them were knowledgeable sailors and enjoyed the evening of conversation.

That pleasant interlude was repeated several days later when Jon again came to dinner at Mrs. Sloan's table. And again the next week. It soon became a habit for them to sit outside watching the harbor after eating one of Mrs. Sloan's dinners. Their conversations always drifted to the subject most interesting to both of them, ships and sailing. Alexis had been at sea most of her life and knew as much as Jon about the advantages and disadvantages of a schooner compared to a brig, or of a cutter to a sloop.

Jon thoroughly enjoyed those nights. He hoped that Alexis enjoyed herself too.

"Jake owned a brig before the English took it, and sailed her all around the Caribbean. Sometimes he said he wanted to change her to a brigantine." Alexis said one evening. "He never did it though. With the wind over her quarter, she could run away from any schooner or sloop. And she could float where bigger ships didn't dare go."

"A brigantine would sail closer to the wind than a brig, but not as close as a schooner. Takes more men to handle the square sails too," Jon commented. "Any way, I love the look a schooner has."

"If you had sailed across the Atlantic a few times like I have, you might know that schooners ain't the best rig for every purpose," Alexis said shortly. She wouldn't accept any hint of criticism of anything Jake might have done.

Jon had no idea why Alexis had replied so snappishly.

"I've sailed off shore enough to know as much as you do about it!" Jon snapped back.

Alexis tossed her head and looked away.

Jon stood up suddenly, over turning his chair.

"It's time for me to leave I see."

And he walked back toward the harbor.

Two days later, while working on the ship, Jon asked her to forgive him for being so abrupt. He spoke in a casual manner, out of hearing of anyone working near them.

"I'll accept your apology," she said without a smile. No one would see her being too familiar with the Captain. "Mrs. Sloan is cooking beef stew for this evening. Would you care to join us."

"I would like that." He tilted his head back and looked at the rigging. "Do you think the mizzen shrouds are set up tight enough?" he said in a louder voice.

"I think they are. They may give a little when we get under way, but we can take care of it then." she replied, more loudly than needed.

Then they went back to their work without another glance at each other. The men who had sailed with them on the Retribution smiled to themselves.

Jon and Alexis, both of them stubborn and opinionated, had repeated confrontations and repeated apologies. Usually Jon made the apologies. On rare occasions, Alexis admitted that she might be too strong in her opinions.

***

Jon had been searching for cannons since they returned to Boston. He approached Mr. Paget for help.

"I think I can get two four-pounders Jon, but the army takes near all we capture. I'm having trouble getting guns for my own ships. There are two more that belong to Morgan. He certainly won't sell them to you."

Jon bought Mr. Paget's guns. He still needed eight more of them, preferably six-pounders.

Finding enough guns for the schooner became even more

of a problem when Scotty pointed out that bow and stern chasers could be more important than a heavy broadside. A long six-pounder, if one could be found, could make the difference between taking and losing a prize. A stern chaser could mean the difference between escape and capture if chased by a large British ship. Mounting heavy guns in the bow and on the stern would require additional work strengthening the decks and hull to bear the punishment the guns would give the ship. Jon considered the problem at some length and finally allowed that a stern chaser could be a valuable asset. The bow chaser might be valuable too, but the extra weight in the bow would be a hazard in heavy weather. He thought of how <u>Retribution</u>'s bow sprit had touched the water in the storm they had encountered just after leaving South Carolina. Even the stern chaser could be dangerous if it kept the stern from lifting as a large sea over took them.

We'll strengthen the deck for a stern chaser Scotty, but no bow chaser for now. Don't cut a gun port in the stern until I decide for sure if we want a stern chaser.

The stern chaser would be mounted under the quarterdeck in Jon's cabin. Strengthening the deck and hull involved work in the cabin so Jon moved to a room on shore.

The second night he stayed ashore, Faith came to his room. By now, Jon knew that she loved money and position more than she could love any man, and he assumed that she regularly slept with Morgan. He thought of Alexis and feebly tried to resist the temptation. When Faith began to remove her clothing the old passions flamed, and he couldn't refuse her. Their lovemaking became intense and hostile, and they both loved it.

They lay in bed side by side, and Jon began telling her about his new ship, the Retribution.

"She's a pretty schooner. I expect her to carry ten or maybe eleven guns without any trouble. I've found a good second mate, and the crew is full of hard fighting men. I know, I've seen some of them fight. We can stand up to any armed merchant man."

"Do you really have eleven cannons?" Faith asked.

Pleased that she showed an interest in his ship, Jon answered her honestly and frankly.

"Well, we only have two now. We might sail with some 'Quakers'."

"What do Quakers have to do with guns. They don't even want to fight."

Jon chuckled. "No, you don't understand. We'll have some tree trunks shaped and painted to look like cannons. That's what we call 'Quakers'. We'll bluff armed British merchant ships into surrendering. Maybe some of those ships will have cannons we can take."

Faith stared at the ceiling for a moment, then she smiled and turned to face Jon again.

"You're so brave Jon." She kissed him passionately. "When will you be ready to sail?"

"I plan to sail next Tuesday if the weather holds."

Faith smiled to herself.

"Now I have to get back to Mr. Morgan's before I'm missed."

Chapter Twenty-Two

The <u>Retribution</u> cleared Boston on the morning tide, armed with two four-pounders and eight "Quakers". From a distance Jon saw Mrs. Sloan waving frantically from the pier.

"Nice of her to walk all the way down to the harbor to see us off. Do you see her Scotty? A fine woman."

When they reached open water, Jon sailed southeast to search for prizes.

Less than four hours out of Boston the lookout sighted a sail.

"Sail Captain," he shouted.

"Where away?"

"Starboard bow. About a point off the bow."

Jon watched from the quarterdeck as the sail slowly grew in size until the lookout in the foretop recognized her as a cutter.

"Gil, come about to put her on our larboard quarter."

Their new second mate, Gil Harper, had the watch. Gil, several years older than Jon, had sailed as mate on a coastal schooner, similar to the <u>Retribution</u>. A British frigate had taken his ship, and he had been imprisoned in one of the hellish prison hulks in New York harbor. A prisoner exchange saved his life.

He stood only a bit over five feet. His short heavy body and small mustache made him seem a comical figure until he stepped onto the deck of a ship. Then he suddenly became a hard bitten ship's officer. He had piercing black eyes that told everyone that he expected to be obeyed without question, and he always was. His experience and seamanship earned the respect of the crew. Within a week, he knew how the <u>Retribution</u> would react as well as Jon did.

"Trim the jib and staysail tighter," Jon shouted, and the fore deck hands hauled on the sheet lines.

Gil smiled as he stroked his mustache. Jon had deliberately trimmed the schooner's head sails too tight. Now she sailed slower than normal. He knew that Jon intended to lure the cutter into close action, hoping she would surrender when she saw what looked like an eleven gun ship.

As the cutter grew nearer, Jon saw the striped American flag through the glass. The attempt at deception didn't fool him.

"We'll clear for action now, Mr. Harper," Jon said in a conversational voice.

"Clear for action," Gil Harper shouted. The sound of the "battle rattle" echoed throughout the ship. Bare feet pounded the deck as the crew ran to their stations. Seamen stationed themselves at the two four-pounders and at the ten Quakers, to lend credibility to them.

"Open the gun ports. We'll show her our teeth."

Then added under his breath, "And hope she doesn't recognize that they're false teeth."

Less than a dozen of the crew had experienced battle other than the action that had resulted in the capture of the privateer now named Gypsy. That had been an easy victory. Now each man feared he might not be able to do his duty in the face of enemy gun fire and reveal his cowardice to his shipmates. The disgrace would be worse than death itself.

"We'll tack now, Mr. Harper. We'll run down on her. Head for her bowsprit."

"Aye, sir. Hands to sheets, ready to tack, hard alee."

The designated men left their stations at the guns and ran to handle the sheets. The Retribution ran toward the smaller ship with gun ports open and Quakers as well as guns run out.

Jon knew the cutter would have seen her gun ports as the Retribution tacked, and expected her to try to run from them. Instead she held her course, closing at a rapid rate. The American flag disappeared to be replaced by the British ensign.

"On deck," the lookout shouted. "I can see her deck now. Five guns. Four-pounders I'd guess. One is mounted as a bow chaser."

"They're a navy ship, and they don't seem to be fooled by our Quakers," Jon said to himself. He didn't have time to pursue the thought further.

"Mr. Harper," Jon shouted, "Bring us up to close hauled."

The cutter tacked to follow them. Now, with both ships on the same tack, Jon expected to run away from the British ship.

"Those cutters can be fast," said Gil Harper. "I've seen them in Boston Harbor once or twice. We'll need to cripple her to get away."

The British cutter began to gain on the heavier ship as the wind slackened.

A puff of smoke followed by a faint report announced that the cutter had begun firing.

Jon watched as a tiny black dot grew swiftly into a cannon ball that hit the water less than one hundred yards astern. Jon stood on the quarterdeck watching the trim of the sails, looking for some way to get another half knot out of her. In a few minutes the British ship fired again. The ball struck the stern, smashing through Jon's cabin and then rolled along the deck, all of its energy spent. Another shot hit the stern. If they hit the rudder, <u>Retribution</u> would be helpless. As the cutter grew closer, the British began firing muskets, although at that range their fire had no effect.

"Don't fire until we're in musket range," Jon shouted to the men in the tops.

Two swivel guns mounted on <u>Retribution</u>'s taff rail began to fire, but the one-and-one-half inch balls had no effect on the enemy ship.

"Load the guns with chain shot on top of the balls," Jon shouted to Scotty. The gunners ran in the two four-pounders and rammed chain shot home.

"We're in musket range now, Captain," Gil said.

"Start firing Mr. Harper," Jon replied.

A volley of musket fire had no appreciable effect. Then Jon heard the distinctive crack of a rifle and the cutter's helmsman sagged to the deck. Fear gripped Jon's chest. He knew beyond a doubt who had fired the rifle. Alexis had fired from the maintop, and he couldn't do anything to protect her.

Before another man could take the helm, the cutter had come into the wind with her sails shivering. It took only seconds for her to recover, but the cutter lost two boat lengths.

A four-pound ball from the cutter struck the rail sending splinters flying. Two of the starboard gun crew fell. Their mates carried them below while others took their places at the gun.

Another ball struck the hull. The cutter grew nearer, slightly to windward of the schooner. Musket balls whistled through the air, some striking the deck nearby. Again the rifle cracked, and a body fell from the cutter's tiny fighting top. The Retribution's muskets kept up a steady, although ineffective fire. Jon prayed that the British would not recognize that a rifle firing from the maintop had caused more damage than all of their musket fire.

"Scotty," Jon shouted, "be ready with the larboard gun. Tell your sail handlers that we're going to tack. We'll cross her bow. Then fire high. We need to cut up her foresails."

Jon waited a few more seconds, then shouted, "Hard alee."

The crew already at their stations eased and trimmed the

sheets as the <u>Retribution</u> tacked. For a moment, it looked as if Jon had waited too long. The two ships came closer and closer. Jon ran to the larboard side, heedless of the musket balls striking around him. As he watched, Jon saw that the cutter's bowsprit would strike the main shrouds, and the two ships would be tangled together. Then the British crew would swarm aboard the <u>Retribution</u>. The fighting would be terrible and the large well-trained and disciplined navy crew would overwhelm his men.

Jon glanced at Isaac Feldman, gun captain for the larboard four-pounder, leaning over the cannon, looking along the barrel. He suddenly stood erect and touched the glowing linstock to the touch hole. The cannon fired.

The foresails of the cutter disappeared in a tangle of flailing shreds. With her head sails gone, the cutter rounded sharply up into the wind, her bowsprit missing the rigging of Jon's ship by only a yard or two. For an instant, the cutter lay broadside to the <u>Retribution</u>, and the British ship fired two four-pound balls into the <u>Retribution</u>'s hull. Then the Americans were past the cutter, running free. Before the British crew could knot and splice the rigging and raise a new jib and staysail, <u>Retribution</u> would be beyond their reach.

In spite of their narrow escape, elation filled Jon's chest. Not fear or relief, elation. More excited and more alive than he had been since their battle for the <u>Mary P.</u> God help me, he thought, I love this.

***

"Chips, sound the well," Jon ordered.

"Aye, sir."

The ship's carpenter ran down the companionway and returned a few minutes later.

"Three feet of water in the well, sir" he announced.

"Rig the pumps, Mr. Harper."

"Aye, sir." Gil Harper replied.

"We can plug the shot holes, but there's some seams started below the water line." the carpenter went on.

"Can you get at them to make repairs?" Jon asked.

"Some of them. Don't know where all of 'em are. The entire hold might have to be emptied before we find it. The pumps will keep her afloat, but the leaks might get worse in a hurry."

"Damn. Mr. Lachlan, we'll run back into Boston."

"Yes, sir," Scotty replied.

***

In Jon's cabin Alexis stood before him, head down and teeth clenched, expecting another tongue lashing.

"You know that you shouldn't take such risks," Jon began. "Fighting ships always try to kill the men in the tops. I saw one of theirs fall just before we crossed that cutter's bow."

"He aimed at the quarterdeck, so I shot him," she said simply.

"Dammit Alex, I mean Alexis, how am I supposed to take care of you if you keep doing things like that?"

"One of the lads in the foretop is only sixteen. Why shouldn't I get to fight too? I own half of this ship, you know. Besides, I'm a better shot than most of the crew. In fact, I'm as good as you are."

Jon abruptly stood up, sending his chair crashing backward. He took Alexis by her arms and shook her. He stopped suddenly. He looked into her eyes, and a sudden cold fear gripped his chest. He pulled her into his arms.

"Oh Lord Alex, what would I do if you . . . ?"

He pulled her closer, and she laid her head on his chest. The top of her head barely touching his chin. Her arms encircled him, and Jon buried his face in her hair. Alexis held herself against him.

Surrounded by sailors during her childhood, Alexis had never paid attention to the stories other girls told. She hid behind a facade of tomboyish actions and speech. The emotions that swept through her, unexpected and powerful, confused her. She lifted her head to look at Jon. He pulled her to him and his lips touched hers. She briefly tried to pull away, looking at Jon's face, then put her arms around his neck and kissed him, so passionately that both of them were shaken.

"Captain, sail sighted due east," Gil Harper shouted from the deck.

Jon cursed and forced himself to step back from Alexis.

She understood and pushed him gently.

"Go," she said firmly.

He ran up to the deck, leaving Alexis standing with her hand touching her lips.

"Lookout, what do you see?"

"A brig sir. Looks to be British."

Jon tucked his glass under his arm and climbed the rigging.

A British merchant ship, armed with four guns, probably small ones from what he could see.

"Crack on all the sail she'll carry Gil. Keep us on course for Boston."

Second Mate Harper's jaw dropped.

"Ain't we gonna take her?"

"You heard my orders, dammit," Jon snarled.

The damaged Privateer could take the fat, slow British ship, but Jon couldn't bear the thought of another battle as long as Alexis was aboard.

Chapter Twenty-Three

When they entered Boston Harbor, Jon saw Mrs. Sloan standing on the pier, wringing her hands and looking at the ship anxiously.

She ran up the gang plank as soon as she could and approached Jon on the quarterdeck.

"Is she alright? I didn't realize what she had done until I found her note. I went to the dock right away, but you had already sailed."

"Yes, she's alright," Jon said somewhat curtly. Then he bawled in his best quarterdeck voice, "Send Miss Archer to the quarterdeck."

Alexis appeared on deck still wearing her seaman's clothing.

Mrs. Sloan led her to the gangway as if she needed help in finding her way. Alexis smiled at Jon as she walked by him. Jon tried to keep a straight face for the benefit of the crew. He failed miserably.

***

The <u>Retribution</u> had been damaged more than Jon had first thought. The cutter's guns had hit her hull only two times, but the hull had been pierced and ribs sprung. The repairs would be expensive and time consuming. They emptied the hull, including ballast, and then hove her down on her side on the beach so that the damaged areas could be reached and repairs could be made properly.

Jon resumed his search for more guns. No guns of any kind except swivel guns could be found. The army's needs came first.

With time on his hands, Jon met Todd every day and had coffee at Franklin's, an Inn they frequented. They had been discussing shipping and privateering, as they usually did, when Todd broke into a smile.

"Jon, I may have a way to get you some cannons."

"I'm interested for sure." Jon replied. "Where are they?"

"Father has a ship expected next week coming from St. Eustatious. They are bringing back some guns for the army. The <u>Mary P.</u> saw them on her return from San Juan. If the British don't catch them, they should be here in about two weeks."

"What about the Army? Won't they insist that we give them up?"

"If I remember correctly, Captain Nestor hoped to find some six-pounders too, just what you want. If you meet <u>Princess</u>

at sea and transfer the guns to your ship, the army won't even know about them."

"Todd," Jon said, leaning over the table and speaking softly, "We need to talk to your father. Don't mention this to anyone except your father. There are too many Tories in this town."

***

The <u>Retribution</u>, still carrying only two guns, but repaired and fully provisioned, swung at anchor in Casco Bay, ready to sail.

Jon paced restlessly along the windward side of the quarterdeck. Scotty stood near the leeward rail idly watching the gulls skim over the water. Jon had ordered the crew aboard. He let it be known that they were expecting some guns to arrive soon from St. Eustatious and would sail as soon as they arrived.

"Mr. Lachlan, we'll sail on tomorrow's tide. We can't wait in port for a ship that might never come," Jon said suddenly.

"Mr. Paget's ship should be in within a week now. If the army doesn't get all of the guns, we'll have twice as many cannon as that British cutter."

"Are you questioning my judgment, Mr. Lachlan?"

"No, sir," Scotty said quickly. "I just . . . ."

He stopped abruptly when Jon glared at him.

"Have the jolly boat manned. I'll sleep ashore tonight."

Jon engaged a room at his old familiar inn and then waited in the taproom until Henry August arrived. They took a table in one corner, away from the crowd.

"Your message said you had important news for me. What

does it concern, Jon?"

"I'll come right to the point. You have a reputation as a patriot, and you helped me when Morgan had me thrown in jail. I need your help again. I'm certain that there are some loyalists here who are spying for the British."

"I know we have some traitors here," Henry August said. "But we don't know who they are. What do you know about them?"

"The <u>Retribution</u> sailed last month with two four-pounders and eight 'Quakers', and they were damn well made 'Quakers'. From any distance, they looked like six-pounders. They would have fooled anyone. A British cutter with only five guns, all four-pounders, attacked us before we sailed a full day out of port. Somehow they knew we only had two guns. No sane person would attack a schooner carrying ten guns with a ship so lightly armed. They not only knew how we were armed, they knew exactly when we would sail. They were waiting for us. I think we were betrayed, and I know who the traitors are."

"I'll give you all the help I possibly can. Tell me what you want."

"I knew you would help. Here's what I'd like you to do."

The two men spoke quietly with their heads close together for several minutes and then Henry August left.

When Jon finished his ale he left the tavern and walked to Mr. Paget's office.

After a quarter of an hour, he returned to his room carrying a tightly wrapped bundle.

That evening, Jon ate a late dinner in the tap room and waited until he saw Faith arrive in the usual closed carriage. He met her at the back door.

"Why ain't you in your room, Jon?" she whispered in his ear, conscious of the other patrons.

Jon laughed. In spite of himself it pleased him that she seemed so eager to bed him.

"I have a thousand things to take care of before I set sail tomorrow. I knew if you came to my room I would never be able to refuse you, and then we might have to lay over another day."

Faith giggled.

"I heard you was goin' to wait for Mr. Paget's ship and get some more guns," she said.

"We can't wait any more for a ship that might never arrive. I'll be able to stay away from that British cutter. I'll go north as soon as we clear the harbor. If he's waiting for us, he'll be to the southeast."

"I hope nothing bad will happen to you this time, Jon. I'll be waiting for you. We'll make up for missing tonight." She gave his hand a quick squeeze and left.

Jon left the tavern and walked up the hill to say goodbye to Alexis and Mrs. Sloan. The sun had set hours earlier, but the light showing in the window told Jon that the two women were still awake.

Mrs. Sloan had seen many such leave takings, but still she had tears in her eyes.

"Come back safe Jon," she murmured and then left the

room. Alexis walked with Jon a few yards down the path toward the harbor. She stopped and pulled him around to face her.

She slid into his arms and kissed him.

"I would like to go with you, Jon," she whispered.

"I would rather die myself than put you in danger. And don't try to stow away either. I've doubled the night guard and told them I'd cut the ears off the man who lets you onboard. No matter what you tell them."

She laughed and kissed him again.

"Be careful, Jon. Please be careful."

**

Before the <u>Retribution</u> sailed, Jon personally conducted a search of the ship to be certain that Alexis had not gotten aboard.

They raised anchor at dawn and sailed southeast as soon as they cleared the harbor.

Scotty nervously paced the quarterdeck. They had taken this same course when the British cutter had found and chased them. He tried to hide his nervousness from the crew, but Jon noticed.

"Mr. Lachlan, we'll have the best eyes in the ship aloft now."

"Yes sir, Captain."

Jon smiled. Scotty never called him Captain unless he disapproved of his actions.

"We are looking for the schooner <u>Princess</u>. She belongs to Mr. Paget. Do you know her?"

"Yes sir, Captain. I know her. I've seen her in port many a

time."

***

Shortly after first light the look out saw a sail on the horizon. A square rigged ship. Definitely not the Princess.

Gil Harper had the watch. "Shall we change course, Captain?" he asked.

He hesitated to suggest any action to Jon, since he didn't know him as well as Scotty did, and he had seen Jon's reaction to Scotty's advice at times.

"No, Mister Harper, we'll continue to look for Princess."

The Princess had made a slower than usual passage, and Jon spent three weeks tacking back and forth across her expected path waiting for her and avoiding other ships.

At last their lookout spotted a familiar sail. The Retribution changed course to intercept her. The Princess changed her course to try to slip away. Jon went to his cabin and retrieved the bundle he had carried away from Mr. Paget's office. He unwrapped it and shook out a white flag with a large black letter P in the center, the Paget shipping company flag. They hoisted the flag. After several minutes, the Princess came about and headed toward them.

"What ship?" the Captain of the Princess hailed.

"Retribution, out of Boston, Captain Weaver commanding," Jon replied. "I have a letter for you from Mr. Paget. I'll come over to deliver it."

***

The ship's boat moved quickly over the water in spite of the five-foot chop. They hooked onto the Princess's main chains and Jon scrambled up the side with no more than one wet foot.

"Welcome aboard, Captain. Honored to have you. I'm Josiah Nestor, master of this ship."

"Thank you Captain. Honored to be aboard," Jon replied. "I have a letter for you from Mr. Paget."

"May I offer you a drink? Wine perhaps?"

"I would gladly accept Captain Nestor, but we have seen two hostile ships in the last two days. I feel that a speedy completion of our business would be wise."

"Of course. Just give me a moment."

Captain Nestor hastily read the letter sent to him by Mr. Paget and then smiled.

"Pleased to help you sir," he said. Then he turned and shouted, "Bosun, get the hatch covers off. Rig tackle to sway out those six-pounders."

"If you bring your ship along the larboard side we can deliver the guns right to your deck. You'll want shot also. I regret that we don't have more guns to give you, but we could only get six of them at St. Eaustatious."

Jon's crew had removed the wooden Quakers from the gun carriages. As the six-pounders came aboard the gun crews placed them on the carriages and moved them to the gun ports. Six-pound shot came aboard, passed hand to hand by a line of seamen. The shot went below into the lowest part of the ship, except for eight or ten shot stowed by each gun.

***

With the guns aboard and ready for use, Jon took the <u>Retribution</u> back toward Boston, exercising the gun crews twice daily as they went.

As expected, the commander of the British cutter had realized he had been tricked and now patrolled near the shore, south of the harbor entrance. As soon as the cutter changed course to chase them, Jon turned toward open sea. The cutter followed them, gaining rapidly, ignoring the schooner's guns and firing her bow chaser.

Jon had cleared for action at the first sight of the British vessel. The gun crews stood at their positions, some tense and silent, others overly animated. All of them alert and praying that they could do their duty and not disgrace themselves.

Now Jon forced himself to stand stiffly erect as he watched the balls from the four-pounders fly toward them. He began to feel the sense of elation at the coming excitement of battle. He couldn't keep a slight smile from his face.

Gil Harper noticed and smiled himself. He felt the same excitement growing within him.

Scotty Lachlan moved among the gun crews, saying a word or two to each man, as calm as on any other day at sea.

When Jon judged that the cutter had come close enough, he shouted.

"Tack now, Mister Harper. Ease the sheets. We'll run down on her. Scotty, have your gunners aim for her mast. Fire as you bear."

As the two ships passed each other, the <u>Retribution</u>'s larboard side guns fired in sequence. Three six-pounders and a four-pounder fired at the single mast of the cutter. The cutter's two guns fired, but they didn't seriously damage Retribution. When the smoke blew away, Jon saw the cutter's two gunports smashed into one opening. Her shrouds cut through and the mainsail sagging as if a halyard had been cut. A long split had opened in the single mast. She still sailed, but slowly and sluggishly.

The Retribution sailed past the cutter.

"Bear up and tack, Gil," Jon shouted, too excited to use the more formal 'Mr. Harper.' "We'll cross her stern and rake her."

The men designated as sheet handlers left their guns and ran to their stations. They eased and hauled the sheets as the schooner came about and then they ran back to their guns.

"Scotty, fire as you bear."

As they crossed the cutter's stern the guns fired carefully aimed shots that smashed the stern and shattered the wheel. Splinters flying along the ship's deck wreaked terrible punishment on the crew. The weakened mast slowly fell over the side.

Jon tacked and once more brought his ship across the stern of the British ship. He backed his topsails to hold her within one hundred feet of the stern of the cutter.

"Hold your fire," Jon shouted to Scotty.

"Will you strike?" he called to the officer standing on the deck of the cutter.

The officer looked at the havoc brought about by the privateer's guns, the mast overboard, the wheel smashed, and the deck littered with dead and wounded. He looked at the muzzles of

Jon's guns, not more than a hundred feet away. Then said bitterly, "Yes, I'll strike."

For the first time, Jon saw that the officer had only one arm.

CHAPTER TWENTY-FOUR

Retribution's crew broke into wild cheering. The few men who had been in battles before, grinned broadly at the relief of the tension. Others were giddy with excitement and relief, they had proven themselves and survived. In their first action against this enemy they had been forced to turn and run. Now they had shown that they could stand and fight. They had done their duty without shirking, and, for the most part, had escaped injury. Their relief gave way to swelling pride. They had faced danger and performed faultlessly, keeping their heads in the midst of roaring guns, smoke, confusion, and enemy fire, served their guns well and sailed the schooner to perfection.

Jon brought the Retribution alongside the enemy. Gil led a boarding party onto the cutter's deck. Their joy and elation over their victory faded abruptly when they saw the carnage on the deck of the enemy ship. Gil and the boarding party faltered and became silent, appalled at the terrible damage done by Retribution's guns. Wreckage from the shattered rigging and mast littered the deck. Blood ran in rivulets back and forth as the cutter rocked in the ocean swells. Wounded and dead lay everywhere. Less than a dozen of the cutter's crew had survived without serious wounds. Dermot O'Neil murmured, "God have mercy on us."

Without waiting for orders, the Americans began giving aid to the surviving British crewmen. The survivors who could walk, made their way aboard the Retribution. Badly injured men came aboard with careful and gentle help from the Americans.

Under Gil's direction, the work party began carrying kegs of powder from the cutter's hold. Another party formed a line and began passing round shot hand to hand back to the Retribution.

The crew worked steadily, hauling ship's stores up through the hatch and carrying them to the schooner. At the same time another work party placed slings under one of the cutter's cannons to sway it aboard the Privateer.

"Sail, Captain," came an excited shout from Colin in the maintop.

"Where away?" Jon shouted back.

"Starboard beam, Captain."

Jon walked swiftly to the starboard rail. From the deck, he clearly saw the topsails of a ship. Colin O'Neil had been late with his warning, careless to the point of endangering his ship.

"What do you make of her Colin?"

"A British frigate. I've seen enough of them to know how they look."

"Scotty, drop that gun overboard. We're going to be chased by that frigate. Gil, set the cutter afire. Quickly now. There's no time to lose."

They cast off from the cutter as soon as all of the crew came back aboard. Jon expected the frigate to sail toward the cutter to look for survivors. Instead, the frigate's captain made a futile attempt to intercept the Retribution. Jon held their ship on a close reach and watched the frigate's topsails slowly drop below the horizon.

A distant plume of black smoke marked the position of the sinking cutter. As Jon watched through his glass, he saw a sudden flash of light and a towering cloud of smoke. After a few seconds, he heard the rumble of the explosion.

"Had more powder left on her than I thought," Gil Harper mused.

The topgallant sails of the British frigate dropped out of sight after only three hours. The royals remained visible as dots of white on the horizon. Colin, still in the maintop and watching through a glass, saw the white dots move together and then separate again.

"On deck," he shouted. "The frigate's come about. Looks like she's heading northwest." "Thank you Colin," Jon called.

Jon held his heading until the British sails were no longer visible.

If the frigate held her new course, she would be near the entrance to the harbor at Boston before Jon's ship arrived there.

He would have liked to return to Boston immediately, particularly with the wounded British sailors aboard, but the probable presence of a British frigate near Boston made him set a course for the shipping lanes east of New York.

***

By sunup the following day, the captured powder and shot had been properly stowed, and the schooner sailed through the sparkling sea with a clear blue sky overhead. The crew had finished knotting and splicing the rigging, patching sails, and repairing minor damage to the taff rail. They returned to their daily shipboard routine, searching for possible prizes.

Jon opened his cabin door and called to Scotty. "Mister Lachlan, send Colin O'Neil to my cabin."

Jon had barely closed the door to his cabin when Colin knocked.

"Come in."

"You wanted to see me, Captain?" Colin asked.

"Yes" Jon said curtly. He looked at Colin sternly and silently. Colin swallowed and cleared his throat.

"I'm sure you know why," Jon said.

Colin swallowed again and bobbed his head.

"You failed to do your duty yesterday," Jon said. "You should have warned us of that frigate long before you did. I'll assume the work on deck distracted you. I hope you know that your duty is to watch for other ships, not to gaze down on the deck."

As he spoke the words, Jon remembered his initial

reluctance to trust Colin and his brother Dermot when the two men had been captured at Charles Towne. Both of the O'Neil brothers had been eager to join their crew and worked diligently when changing the captured ship into the schooner <u>Retribution</u>. There had been no hint of disloyalty to Jon and the ship, but a flicker of doubt had remained in Jon's mind.

"I hope you didn't have some other reason . . . ." Jon let the sentence hang in the air. Colin had begun to perspire heavily, but his voice didn't waver.

"I was careless Captain, but me and my brother are loyal Americans now. We'd both be hung if that British ship caught us. Letting that frigate get so close might have been the death of me 'n Dermot. We lived under British rule in Ireland. We know 'em too well to have any love for 'em."

"We'll say no more about it then. You may go."

After Colin left, Jon went on deck and stood at the rail, staring at the horizon, trying to organize his thoughts. Colin's speech sounded convincing, however, the safety of the ship and crew depended on Jon's judgment. He would say no more, but keep a watchful eye on both of them.

***

When Jon came on deck the next morning, the sun had just cleared the horizon. A comfortable, brisk breeze carried them swiftly toward the shipping lanes off New York.

A voice called to him from the deck

"May I come up onto your quarterdeck sir?"

The Lieutenant who had commanded the British cutter

stood on the deck a few feet away.

"Please do, Lieutenant," Jon replied.

The British officer climbed the ladder to the quarterdeck with no apparent trouble in spite of having lost one arm at the shoulder.

"Allow me to present myself," the officer said stiffly. "I am Lieutenant Garvin Kendall Kendrick, formerly Master and Commander of His Majesty's cutter Star."

The lieutenant's uniform had been cleaned as well as possible but still showed black powder streaks and small rents in the fabric. His face bore signs of the combat that had taken place just hours earlier. His cheek and ear were reddened from a powder burn that had also singed his dark brown hair. His right hand, the only one he possessed, had been scraped deeply and dried blood covered the knuckles. Nearly as tall as Jon, he held himself stiffly erect.

"I am Jon Weaver, Captain of this schooner, as I imagine you know," Jon replied. "I feel that I must tell you that I may have been responsible for the loss of your arm. I think it is better to clear the air on that."

Lieutenant Kendrick stiffly nodded his head.

"Yes, it is better to clear the air as you say though I knew of you before this battle. The wound didn't amount to a great deal. It would have healed with just a few stitches, if our surgeon hadn't botched the job."

"You only did your duty as you saw it," he went on. "If I needed someone to blame, it would be that surgeon. In any event, a good visible wound is an advantage in our navy." He smiled bitterly. "I try not to complain."

"If you hold no malice toward me, why did you chase my sloop so far and risk your frigate in shoal waters off South Carolina?"

"You must know that a mere Lieutenant would not be in command of a frigate," the British officer replied sarcastically, momentarily losing control of his emotions. Then he continued in a more conciliatory tone. "The Captain of that frigate is my uncle, Kendall Kendrick. He has some idea about family honor, that sort of thing. The whole episode turned into a fiasco."

After a pause, he continued. "I heard that you lost your ship."

The last phrase seemed sympathetic.

Jon nodded. "As well as my entire crew. Six of us survived the wreck, but injuns killed four. Scotty Lachlan, our first mate, and I hid out in the woods and finally reached friendly forces near Charles Towne." He opened his mouth to tell the rest of the story, then stopped. The story might be too useful to a British naval officer.

Lieutenant Kendrick's attitude toward his captors surprised Jon. He had expected the British Lieutenant to complain bitterly and display the over-bearing airs of the typical upper-class Englishman. If the captured officer felt any class superiority, he concealed it well.

When Jon related how the British had bombarded Boston, the Lieutenant shook his head.

"It seems a pointless thing to do. I suppose they felt justified. You colonists are in rebellion you know."

"I suppose the Tories in the Mohawk Valley felt justified in turning those savages loose to kill my family?"

Lt. Garvin Kendrick's face reddened. He turned away and stared at the horizon.

"I would be the last to say that we have any claim to moral superiority, Captain Weaver." Then he turned away and left the quarterdeck.

The confines of a sailing ship forced the ship's officers and Lieutenant Kendrick into close proximity. Lieutenant Kendrick avoided conversation concerning the war, and Jon and Scotty accepted "Garv", as he preferred to be called, with stiff politeness as an unavoidable guest on board their ship. Gil, however, refused to accept the prisoner as any thing better than an unwelcome intruder. His experience in the prison ship had left him with a glowing-hot hatred of anyone or anything British.

***

Lieutenant Kendrick observed the easy discipline aboard the <u>Retribution</u> with wonder.

"How do you get your crew to perform their duties so well without any threat of punishment? In our navy we must use the cat frequently to keep the men sharp. You seldom even need to speak harshly to anyone."

"These men are here because they want to be here. We don't have to 'press' anyone. They can reap great rewards in prize money as your seamen can. However, most of our crew are patriots as well. If a ship hadn't been available, they would most likely have joined General Washington's army."

The British officer looked skeptically at Jon but said nothing more.

***

Lieutenant Kendrick joined the other officers in Jon's cabin every evening for supper. Either Scotty or Gil would have the watch, so only three men dined at any one time. If Gil dined with them, he invariably found an excuse to leave as soon as he could without being too offensive. His hatred for the British made it difficult for him to be polite in the presence of one of their officers. Scotty and Jon, on the other hand, actually enjoyed conversing with Garv. His stories of life in the British Navy were interesting and enlightening, at least until he had drunk an excessive amount of wine. Then he became sullen and morose. Garv frequently steered the conversation around to the subject of business opportunities in America.

"You sound as if you want to go into business in America," Jon said. "You'll surely be allowed to give your parole when we reach Boston, and you're certain to be exchanged soon."

"Jon, let me instruct you about the conditions I face. Whenever a British Naval vessel is lost, her captain must face a court marshall. In most cases the commander is found innocent. However, I carelessly let you trick me into fighting your larger and much more heavily armed ship. I would almost certainly be found guilty of negligence and probably cashiered. You not only took my arm away from me, you took away my career." He could not keep the bitterness out of his voice. After a pause, he sighed resignedly and then continued. "You can understand that returning to England is not my desire."

"You must have family and friends there. Surely you want to see them again."

The lieutenant smiled ruefully. The bitterness in his voice changed to resignation.

"In the colonies a man's family is not as important as it is in England. I would bring disgrace on generations of Kendricks to come if I returned to England as a cashiered Naval Officer. My father is an Earl, and by law, my oldest brother or his son will inherit that title and all of the estate. My next oldest brother also has a son, so I stand fifth in any possible inheritance."

"As for friends, I have been in the navy since the age of twelve, most of the time aboard a ship. I have few friends other than in the service. Now I would be an embarrassment to them."

"I like the active life of the navy, but I will never get another command. My father will send me an allowance, and," he paused for a moment, "if I promise not to return to England, the allowance might be a bit larger."

"After the war, I'll probably find some use for my talents in the Colonies."

"Even if we win our freedom?" Jon asked.

"Yes, even if you are no longer English!"

"If you want to succeed here," Jon said with a slight smile, "you'll have to call our country America, not 'the colonies'."

***

The <u>Retribution</u> cruised along the shipping lanes for three weeks before they saw any suitable prizes. Then they captured two ships in two days, both of them loaded with ship's stores, powder, and shot. With his crew depleted by the assignment of prize crews, Jon decided it would be foolish to stay at sea any longer than necessary. Even if the frigate had sailed to Boston, Jon didn't believe that she would be waiting for him after so long a time. The <u>Retribution</u> escorted the prizes back to Boston. As he expected, the blockade didn't cause them any trouble.

***

Jon left the care of the ship to Gil and Scotty and went ashore as soon as the anchor dropped. As he walked toward the office of Henry August, he notice several people looking at him and smiling.

"Good afternoon, Captain Weaver," a well-dressed stranger said as they passed each other. Jon smiled and touched his cap. He didn't have any recollection of seeing the man before.

No more than one hundred paces along the street, a second man dressed in black and carrying a bible in his hand stopped Jon.

"God bless you, Captain Weaver. You're doing the Lord's work."

Jon didn't know how to reply. He mumbled thanks, and walked away.

Before he reached Henry August's office, three more people greeted him politely and with great respect. He scarcely knew any of them. They had all addressed him as "Captain Weaver". Jon wondered why he had become so popular. It didn't occur to him that he had become a hero in the eyes of the residents of Boston.

Henry August greeted Jon with a wide grin.

"We got them, Jon. All three of them. They did exactly as you thought they would."

"Three of them?" Jon had expected that only Faith and Mr. Morgan would be involved.

"Oh yes," Henry August said. "Jakob Braun. A notorious Tory. He carried the message to the boat the British sent in."

"We've been waiting for you to get back. I think you might have to testify to be sure of convicting them."

Chapter Twenty-Five

Unloading cargo and figuring the shares for everyone in his crew, demanded Jon's complete attention for more than a week. The cargos proved to be more valuable than expected. A frugal crewman could live well for many months on his share from these two ships. Alexis received her share as half owner, and Jon received the captain's share as well as half the owner's share. They both had enough to live comfortably for several years.

Alexis and Jon spent most of the evenings on the lawn outside her house as they had weeks earlier. Leaving her, to return to his ship every night, seemed like a tremendous hardship to Jon, but, of course, anything else would be completely unacceptable.

The trial could be delayed no longer. Papers had been served and a date selected. On the day of the trial, Jon took the stand as the first witness for the Government. He asked that he be allowed to testify in private, but the court refused his request. As he waited for the trial to begin, he saw Alexis seated among the spectators. Scotty, Garv, and Mrs. Sloan sat with her.

"Please tell us how you found out about Faith Crawford's traitorous actions," the Judge intoned.

"I had told her that our ship had only two guns and eight 'Quakers'. Then I told her when we would leave, and how we planned to avoid the English ships. When we set sail that British ship found us right away. They knew where we would be. I thought we could bluff them with our 'Quakers'. Instead they came right at us. They only had five four-pounders, but we looked like we had eight six-pounders and two four-pounders. We appeared to out gun them by more than three to one as far as weight of shot goes. They knew before hand that we had fewer guns than they did. If it hadn't been for good gunnery that took out the cutter's foresails, they would have taken us."

"That isn't proof," Mr. Morgan's lawyer shouted. "Where were you and Miss Crawford when you confided in her this important information?"

"In my room at the Inn," Jon mumbled.

"Speak louder Mr. Weaver. Let the Court hear what you say."

"She came to my room at the Inn," Jon said in a loud voice. He glanced in the direction of Alexis. As the implication of Jon's words became apparent to her she gasped audibly and her face began to redden.

"Had this happened before? Did you entice her to your room before?"

"No, sir."

"Do you expect us to believe that she came on her own accord? With no invitation from you."

"Yes, she came of her own accord. She started it a long time ago."

Alexis' face grew redder still.

"Did she share your bed all of those times?"

"Yes," Jon replied, quietly.

Alexis' mouth tightened in a grim line. She spoke to Mrs. Sloan in a low, intense voice. Mrs. Sloan touched her arm and whispered in her ear. Alexis shook her arm loose and glared at Jon.

He lowered his eyes to the floor in front of him, his face hot with embarrassment.

"Gentlemen," the defense lawyer said, "We have here a man who admits that he lured a young lady to his bed, and now he wants to shift blame for his lack of common sense and seamanship from himself to this innocent girl."

Alexis tried to rise to her feet. Scotty didn't know if she intended to leave or to attack Jon. To be safe he held her in her chair.

"I must object to that statement," said Henry August. "We will show that Jon Weaver is an excellent seaman and a great patriot as well."

The questioning continued for another hour. The attorney restated the idea that Jon had lured Faith to his room. That she had not come of her own accord.

Eventually Henry August rose to question Jon.

"Between the voyages of the Mary P., how many times did Faith Crawford come to your room?"

"I can't tell you exactly. Whenever the Mary P. brought us into Boston, she spent at least one night with me," Jon answered.

"Before you sailed on the sloop Savage that later went aground in a storm, did she visit you then too?"

"Yes, she did," Jon mumbled, not daring to look at Alexis.

"And did you tell Miss Crawford of your plans?"

"I think I might have told her when we planned to sail."

"When you sailed, what happened outside the harbor."

Jon thought for a moment. "Well, a British frigate spotted us about four hours out. Chased us a long way."

"And did you say anything to Miss Crawford about your plans before the Retribution sailed? The day the British cutter attempted to capture you."

"Yes," Jon mumbled, embarrassed that he had been stupid enough to give that information to Faith.

"You saw her again before this last battle did you not?"

"Yes, in the tavern's taproom. We talked only briefly."

"Did you tell her your plans?"

"No, I didn't. I told her that we would skirt the north shore, but instead we went southeast. I told her that we still had only two small guns and eight 'Quakers'."

"Did you have more and heavier guns by then?"

"No, but we met Mr. Paget's ship Princess and took some guns from her cargo."

"So you took your ship, now more heavily armed, and you went looking for the British cutter."

Henry August turned away from Jon to address the court.

"As we all know, Captain Weaver destroyed that British cutter and furthermore brought back two prize ships. I believe his actions speak for themselves. His seamanship and bravery are above reproach."

"Now I will tell you what transpired the night before the <u>Retribution</u> last sailed. Captain Weaver had given her the false information. She went straight to the Morgan residence. Shortly after that, Mr. Morgan, himself, left the house. He walked to the home of Jakob Braun, a man who has long been suspected of Tory sympathies. He handed Mr. Braun a piece of paper and then Mr. Morgan returned to his home. Later Jakob Braun walked to the shore carrying a shielded lantern. We followed Mr. Braun. At the water's edge he flashed a signal and soon a small boat rowed to the shore. He gave the piece of paper to the men in the boat, and they rowed back out to sea."

A sudden babble of excited conversation broke out in the courtroom.

The judge banged his gavel until the crowd became silent.

Henry August continued.

"I have two witnesses beside myself that saw the transfer of that scrap of paper to the boat. After Mr. Braun returned to his home, we called on him. The young men persuaded him to explain his actions. He admitted that he had both sent and received messages in the past. All of them from Mr. Morgan to the British or from the British to Mr. Morgan."

The spectators in the courtroom began talking loudly once more, and the judge banged his gavel for a full minute before the crowd became silent.

The lawyer for the defense didn't bother to speak. He picked up his papers and left.

***

The Court found all three of the defendants guilty and sentenced them to jail for ten years. For a man of Christian Morgan's age and poor health, it amounted to a death sentence.

As the prisoners filed out of the courtroom, Jon saw Faith looking at him, her face distorted with hatred. He would have been sorry for her, but she had nearly destroyed his ship and killed him and Alexis as well. In ten years, if she lived that long, Faith would be a changed woman and not for the better.

Outside the courtroom a crowd of well-wishers gathered.

"Congratulations, Jon," Mr. Paget said, shaking Jon's hand. "I know I speak for every patriot in Maine Territory when I say we are proud of you. You have gotten rid of a nest of traitors. Everyone who sails out of Boston owes you a debt of gratitude."

"Even I congratulate you, Jon."

Jon looked at Garv in surprise.

"After all, no one likes a spy," Garv said, extending his hand.

Mr. Paget insisted that they repair to the tavern for a small celebration, and everyone agreed. Jon less enthusiastically than the others. He had been trying to find Alexis in the crowd, but she had left with Mrs. Sloan as soon as the trial ended.

Chapter Twenty-Six

The Retribution swung idly at anchor in BostonHarbor full of stores and ammunition. Two more four-pounders had been found, and she now carried ten guns. Six six-pounders and four of the smaller four-pounders. She could sail when the tide turned, but none of her officers had come aboard, and no one expected them until early morning.

Jon, Scotty and Gil had been invited as guests of honor to a dinner party given by Mr. Paget. The party had been arranged to celebrate Jon's victory over the British cutter as well as the downfall of the three spies. To the surprise of many citizens of Boston, Lt. Garvin Kendall Kendrick also received an invitation. He had given his parole and seemed to be a likable man. As an enemy officer he would always be suspect, but as the son of an Earl, his value as a guest at Mrs. Paget's table could not be ignored.

Jon, Scotty, and Gil had mixed feelings about the party. They had spent the better part of their lives on board ship and had gained their positions because of their seafaring knowledge and skill gained by years of hard work. They had become excellent seamen, but social graces had never been part of their training. They had little opportunity to develop skills in polite, "drawing room" conversation.

Scotty tried to say he had to stay aboard the <u>Retribution</u> to keep order, but Jon wouldn't allow that. Gil Harper resigned himself to the dinner because his wife thought it would be the most exciting event of the decade.

None of the <u>Retribution</u>'s officers had any clothing suitable for the party. Garv solved the problem by taking the three men with him to the best tailor's shop in Boston. The shop produced four sets of clothing in an amazingly short time. Now, thanks to Garv, they arrived at the Paget home confident of their appearance, if nothing else.

As they entered the dining room, Jon saw a remarkably beautiful woman in the far corner of the room. He inhaled sharply when he realized he was looking at Alexis.

"My God," he gasped. He had fallen in love with her when she wore boy's clothing and climbed through the rigging like a seaman. Now when he saw her in the gown that Mrs. Sloan had picked out for her, her beauty stunned him. Her cheeks were lightly tinged with rouge and her hair shone in the light of the candles. He stared at her for several moments. His mouth became dry, in part because it hung open. He recovered his composure enough to close his mouth and began moving toward her through the crowd. Mr. Paget stopped him and began introducing him to the cream of Boston society. He couldn't escape without giving offense. After several minutes of forced conversation, he looked for her again. She had disappeared.

The guests began looking for their places at the table. Jon found his place but didn't stop searching until he found Alexis' place card. He would have exchanged her card with one next to himself, but both chairs adjacent to his own had been occupied.

After Jon seated himself, the women on either side of him began vying for his attention. After his years at sea in all male company, he hardly knew how to talk without swearing, let alone make pleasant conversation with two women who were total strangers.

"Oh, Captain Weaver, I've so wanted to talk to you," the woman on his left gushed. "I'm absolutely fascinated by your courageous actions against the British."

"You should be," said a familiar voice. Garv sat across the table from them. "He is an extremely brave and intelligent mariner."

Garv's comment saved Jon from making an awkward reply and allowed him to recover somewhat.

"Lt. Kendrick is very kind. We had a great advantage over him in number and size of our guns. He fought bravely."

"Yes, you did have an advantage," Garv said with an edge in his voice. "The result might have been different if it had not been for your trickery."

"Quite so Lieutenant. But then 'all is fair in love and war'."

This weak hackneyed response was greeted with laughter from both sides of the table as if it were the wittiest comment ever.

Garv glared and then turned away from Jon to strike up a conversation with the woman on his right.

The woman who had first spoken to Jon tapped his arm with her fan.

"Well said, Captain," she whispered.

Jon's apprehension vanished and he conversed with her, as well as the woman on his left, easily and confidently.

Even his inability to manipulate the silverware with skill seemed unimportant. He noticed that Scotty and Gil had similar problems, and neither of them showed the least bit of embarrassment. What would anyone in Maine Territory expect of seafaring men?

Garv, completely at ease, appeared to be enjoying himself immensely. A widow, three times his age, sat at his left, and a young, plain girl at his right. Both of the women smiled all evening long, completely captivated by the young Englishman.

***

In contrast to the officers of the <u>Retribution</u>, Garv had looked forward to this dinner. He wanted to become more broadly acquainted. He had listened closely to the opinions of the merchants, bankers, and sailors he spoke with before the meal, hoping to find some exciting and profitable venture that he could take up after the war. As a captive British Officer, it would be a severe breach of ethics to enter into any commercial venture until after the war ended. At least, not openly.

***

The meal ended at last and to Jon's relief, he had not made any major mistakes at the table. In fact, except for a purple wine stain on Scotty's waist coat, all three of the Retribution's officers had survived unscathed.

The ladies left the room and servants passed cigars and brandy around the table. The men talked mostly of commerce, taxes, and business, subjects that bored Jon but fascinated Garv. Jon thought of Alexis and how he would explain away his relationship with Faith. He knew that Alexis would understand if only he could talk to her.

After twenty minutes of boredom, Mr. Paget rose from his chair. "Gentlemen," he said. "I think it is time we join the ladies."

Jon, Scotty and Gil dutifully followed the other guests into another room where the ladies sat, chatting among themselves. Alexis had seated herself near an open French door that led to a grass covered terrace. When Jon entered the room, she left and walked out onto the terrace. Jon moved through the crowd as quickly as good manners allowed.

On the terrace, he paused for a moment letting his eyes become accustomed to the dark. He saw her standing near a small pond. Moonlight gleaming on the water brought to mind that evening on the deck of the Retribution in South Carolina. Jon's confidence began to fail him. He walked hesitantly toward her, clearing his throat nervously.

"Alex, . . . ," he began. His throat seemed to close and he

couldn't speak.

"Yes, Jon," Alexis said in a soft encouraging voice.

"I've wanted to speak to you for so long."

Jon reached for her and took her hands in his.

Alexis copied her father's bosun's actions when he dealt with a belligerent drunken crewman. She raised her knee quickly and forcefully into Jon's crotch.

"Were you going to tell me about your whore?" her voice hard and grating and her eyes filled with fury. She kicked him as he lay gasping for breath. Jon took the blow in his stomach, and rolled over in pain. She tried to kick him again, but her shoe caught on the hem of her dress. She turned away with a quietly spoken, venomous and salty oath and walked back to the house.

Jon had raised himself to his knees in time to see Alexis enter the door of the Paget house.

She approached the first man she saw. "Lieutenant, would you mind escorting me home," she said demurely as she slipped her arm under Garv's. "I feel a sudden chill."

Garv gallantly made their excuses to Mr. Paget and led her through the crowd to the door. He hailed a carriage and assisted her as she climbed in. They had traveled for only a short distance when he realized she had started to weep.

"Are you troubled, Miss Archer?" Garv asked in a quiet, kind voice.

"Oh what the hell," she said, dropping back into her seagoing vocabulary. "Jon wanted to tell me . . . ."

"What did he say to hurt you so?"

"I didn't let him say anything. I kicked him when he came close. I left him laying on the ground."

Garv choked, trying to stifle a chuckle. He soon gave up and began to laugh, quietly at first. The laughter grew uncontrollably until tears came to his eyes. The image of Captain Jonathan Weaver, "Fearless Colonial Captain of a Privateer," struck down by this beautiful woman seemed too absurd to be true, but somehow not overly surprising from his own class conscious outlook.

"Stop laughing dammit," Alexis shouted. The carriage driver leaned over from his seat and peered in the window.

"Is everything alright ma'am?" he asked.

"Mind your own damn business," Alexis snarled.

Garv's laughter died away to a chuckle. A chuckle with some overtones of smugness.

Chapter Twenty-Seven

"What course, Captain?" Scotty asked Jon as they cleared Boston Harbor.

"The usual, Mr. Lachlan," Jon replied in an indifferent and careless manner.

Scotty looked around in embarrassment to see if other crew members had heard Jon's voice.

"South by east Dermot," he shouted to the helmsman.

Physically Jon had recovered completely, however his mind would not stop dwelling on Alexis' unexpected and unjustified action.

"Why should she care what I did before I met her?" he mumbled to himself.

"After we brought the <u>Retribution</u> into Boston, Faith came to my room. I didn't go looking for her."

Jon paced two more circuits around the quarterdeck.

"Watch your heading," he snapped at the helmsman who had been holding the course quite well.

"And I only talked to Faith that last time so we could trap her," he continued mumbling to himself, as if rehearsing lines to say to Alexis. "She knows that. Why is she so angry?"

He continued pacing the quarter deck, eyes on the deck, muttering terse replies to anyone daring enough to speak to him.

***

The demanding task of commanding a Privateer overcame his sulk before sunset. At night in his bunk he thought of her again and again. How intensely attractive she had been that warm night in South Carolina on the Retribution's deck. Her firm young body against his for a brief moment.

He remembered her courage when she led the panicked crew into the foretop to set Retribution's fore topsail in the gale off the Carolina coast. He thought again of his horror when he realized that she had climbed to the Retribution's maintop and began firing his rifle at the British cutter, and the wave of desire that had swept over him when he called her to his cabin to rebuke her after the battle.

He would lay in bed thinking of her beautiful face and firm lovely body. He imagined his hand touching her breast and even dreamed that somehow she might not object.

He saw her again as the fantastically beautiful woman at the dinner party, and then he remembered what had happened on the terrace that evening and lapsed into hopeless resignation.

He tossed in his bunk unable to sleep.

Before first light, Jon had given up. He left his cabin and came up to the quarterdeck.

"Lookout, what do you see?"

"Can't see nothin' Captain. Can't make out the horizon yet."

Jon continued to pace with his head down, as if something on the deck held his attention.

The sun cleared the horizon before he stopped.

Gil Harper had the watch, as reliable a man as any captain could want. Jon went below to his cabin.

He tried to rest but had no more success than he had the night before. He sat at his table staring at his logbook. Eventually, he dozed.

Jon awakened to the shout, "Sail ho."

"Where away?" Gil Harper responded.

"Fine on the larboard bow."

Jon came on deck before anyone could reach his door to knock.

"What do you make of her?" he shouted to the lookout.

"She ain't no navy ship. Look's like a brig."

Jon ran up the shrouds with his best glass, one he had taken from a British merchantman. His testy mood forgotten.

"She's a brig alright," he said.

He looked around the horizon and saw no other sails.

"Mister Harper, set a course to intercept her. We'll close with her and see if she's theirs or ours.

The schooner closed with the brig quickly. By midmorning

the ship could be seen from the deck, hull up on the horizon. By noon Retribution's guns could reach her.

As they grew nearer, it became apparent that Jon had been too optimistic. With her wide bottom and bluff bows, the brig looked like a slow and clumsy merchant ship, but she had five gunports on each side.

They closed to within a quarter mile when the ship turned to starboard and fired broadside at Retribution. The shots went wild.

"We know she's British for sure. She needs to shoot better than that if she wants to scare us off," Scotty said.

Jon held their course, closing rapidly with the brig.

Once more the merchant ship turned and fired a ragged broadside. Two of the shots hit the hull, well above the water line.

They continued to close with the enemy ship.

"Now we'll see how well she sails. Cross her stern, Gill." The Retribution turned to larboard. The merchant ship began to turn to avoid Retribution's raking fire, but she started too late and turned too slowly. As they crossed the stern of the enemy ship, Retribution's guns fired in sequence, sending lethal splinters flying along the deck and dismounting two of her guns.

"Bring her alongside, Gil. One broadside and we'll board her in the smoke."

The merchantman tried to turn to cross the Retribution's bow. The slow and awkward ship didn't respond fast enough.

Jon jumped down to the main deck and seized a cutlass from the barrel lashed to the mizzen mast.

The starboard guns crashed out again, and they felt the jar as the ships came together.

Before the grapnels caught the brig's rigging and rail, the Americans had already crossed to the brig's deck. The heavily outnumbered British merchant sailors threw down their arms and surrendered. The officers accepted the inevitable and struck their colors.

The prize had suffered superficial damage, but Retribution's guns had killed two seaman and wounded seven more. The Retribution's crew had no serious injuries.

The Americans set about repairing damaged rigging and sails of both ships even before the prisoners had been led below. Jon made a quick inspection of the cargo hold. The ship carried a mixed cargo that would be valuable in Boston. Bolts of cloth, knives, scissors, thread, needles, as well as tar, sail cloth, rope, and ship's tackle. Items prized by both New England housewives and shipyards.

Jon gave command of the prize to Gil, and they picked a crew to sail her back to port. Jon ran the rail intending to return to his ship. His foot slipped in a pool of blood where one of the British crew had died from a massive wound. His feet went out from under him and his head hit the deck with a resounding crack. Several crewmen rushed to his side. Although unconscious, he breathed normally. His crew rigged a sling and took him aboard the Retribution as gently as possible. In spite of their best efforts, Jon's inert form had been pushed and rolled over in the blood on the captured ship's deck.

Dermot O'Neil hadn't seen the accident. He came up out of the prize's hold in time to see Jon's limp body moved to Retribution's deck and taken below, bloody clothing and all.

"Lord have mercy," he murmured. "Lord have mercy on us all."

Gil took command of the prize and Scotty took command of the Retribution until Jon could recover.

"D'you want us to stand by to help you?" Gil shouted to Scotty.

"Ain't nothin' you can do for him. He didn't do no real damage to his self. He'll wake up with a wonderful headache, but he'll be alright I think."

"We can stand by if you like," Gil called back.

"Sail ho. Larboard quarter," came a shout from the mast head.

"We'll take a look at that ship, Gil. Set a course for Boston. If that ship we just sighted is British, we'll keep her away from you. Captain Weaver might not wake up for a few hours, and like I told you, there ain't nothin' you or me or anybody else can do. If we take him into port, some fool doctor will get at him. God knows they do more harm than good. You head for Boston. We'll go hunting for more prizes."

The strange ship tacked and tried to run from Retribution. Scotty kept chasing her until she proved to be an American ship headed for Boston.

Jon recovered consciousness before the merchantman had disappeared over the horizon. He suffered a splitting headache for two days but no permanent damage.

Chapter Twenty-Eight

Gil brought the prize ship into the harbor at Boston, aided by a flooding tide. Contrary winds and the poor sailing qualities of the brig had delayed them for over three weeks. The militia took charge of the captured British seamen and officers. The prize crew directed the emptying of the hold and went ashore to do whatever pleased them.

Alexis stood in the doorway of their house dejectedly watching the action in the harbor.

"Alexis, let's walk down to the harbor and see where that ship is from," Mrs. Sloan said. "You've been moping around too long. The walk will do you good, and they might have news about Jon."

The two women walked at a brisk pace toward the harbor.

They reached the wharf when they saw Dermot O'Neil on the other side of the street.

"Dermot," Alexis called.

Dermot trotted across the street and removed his hat before he spoke to her.

"Yes, Miss Alexis?"

"Did you come in on that ship there." She gestured toward the ship moored alongside the wharf.

"Yes, Ma'am," he replied. "She's a prize we took."

"How is Captain Weaver?" Mrs. Sloan asked.

"Ooh, I can't really say Ma'am."

"Has he been hurt?" Alexis asked quickly. "How badly is he hurt?"

"I don't rightly know ma'am. A right bloody mess he looked, too."

"Is he . . . ?"

"Alive you mean? Oh yes, at least when last I saw him."

The women hurried on, looking for someone with more information. At the next corner they saw Gil Harper leaving Mr. Paget's office, walking back toward the harbor.

"Gil," Alexis shouted.

Gil turned and saw Mrs. Sloan and Alexis. He smiled warmly and walked toward them.

"For shame, Mr. Harper." Mrs. Sloan said. "Walkin' about and smilin' as if nothing had happened, and poor Jon wounded so bad on that schooner of his."

"I don't . . . ." Then Gil looked at Alexis and saw the pain and worry in her eyes. So this is the woman who kicked Jon and left him lying on the ground, he thought. Gil Harper had come to respect and like Jon, and resented this woman who had caused him so much pain.

"I'm sorry if I appear hard hearted," Gil said. "The truth is, Jon didn't want anyone to bother you with it. For some reason, he wouldn't hardly talk to anyone after Mr. Paget's party. Didn't sleep or eat much. He sort of came alive when we sighted that brig." He vaguely motioned toward the pier. "Jon took a lot of risks when we fought her. He led the boarding party onto the prize. He fell while on the prize's deck."

"You mean they shot him?" Alexis said, nearing hysteria.

"Oh, the poor brave man," Mrs. Sloan wailed.

"I didn't see the wound. Before I got there, Scotty had him carried down to his cabin, but the deck ran with blood. Scotty wouldn't let us take him off of the Retribution. Said he didn't want to move him."

Alexis closed her eyes and groaned.

"Come child," Mrs. Sloan said gently. "We should go back to the house. Here, take my arm."

Gil watched the two women wondering if he might have gone too far with his tale.

CHAPTER TWENTY-NINE

Garvin Kendrick idled away his time on shore in Boston. He could have traveled into Boston on his parole, but he might have seen some of his old acquaintances, also on parole. The way he had lost his ship and been captured embarrassed him. Blindly attacking a ship with far superior armament and a crew three times the size of his own, would be hard to explain.

Garv used his considerable charm to become a friend and confidant of Isaac Miller, the man who had taken over Mr. Morgan's bank.

Miller had been reworking the books so that he could legally claim most of the bank as his own. Fishermen, ship owners, local businessmen, all came to him for loans when they needed more cash. Garvin approached him for a loan against his soon to be received remittance, and Isaac readily agreed to lend the money at an unreasonably high interest rate. Then he happily loaned more when Garv ran through it all before he had received anything from home.

Garv didn't lack for entertainment in Boston. Wives of local merchants and ship owners vied for his presence at their dinners and parties. When he had idle evenings, he entertained himself in the less reputable inns and with the still less reputable ladies along the waterfront.

After some weeks, the novelty of a British Officer wore off and invitations to parties came less frequently. In his idle moments his thoughts frequently returned to the beautiful Alexis. She had looked absolutely lovely that night, he thought. Many of the society beauties in London would envy her. If only she didn't use such coarse language. Of course, the manner in which she repelled Jon would scandalize polite society. Still, she would be a pleasant diversion. Jon must be a compete fool to let her treat him so. Women needed a firm hand Garv knew. Especially those of her class.

***

Garv had seen and spoken to Alexis several times since the dinner at the Paget's home. She remembered him as the kind man who had escorted her home after her confrontation with Jon.

Alexis and Mrs. Sloan met Garv on the street one day while shopping. Alexis smiled and spoke to him.

Boston had become a lonely place for her. She didn't fit into the local society, made up of young, brainless school girls and old stern-faced mothers. After a short conversation, she asked Garv to dinner with them in their cottage.

The two women enjoyed their evening with him, and Garv enjoyed being near Alexis.

His conversation and wit amused them and they asked him back the next week. They fell into a pattern of having Garv visit every Saturday night. The women enjoyed his company, and he enjoyed the meals and the growing friendship between himself and Alexis.

On one of these Saturdays Garv steered the after dinner conversation to the subject of the cheap land available in Kentucky.

"I have it on good authority that land prices are so low that I could buy a tract of land larger than my father's estate in England. My remittance will be enough for a good start. It will take time, but the result will be well worth it."

The women listened with polite attention. Neither of them understood his preoccupation with owning a large tract of land. Both of them would have been more interested in ships and trading in the Caribbean.

***

Garv had heard the story about Jon's wound as told to Alexis by Gil Harper. But he had also heard other stories from seamen along the docks. They all knew that Jon hadn't been seriously hurt. Apparently, no one had passed that information along to Alexis and Mrs. Sloan. When the subject arose after dinner one Saturday, Garv thought he saw a chance to cement his budding friendship with Alexis.

"Perhaps he isn't hurt as much as you fear," he said to the

women.

"Have you heard something we haven't?" Alexis asked eagerly.

"No, I didn't mean to imply that. It's just that he might be trying to . . . ah, perhaps retaliate is too strong a word. Well, you did treat him somewhat . . . er, harshly at Paget's party you know."

"You ain't implying that Jon had Gil Harper tell us a lie are you Lieutenant Kendrick?" asked Mrs. Sloan in a stern and threatening voice.

"Oh, no. That would be quite unacceptable. No, no, nothing like that. I apologize if I gave you that impression," he said hurriedly.

The conversation lagged after that, and Garv soon excused himself and left, cursing himself for making such a hash of the evening.

The next week he left with a guide and two packhorses, heading for Kentucky.

***

The <u>Retribution</u> entered the harbor at Boston, escorting another prize, one month to the day after Gil had dropped the anchor of his first prize.

Alexis watched from her doorway. She couldn't see clearly enough to recognize Jon, but she did see that the <u>Retribution</u> had been in a serious fight. Cannon fire had smashed the bulwarks in places, the sails had been patched, and her crew maned the pumps continuously. She called to Mrs. Sloan and the two women set off for the docks.

When they arrived, they saw the Retribution lying alongside the wharf. They waited at the gangway while a party of men carrying stretchers went by.

Alexis watched them and breathed a sigh of relief when she didn't see Jon among the wounded.

As soon as they saw a break in the line of men leaving, they ran up the gangway onto the ship's deck. Scotty Lachlan stood on the quarterdeck directing a work gang bringing ship's stores out of the privateer's hold and transferring them to the dock.

"Scotty," Alexis shouted, "Where's Jon?"

Her shout startled Scotty. He disliked distraction while swaying heavy stores up out of the hold. Particularly, since Alexis had caused Jon so much unhappiness.

"Captain Weaver is in his cabin," he said abruptly. "Ma'am," he added pointedly.

Alexis didn't notice the coolness in his reply.

He's hurt too much to come on deck, she thought.

"Can we go see him?"

"Yes," he said curtly.

She ran down the companionway and stopped before Jon's cabin door to compose herself.

She knocked on the door and heard a low growling voice say, "Come in."

Jon sat at his table with his back to the door and a thick pile of papers before him.

"Jon," Alexis said tentatively.

Jon jumped to his feet, dropping his pen and spattering ink

over the documents. He started to move toward her and then, remembering their last meeting, stopped before reaching her.

"It's good to see you again Alex," he said, using the name he had first known her by.

She stepped closer to him.

"Is your wound healed now?" she asked.

"Wound? I don't have a wound."

"Gil said they carried you below, covered with blood."

"Oh yes, I slipped in some blood on the deck and hit my head. Nothing serious."

"They said you had blood all over you."

"I suppose I had a lot on me. Not my own though."

He smiled. Her concern raised his spirits tremendously.

Alexis stood dumbfounded. Garv had tried to warn her, but she had run up the gangway like a stupid child, filled with fear for Jon. He didn't have a scrap of a bandage on him.

"You scum," she shouted. "You had Gil tell me you were hurt so you could see me make a fool of myself?"

"I didn't tell Gil anything. I got a bump on my head. Knocked me out. Gil took the prize, and he started off with it before I woke up."

He involuntarily took a step toward her, reaching out for her hand. Alexis batted his hand aside and swung her fist in a hard right cross that caught Jon squarely on the nose. Alexis had grown up knowing how to use her weight when working on board her father's ship. The blow wasn't an ordinary one that might be expected from so small a woman. When her fist hit him, it came with all of the weight and muscle in her small body behind it.

Jon staggered backward. Blood spattering down his shirt. Alexis calmly opened the door and walked out.

"Don't bother to come calling either," she said over her shoulder, and slammed the door.

Jon sat on his bunk, holding his bloody shirt against his face, trying to stop the bleeding.

A knock on his door and Scotty's voice saying, "All of the stores are on the dock. Chip says he still can't find the leak. He wants to beach her so he can get at it better."

"Take the guns off. Put them under guard when you do."

Jon's voice sounded muffled and difficult to understand. Scotty considered asking if he needed help. Then he remembered the look of fury on Alexis' face as she left the cabin. He went back on deck.

***

Jon's nose had stopped bleeding, and he wore clean clothing as he walked toward Mr. Paget's new warehouse and office.

"Good day Captain Weaver," said a passer by.

A block later another man said, "Happy to hear you made another successful cruise, Sir."

Jon knew none of the people who addressed him. Todd had called them hangers on. Some of the most offensive and persistent of them wanted him to invest in schemes that would be "certain to show huge profits".

"Captain Weaver, may I have a word with you?" A neatly

dressed young man, or perhaps "boy" would be a better description, stood in his path.

Jon tried to push past him, but then he saw the look of desperation in the boy's eyes.

"Of course," Jon replied.

"I would like to go to sea on a privateer, and you have the best reputation of anyone in Boston. If you have a place for a landsman in your crew, I would like to be considered."

"I take it you have no experience."

"That is correct sir. But I'm healthy and strong. I can learn quickly."

"We have a full crew. What is your name in case I want to find you," Jon said.

"Timothy Braun, sir, and yes, Jakob Braun is my father. That's why I've come to you. My father has never been an admirable person. He neglected his family even when mother lay dying. I hate him. People in Boston expect me to be a traitor because my name is Braun. If I could serve with you . . . ."

His voice trailed off as Jon looked at him closely.

"So you want to reclaim your reputation by going privateering. Have you ever thought of joining the navy?"

"I have a sister to support. The navy doesn't pay well enough. This war won't last too long, and if I can save enough, I'll be able to open a shop in town."

"What sort of a shop?"

"Probably a book shop. More and more people know how to read it seems."

"Do you know how to do sums as well as read?"

"Yes, sir, I do."

"Your father deserted your family, and your mother is dead, yet you seem to have been educated well. How can you explain that?"

"My mother had been well educated for a woman and taught my sister and me to read and write. She died last year, God rest her soul."

"Alright, Mr. Braun, I'll keep you in mind."

He touched his cap and resumed walking toward Paget's warehouse.

***

"Jon," Todd Paget shouted from across the wide expanse of the Paget warehouse, startling one of the clerks who upset his inkwell. "How are you. We've had some confused reports about you. Some said you had died. You look healthy enough now except for that nose. Did you get hit by something?"

"It's nothing serious, Todd. That sort of thing happens on board a ship."

"We brought in a second prize beside the one Gil brought in. I'd appreciate your help again in selling both of them."

"We can take care of that for you, Jon. Don't give it another thought. I see that the Retribution looks pretty beat up. Did you have a tough fight?"

"After Gil left us, we did have a brisk fight with an armed merchant ship," Jon said, happy to shift the conversation away from the appearance of his nose. "We hit her hard. Raked her twice and they still kept on fighting. She caught fire, and it spread so fast we couldn't board her. I stood off to windward and waited to take survivors aboard. I think her timbers must have been rotten the way she caved in when our shot hit her. We searched for an hour or so. Didn't find but five survivors."

"The prize we brought in with us just fell into our laps. She showed up one morning at first light, only about a mile from us. Helps to have Dame Fortune on your side."

"Let's go talk to my father. He'll want to know all about the action. You bring a lot of business through Paget and Sons." Todd smiled proudly as he said the words.

"Paget and Sons you say. I guess congratulations are in order. You deserve it."

As they climbed the stairs to the private office of Mr. Paget, Jon began telling Todd about the damage to the <u>Retribution</u>.

"She's going to need a lot of work. The hull is leaking bad enough that we have to pump the bilges for twelve hours a day. She might have to be hove down to get at the damage," Jon said as they walked toward Mr. Paget's office.

Todd knocked on the office door and heard a voice telling them to come in.

"Welcome back, Jon," Mr. Paget said as he walked around his desk to take Jon's hand in his own. "Tell me what happened to you when you took that first prize. A valuable prize I might add. We heard you had been wounded. I can see by the swelling that still shows around your nose that you were hit hard by something."

"No, I wasn't wounded. I slipped in a pool of blood on the

deck of the first prize and hit my head. I was out for most of a day, but it wasn't serious. Not everyone saw how I fell, and some thought I had been wounded. Scotty took command until I recovered. I had a headache for a day or so. Nothing permanent."

"Just a broken nose, eh?"

"No, it's not broken," he said with some asperity. "Just a minor shipboard incident."

"To get back to business, the <u>Retribution</u> has been damaged seriously. Another ship we tried to take shot us up. Several shots hit at the water line and one or two below it. Judging from the way she's leaning, she'll need to be hove down again, if only to clean her bottom and to check for rot and shipworms. A good clean bottom would help our speed. It will be a month or more before we finish."

Mr. Paget smiled to himself.

"Jon, the funds I invested in fitting out your ship have been repaid many times over. Captain Rob Clay also brought in two prizes this last month. Don't worry about hurrying back to sea."

"And by the way, your comment about the ship's bottom reminded me that part of the cargo of one of Rob's prizes is a large amount of copper sheet. It's in the warehouse now. Not enough for Rob's ship, but perhaps enough for <u>Retribution</u>. It is frightfully expensive, but it might give your ship a bit of extra speed."

No ship's captain could refuse the opportunity to improve his ship's speed. A merchant ship would benefit from faster passages, and a Privateer's survival might depend on it.

***

The next morning Jon brought the <u>Retribution</u> into the ship yard for extensive repairs and for coppering her bottom.

CHAPTER THIRTY

<u>Retribution</u> lay on her side on the sand, hove down so that workmen could reach the damaged area on her hull. Some of the planking had been smashed, and two ribs sprung. Jon watched apprehensively while the carpenters pulled and cut the damaged wood away from the hull.

"You look as if you are watching a funeral, Jon," Todd Paget said.

Jon and Todd looked on as the repairs began.

"I feel that way Todd. She is a good ship, and I hate to see her treated so roughly. Look at that, they're cutting right through her hull."

"They're doing what needs to be done to get rid of the damaged wood, Jon. The <u>Retribution</u> is in good hands. Don't worry so much."

"Well . . . I guess you're right. Let's walk back to the warehouse. I don't want to watch this."

The two men walked toward the chandlery talking idly.

"Where is Garv? I haven't seen him since we left port."

"He decided he could make a future for himself in Kentucky territory. He said he could buy cheap land there and watch it grow more valuable as more families moved west."

"He broke his parole then?" Jon asked in surprise.

"I suppose he did. He'll be back I expect, either to show us how rich he is, or to borrow more money from Miller's bank."

"Didn't he get his remittance from his father then?"

"No, I don't think so. The bank gave him a loan. He and Miller are friends these days."

"You think he'll get rich in Kentucky?"

"I don't know any more than you do. It sounds too good to be true."

Jon could only nod.

Then, in a carefully casual voice Jon asked, "Have you seen Alexis lately?"

"She hasn't been active in our little society in Boston. Particularly since Garv left. They went to several dinners and parties together, but now that he is away she stays at home except for church and the like."

They walked in silence toward the Paget and Son warehouse.

"She is a very special woman, Jon. She shouldn't stay hidden in her house like she is."

"Well . . . I don't think she wants me to take her anywhere. As I'm sure you know, I can't get close to her without getting hurt.

Why don't you escort her around. Maybe she'll be less likely to injure you."

Todd laughed. He wanted nothing so much as to do exactly that, but Jon had been his closest friend for many years.

The two men walked on toward the Paget warehouse where Jon had been given space for a small desk.

The conversation had lagged when Jon asked, "Do you know Timothy Braun, Todd?"

"Yes I do. He worked for us for a short time, but I didn't get to know him well. His mother died sometime back, and he seemed to be stricken badly by it. He quit to care for his sister for awhile. Why do you ask?"

"Can he write and do sums accurately?" Jon asked, ignoring Todd's question.

"Yes, he has a good hand. And his work at sums is careful and accurate."

"Why does he have trouble getting work?"

"We filled his position when he left. Otherwise we would have taken him back. His problem is that he is Jakob Braun's son, sort of 'The sins of the father' thing."

"I'm thinking of hiring him to relieve me of the paper work," Jon said. "There are more orders and deliveries and payments than I thought possible."

"You won't regret it. We hated to see him leave."

***

Timothy, or Tim as he preferred to be called, worked diligently for Jon. He attacked the paperwork with a will, and each day he went to the shipyard to inspect the material as the teamsters delivered it. If the quantity or quality didn't match the orders, he reported it to Jon who then had words with the owner of the ship yard.

"Captain Weaver," Tim said hesitantly one day. "Would you mind if I brought my sister here while I'm working? She's only seven and she's by herself all day in our rooms."

"Don't you have anyone to look after her?"

"No, sir. We don't have any family left, and we have to pay off some debts my father left. I can't afford to have anyone stay with her during the day."

"Then by all means bring her with you tomorrow."

***

Grace Braun, a pretty little girl wearing an old worn dress, peered shyly around her brother's side. Tim held her hand and stroked her long, blond hair. He spoke softly to her, and Jon saw her shake her head.

"Let her get used to the office and to me for a bit. We'll get acquainted soon."

Other workers in the warehouse stopped by to see and talk to the girl, but she shyly refused to speak. When she thought no one saw her, she gazed at Jon.

The following day Jon hired a carpenter to build a small child's desk for her so she could play at being in school, and Tim used his lunch time to give her lessons.

After a week, Grace began to lose her shyness. Then she became too boisterous, like any normal seven year old, and disturbed some of the clerks at their work.

Jon could think of only one solution. Mrs. Sloan might care for the girl, Jon hesitated to go to the house to talk to Mrs. Sloan, but he saw her on the street the next day. She had just finished her shopping and sat on a bench resting before her walk back up the hill to the cottage.

Mrs. Sloan did not accept the idea with any enthusiasm.

"I'm not so young any more Jon. Caring for a little girl might be more than I want to take on."

"Well . . . I could pay you a little more perhaps."

"How much more?" she asked, surprisingly quickly.

The figure Jon named didn't seem to satisfy her.

"There is a lot of work caring for a house like this. Cooking, washing, splitting wood and tending the garden."

"Doesn't Alexis help?"

"Oh yes she helps out quite a bit. She's just too delicate for the heavy work. She's a small woman you know."

Jon struggled to keep a straight face. The idea of Alexis, one of the best topmen he had ever seen, being too delicate for heavy work nearly made him laugh out loud.

"I'll hire a man to split the wood and tend the garden."

"It won't be easy to boss some old incompetent man either."

"Well, maybe I could pay you a bit more. If I gave you one half of a seaman's share out of my half owner's share of prize money, would that be enough?"

"Well alright. I'll do it as a favor to you, Jon."

As he walked back to the ship, Jon had a pleased smile on

his face. The small fraction of prize money Mrs. Sloan would receive, along with the generous salary Jon already paid her, might well be enough to take care of her for the rest of her life. And it had been arranged without Mrs. Sloan feeling embarrassed for asking for special favors.

Best of all, Grace had a home at last. Her father had deserted his family and her mother couldn't take time from trying to fill their need for food and shelter to give her all the attention she needed. Now Mrs. Sloan, always ready to give her a smile and a hug, filled the role of grandmother.

Alexis fell under the little girl's spell also. The three of them spent hours shopping for clothes and a few toys for Grace. She became the best dressed seven year old in Maine Territory.

Tim came to the house each day after work to take Grace home. On occasion, Jon and Todd accompanied him. Grace and Mrs. Sloan greeted them happily. Alexis greeted Todd cordially but remained cold and distant toward Jon.

"Why doesn't Miss Alexis like Mr. Jon?" Grace asked Mrs. Sloan one afternoon.

Mrs. Sloan sighed. "I think she does like him. She's angry at him and stubborn. He's a fine man, brave, honest, and a real patriot."

"He's rich too," Grace said.

Chapter Thirty-One

Rob Clay brought the schooner Gypsy into port after a long privateering cruise. He had sailed across the Atlantic and raided merchant ships along the western shores of England and in the Bay of Biscay. Two large prizes and ten smaller ones had been taken and sold off in French ports. In addition, three small sloops had been sunk after the choice parts of their cargos had been transferred to Gypsy's hold. Now Rob's ship needed to be repaired and refitted, and he needed seamen to replace crew members who had been seriously wounded or killed. He would be ready to sail within the month.

***

"Jon," Rob called when he saw Jon and Tim on the street. "We need to talk." He broke into a trot as he crossed the street to be by Jon's side.

"Let's stop at the tavern and have a mug of ale."

Tim excused himself so that he wouldn't be late to pick up

Grace.

Both Jon and Rob had become fairly wealthy from privateering, and the servants in the tavern rushed to attend to them.

"I heard you had a good cruise, Rob."

"It could have been better," Rob replied.

Jon laughed at Rob's comment.

"You're a hard man to please. How could it have been better?"

"Twice we had a ship beaten when a British Navy ship showed up. Not particularly big, but still a navy ship. Combined with the merchant ship they out-gunned us considerably."

Rob took a long pull at his ale and wiped his mouth with the back of his hand.

"If another ship had been with me, we could have beaten those prizes so quick that the British Navy wouldn't have been able to stop our taking them. Two ships have a great advantage. Fast nimble ships like yours and mine could engage from both sides of a prize or even a small navy ship. Most of them are short of men. They have each gun crew serve both sides. After the first broadside they can only load half of their guns at one time."

"Are you certain about that?" Jon asked.

"I've heard it from a lot of people. Mostly captives from our prizes."

"I have to think about this. How long before you sail again?" Jon asked.

"I'm planning on four weeks, but I could be ready sooner. I

have to get some minor repairs finished, and I have a desk covered with papers and letters to answer. By the way, do you still need some guns? We have a couple of six-pounders we took from a prize."

"I'll take the guns. Name your price. And about sailing together, are you going back across the Atlantic again?"

"Yes I am. There are plenty of prizes and fewer navy ships over there. They are all blockading our coast and sailing around in the Caribbean."

"I can help you get through your paperwork. That young man who was with me is Timothy Braun. His father is Jakob Braun, but this lad is a patriot. Jakob abandoned his family, and now Tim is supporting himself and his sister by working for me."

"He's a good honest lad and good at writing and doing sums. He might help you with your paperwork. I don't like leaving him here without a job while we're at sea. If we send some prizes back, he'll be kept busy making out cargo lists and figuring up the shares."

"Send him over to me. I'll make good use of him."

Jon drank deeply from his mug.

"I like your idea of sailing together. Don't say anything about this to anyone. If we sail together, we should meet at sea. No sense in letting the whole world know of our plans."

Rob nodded his head in agreement.

"Let me know what you decide," Rob said.

Then he left the tavern to attend to his ship.

Jon sat staring into his ale, thinking of a long cruise to the coast of Europe. Six months or more at sea might help him recover from the lonely desolation that settled over him when Alexis turned him away.

The following day the two new six-pounders came aboard. The <u>Retribution</u> now could boast of ten six-pounders and two four-pounders. At the end of the week the repairs had been completed, and she swung at anchor in the harbor, ready for sea.

At the end of each day Jon and Tim walked to Grandmother Sloan's house. The title "Grandmother" seemed appropriate for Mrs. Sloan. She didn't object. Soon everyone knew her by that name.

Grace fairly bounced with delight when Jon gave her a doll he had bought for her. She ran to show it to Alexis and insisted that she come back into the room with everyone else.

Jon had been talking with Tim about working for Rob Clay when Alexis entered. Jon stopped talking in mid sentence, then leaped to his feet.

"Good day, Captain Weaver." Her voice cool and disinterested. Then she sat on the couch with Grace helping her play with her new doll.

Alexis had dressed carefully for this day. Jon would be sailing soon she knew. She had set her hair and applied a tinge of rouge. Her dress had been purchased for the occasion. Jon stared at her, his heart aching. She looked so incredibly beautiful. He remembered her climbing the rigging during the storm off the Carolina coast, and how his heart had jumped into his throat. Then she wore seaman's clothing, her face weathered and her hands calloused and dirty, but she looked no less beautiful to him then than she did now. He knew that he had fallen in love then. Now her beauty paralyzed him.

"Jon, what does Rob Clay want me to do?" Tim asked.

"Oh, yes," Jon said, startled back to his senses. "He has some letters to write and some shares to figure."

"Where can I find him?"

Jon didn't hear him. He walked across the room to Alexis and took her hand.

"Walk with me Alex."

She carefully kept her face blank and allowed him to lead her out of the house.

Jon held her hand with both of his until she pulled it free.

Jon stopped staring into her eyes and instead looked across the bay at distant clouds.

"Alex," he began.

"Alexis if you please," she interrupted coldly.

Jon's shoulders slumped a little.

"Yes . . . Alexis. I understand why you dislike me so, but that woman didn't mean anything to me. And then I discovered how I feel about you . . . ."

Alexis looked at the ground in front of her, waiting expectantly. Jon kept staring at the horizon.

"I can't change what I did, and I guess you can't forgive me. I won't bother you again."

Then he walked away, leaving Alexis standing open mouthed, a sudden empty feeling in her breast.

Just before dusk, Alexis and Mrs. Sloan heard the clanking of the <u>Retribution</u>'s windlass as she weighed anchor. From their home on the hill overlooking the harbor, they saw <u>Retribution</u>'s sails filled by the offshore breeze and begin moving toward the harbor entrance.

"He's leaving!" she said.

"What did you expect?" Mrs. Sloan muttered. Alexis suddenly turned away and ran back to her room. Mrs. Sloan remained at the door watching the harbor scene. When the <u>Retribution</u> cleared the harbor, she went to the door of Alexis' room and stood listening. She heard Alexis' muffled sobs. When she opened the door, Alexis turned away trying to hide her tear-streaked face. Mrs. Sloan pulled her to her feet and then put her arms around the sobbing girl.

"He's gone Mrs. Sloan. He might get hurt or even killed, and he still thinks I hate him," Alexis wailed.

"Yes he does child. You as much as told him that."

"No, no I didn't. I love him."

"Then why did you kick him and hit him?" asked Mrs. Sloan crossly. "Yes, I know about that. Everyone in Boston has heard the story. And a few days ago you acted so cold toward him that little Grace asked me why you didn't like Jon."

Alexis threw herself across the bed, sobbing louder.

"About all we can do is talk to Rob Clay and have him take a letter to Jon," Mrs. Sloan said.

"He might not see Jon's ship for months or years."

"Don't worry about that dear. They are going to sail

together, so they can take bigger ships. Rob and Jon tried to keep it a secret, but everyone in Boston knows Rob will meet Jon at sea and then sail across the Atlantic."

"He could be gone for years," Alexis began crying again.

"You're thinking of yourself Alexis. How do you imagine Jon feels? And don't count on him coming back ready to make up either. They will probably sail into ports in Spain or France to get supplies and leave their prizes. Don't think that the women there won't be after him."

"Besides that, privateering is a dangerous business. A lot of ships have been lost to the British."

"What can I do now?" she wailed.

"Stop crying and do whatever you have to do." Mrs. Sloan's voice grew louder and more emphatic. "My husband was popular with the ladies before I married him. But that didn't stop me. And we had a good marriage."

"Why didn't you say something to me?" Alexis wailed.

"You wouldn't have listened. I know how stubborn you are." She stood silent for a moment. "But I didn't know how foolish Jon is," she said and walked out of the room.

***

The Gypsy, loaded with water, stores, shot, and powder lay at the pier, ready to be warped out to anchor in the harbor. Tim Braun walked briskly toward her, carrying Alexis' letter for Captain Clay to take to Jon. Tim, a frequent visitor to the ship, went down the companionway without so much as a glance from any crew member. No one noticed that he didn't return.

Chapter Thirty-Two

Tim found a small narrow space barely big enough for his thin body. He pulled a bag of ship's biscuits after himself to hide the opening. If he stayed hidden for two days, Captain Clay wouldn't return to Boston to get rid of him. He would then be able to fight the British and erase the memories of his traitorous father. Tim took Alexis' letter from his coat pocket and tucked it into his shirt. He folded his coat to use as a pillow.

He fell into restless sleep. The motion of the ship awakened him. The rolling and pitching began to have its well know effect on him and his stomach rebelled. In his cramped hiding place he had to lay in his own vomit. The stench made him sicker still, and even though his stomach had completely emptied itself, he still had racking spells that produced nothing but small amounts of yellow fluid. Tim survived the day in his filthy squalid condition. Only the thought that he might get an opportunity to fight for his country and erase the blot on his family name made him stay hidden. He heard someone moaning and realized that it was himself. Gritting his teeth to hold back the moans he closed his eyes and tried to concentrate on more pleasant times.

The next day Tim felt surprisingly better, although more hungry and thirstier than he thought possible. He heard shouts from the deck above his head and the sound of men running and the guns being run out. He pushed the bag of ship's biscuits out of the way and crawled out into the open. He staggered to his feet just as _Gypsy_ came about and heeled in the opposite direction throwing him off balance. His head struck the deck and the blow momentarily stunned him. A cannon ball crashed through the ship's hull a few yards from him. _Gypsy_'s guns began to roar and the noise became unbearable.

He saw a group of boys, even younger than himself, running up the companionway carrying bags of gun powder. Tim staggered to his feet and followed them.

A gun fired as he stepped onto the deck. The shock of the explosion made him stagger and he slipped and fell. Blinded by smoke and deafened by the noise Tim lay still for a moment. A heavy foot smashed his hand. He crawled away from the companionway. Blood covered his hands and stained his clothing. He dimly realized that blood had made the deck slippery. Another terrible crash and flying splinters sang past him. A gun from a smashed gun carriage slid along the deck. Through the cloud of smoke, Tim saw a seaman under the dismounted gun, the man screaming with pain, his mates struggling frantically to free him.

Tim ran to help. As the men lifted the gun, Tim pulled the injured man free.

A boy reached for the wounded man and shouted, "Help me carry him below."

Tim helped the loblolly boy carry the injured man down below deck where the surgeon worked. In the relative quiet, Tim's head began to clear. He remembered his resolve to fight bravely and ran back on deck, a seaman with a blood soaked rag wrapped around one hand worked at one of the guns, awkwardly trying to ram a powder bag into the barrel.

"Tell me what to do, and I can help you," Tim shouted.

"Here boy, take this ram rod and ram that powder bag in as hard as you can," the wounded man shouted.

"Good lad, now the ball. Ram it home and then ram in some of this wadding. Harder. Hard as you can."

"Now stand aside while they run the gun out and fire."

Tim stood aside as the gun crew hauled on the lines to move the gun up to the gun port. The gun roared and leaped back against the heavy breech lines. Tim dipped the swab in the water bucket and swabbed out the barrel. Then he rammed the powder bag home. He drove the ball and wadding home and stepped aside as they ran the gun out.

The loblolly boy pulled the wounded man away from the gun and helped him below deck to the surgeon.

The gun fired again and leaped back against the breech lines.

Tim dipped the swab into the water bucket and swabbed

out the barrel. Then rammed the powder bag home. A seaman put a ball into the barrel and Tim rammed it home. Next the wadding.

He stepped aside as the gun rolled up to the port. It roared again and flew back. Tim started again, swab the barrel, ram the powder bag, ram the ball, then the wadding, stand aside as they ran the gun out and fired. Then he started again, mechanically going through the motions, not thinking of or even hearing the tremendous roaring of the guns.

Retribution had joined the Gypsy in the fight and sailed across the stern of the British ship, but Tim thought only of the gun he was serving. Swab out the barrel, ram the powder home, ram the ball and wadding home, stand aside as the gun was heaved up to the port. The gun roared and leaped violently backward against the breech tackle. The intensity of the enemy fire decreased drastically. His own gun roared again and leaped back. He saw the rail of the British ship shatter into splinters. He dipped the swap into the water bucket again and swabbed out the gun.

A six-pound cannon ball struck Timothy Braun full in the chest. He died instantly, and the letter mutilated beyond recognition, could never be delivered.

***

Gypsy and Retribution won their first battle while working together. The enemy ship had put up a strong fight for a merchantman, but the two Privateers out gunned and out maneuvered her. Her captain wisely surrendered before more good men died.

The butcher's bill listed two dead and ten wounded who

were expected to recover. Tim Braun wasn't identified until the sail maker recognized him as he sewed his remains into a sail cloth bag for burial.

When repairs had made the prize seaworthy, a prize crew took command of her and started for Boston.

Chapter Thirty-three

Mrs. Sloan and Alexis kept Grace with them when Tim failed to return. The little girl at first thought she had been given a special treat, staying over night with Mrs. Sloan and Alexis. When Tim didn't come to the house to pick up Grace after <u>Gypsy</u> sailed, Alexis and Mrs. Sloan realized that he had sailed on her.

Two days later a ship sailed slowly into the harbor. Her shattered railings, patched shot holes in her hull, torn and patched sails, showed that she had been in a fierce fight. Jon and Rob had sent in the first prize of their cruise.

If Tim had sailed on <u>Gypsy</u> as a stowaway, surely Rob would have sent him back with their first prize. Alexis waited for Tim to bring her some word about Jon and her letter.

If Rob gave the letter to Jon, then Jon must know how she felt. There would be an answering letter.

Without waiting for Mrs. Sloan, she set out for the harbor.

She expected to see Tim in the crowds of seamen leaving the dock. Instead she saw a tall, thin, sober-faced sailor walking to meet her.

"Do you know Timothy Braun?" she asked before the man had a chance to say anything.

"A fine, brave young man," the sailor replied.

"Where can I find him?"

"I'm Jon Patrick. A prize master from Captain Clay's ship." He paused momentarily. "He asked me to see you as soon as we got our prize into port." He paused and swallowed, his Adam's apple bobbed. "Tim Braun stowed away on <u>Gypsy</u>. He came out of hidin' when we started to fight that ship."

He gestured toward the battered ship.

Alexis suddenly knew what he would tell her.

"Tim helped serve one of our guns. One of the regular gun crew got hit by a splinter, near took his handoff. Tim took his place. They kept the gun firing, and Tim hadn't never even seen one fired afore."

"Is he alive, Mr. Patrick?" Alexis asked hopelessly.

"No, Ma'am. He died 'fore the prize struck. A ball from a British cannon hit him. He didn't suffer one bit, Ma'am," he added. "No, it were right quick." He shook his head sadly.

Alexis stared at Jon Patrick without seeing him. She thought of her friend Tim, Grace's brother, who would never come ashore again, never see his sister grow up, or find a girl he could love.

"Miss Archer, are you all right?" Jon Patrick asked. "Here let's stop at this here shop for a cup of tea. You can rest for a bit."

Alexis sat at the small table Jon Patrick indicated. She fought to control her tears. Poor Tim. Poor Grace. At least she could take care of Grace. Jon's success had made her wealthy. Grace would lack for nothing, except for a brother.

"Tim had a letter from me for Captain Clay. Do you know if Tim gave it to him before . . . ."

"I don't know for sure Miss Archer, but I doubt it. The loblolly boy told me that Tim helped him carry a wounded man below when he first came on deck. Then he started servin' the gun. He didn't have no time to give a letter to Captain Clay."

Alexis suddenly stood up, holding her handkerchief to her eyes. "Thank you," she said in a choked voice. Then she began the long walk toward the house.

***

The little girl and the two women stood on the shore watching the tide carry a wreath out to sea. The memorial service for the men who had died was over, and all of the few friends and relatives had left.

"Who were all of those people?" Grace asked.

"People who were friends of your brother," Alexis answered.

"Why didn't they help us before Jon gave Tim a job?"

Alexis couldn't think of a reply.

***

Grace recovered from her grief more rapidly than Alexis did. The little girl knew that Tim would never come back, and she would never see him again, but she accepted that.

Alexis had more difficulty with Tim's death. Mourning for Tim and worried about Jon, she withdrew from her friends and neighbors after the memorial service. She hoped that Jon's ship would appear on the horizon some day, and she could explain to him how she felt.

Days dragged into weeks and weeks into months. She stood on the lawn in front of the house searching the horizon every day hoping to see his ship. At times a sail would look familiar. But as it grew nearer, she would see that the ship didn't resemble <u>Retribution</u>.

Occasionally, a ship docked at Boston after sailing across from France or Spain. They brought little or no news about the two privateers. Sometimes they carried mail for families of the two crews, but nothing for Alexis. Even Mrs. Sloan received a short letter. Jon and Rob had great success and captured several prizes. The ships and cargos had been sold in French ports for the most part, but some sailed to Spain. In Spanish ports, they repaired and provisioned the two schooners.

The only reference to Alexis in Mrs. Sloan's letter gave an accounting of Alexis' share of the prize money and noted that it had been sent to her bank in nearby Portsmouth.

Chapter Thirty-four

Gradually Alexis learned to accept Tim's death, but she became quiet and withdrawn. She thought that she had somehow been the cause. If she had only talked to Jon honestly and openly, perhaps Tim would still be alive. She knew that Tim stowed away on the Gypsy so he could clear his name, but her letter might have been the excuse he needed. She rarely left the house and yard except for church on Sunday. All of Mrs. Sloan's urging could not persuade her to be more active socially.

Only Grace could make her smile. She frequently took Grace with her on long walks. Sometimes they would stop and have tea at one of the shops or look for new clothes for Grace. Most of these walks took her past the docks where she might hear some gossip about Jon and his ship.

She heard talk that Jon and Rob had been fortunate. They had sent fifteen prizes into French or Spanish ports and had refitted and provisioned three times. Mrs. Sloan's warning about Jon meeting French or Spanish women lingered in the back of her mind.

***

A tall muscular figure walked along the street toward the newly built building, now occupied by the Miller Bank. He wore buckskins stained with dirt and grease and smelling strongly of sweat and smoke. His long hair brushed against his shoulders. In his belt he carried two pistols and on his right side a large knife. On his left side he carried an Indian tomahawk in his belt situated in such a way as to be easily reached by his right hand. He didn't have a left arm.

Lieutenant Kendrick of the Royal Navy, paroled prisoner of war, walked along the street to the Miller Bank building and pushed open the door.

"I would like to take ten pounds out of my account," he told the teller.

The teller looked up from counting the contents of his cash drawer, gasped and turned deathly pale. A dirty unshaven man armed to the teeth had asked for ten pounds. He began to stammer and stutter.

"Hello Garv," a voice said. Garv turned around and found himself looking at Todd Paget.

"You have changed, Garv. You look like one of the meanest bandits in the country." Then to the teller, "Don't worry, he's not going to rob you. He's probably one of your best accounts. Give him his ten pounds."

**

Later Todd and Garv sat at a table in a waterfront tavern.

"What is Jon doing now?" Garv asked.

"He's at sea on a voyage across the Atlantic. Rob Clay and Jon both sailed eight or nine months ago. The rumors we've heard say that the two of them have sent twenty or more prizes into Spanish and French ports. No doubt that's an exaggeration, but even so they have been more successful than anyone expected."

"What have you been doing out on the frontier, Garv?"

"I found the biggest stretch of land I've ever seen. It's cheap too. I bought enough of it to build an estate three times as large as my father's back in England. It will need to be cleared. It's wild and hostile now, but in a few years it will be tamed, and I'll start building my estate. I've bought deeds for over a thousand acres," he boasted.

"I haven't heard much about Boston though. News doesn't get out to Kentucky. How are Alexis and Mrs. Sloan getting along?"

Todd took a long pull on his ale.

"Well, . . . I think you could say they are doing well, all things considered. She hasn't been seen around much since Jon left and then Tim Braun got killed in a fight on the Gypsy."

"Who is Tim Braun?"

"The son of Jakob Braun. You remember him surely."

"Oh yes, the Tory who tried to have Jon killed. How does this 'Tim', affect Alexis?" Garv asked.

"He and his sister, Grace, had been having hard times.

Everyone expected him to be a Tory too, like his father. He couldn't get any work. Jon finally hired him."

"Tim thought he had to prove himself, so he stowed away on Rob's ship. He died in their first battle, not far off shore. They sent the prize back here. That's when we found out about him."

"Alexis doesn't do much now," Todd went on. "She goes to church and prayer meetings and the like with Mrs. Sloan. Most of the time she watches for ships arriving, hoping one of them might bring news about Jon. She's lonely. I've asked her several times to go with me to parties or just take a walk, but she would rather stay at home. That little sister of Tim's is about the only person who can get her to smile. She never leaves the house except when they go to church or when she takes the little girl for a walk."

"I'd like to go see her," Garv said.

"I'm sure she would like that. She thinks highly of you as I remember. Maybe you could cheer her up."

They finished their drinks and walked outside.

"I think I'll make a call on Alexis right away. Do you think she would like that?"

Todd laughed. "I think she would be hurt if you didn't. But take my advice and get some new clothes and take a long bath before you call on anyone."

***

The next afternoon Garv arrived at Alexis' home, dressed in new clothing, shaved, bathed, and with his hair cut short.

"Garv!" Alexis cried when she opened the door. "Come in. What a surprise! Where have you been all this time?"

She chattered on, so excited to see someone she could talk to openly. Garv could scarcely get a word in though he tried several times. Alexis didn't stop talking until Mrs. Sloan and Grace entered the room.

"So this is Grace that everyone has been telling me about," Garv said. "My, but you are a pretty girl. Did Miss Alexis pick your dress out for you?"

"No," she said firmly. "I picked it out myself." After a short pause she said, "Were you a friend of my brother?"

Garv looked into the little girl's eyes. "No, I never met your brother. I wish I had. I've heard of him and know he was a smart man and very brave."

Grace nodded solemnly.

***

Long after Grace had been put to bed, the two women sat in the living room while Garv told them stories of the frontier. The friends he had made, both white and Indian, and the rich soil and low land prices. The wonderful feeling of independence and self-reliance he had gained while living in the wilderness, miles away from other white men.

***

Alexis and Garv saw each other frequently over the next few weeks. He finally received his remittance from his father, so he lived in relative luxury.

Garv, because of his engaging manner, frequently received invitations to dinners and parties hosted by wealthy residents of Boston. He always invited Alexis to accompany him. They enjoyed each other's company. To Alexis, Garv took the place of an older brother, someone who would listen when she spoke and a friend to lean on for support. She could never have any deeper feelings toward him.

Garv had feelings of a different sort. He treated Alexis in a friendly and considerate manner, but couldn't rid himself of his elitist feelings. She had grown up on a ship without a mother. Her family background, no better than that of a common laborer's or even a seaman on one of Jon's ships, kept her from being totally acceptable. For that matter, all of the Colonists in America fell into that category. However, Alexis' beauty and intelligence warmed his heart, and his feelings grew stronger as he spent more time with her.

Chapter Thirty-Five

A thin, wiry man sat leaning back in his chair with his feet in the bottom drawer of his huge desk. His bearded chin nearly rested on his chest, his eyes nearly closed. A half filled bottle of rum lay in another drawer, and he occasionally sipped from it. A bright cheerful morning sun shone through the window.

A loud knock on the door roused him from his lethargy. He quickly closed the desk drawer and arranged himself in the posture of a man hard at work, inspecting some papers on his desk. Before he could respond to the knock, Lieutenant Kendrick walked into his office. Isaac Miller rose to his feet and arranged his face in a congenial smile.

"Some day you're going to walk in on something you'd rather not see, Garv. I might be counting our gold here on my desk and packing it into bags ready to abscond," he chuckled easily.

Garv smiled coldly. "You wouldn't do that, Isaac. You

know what I'd do, don't you?"

Garv's smile didn't reach his eyes. He looked steadily at Isaac until the man lowered his gaze.

"Let me pour you a drink," Isaac said as he took the bottle and mug from his desk drawer.

"How much do you have now?" Garv asked quietly as he took a generous gulp from the mug.

"Nearly fifty thousand. Some in English pounds and some in gold and silver coins. When do we take it?"

"I'll tell you when it's time."

"I'm going to enjoy thinking about these fools when they find out that quiet old Isaac Miller has left with their money."

"Half of their money, Isaac. Only half," Garv said coldly, looking at him over the rim of his mug.

"Of course, Garv. Half. That's what I meant. It's too bad you lost that land in Kentucky." After a short pause, he continued, "That thieving land agent took most of what you had didn't he."

"I'll get it back, with your help." He held out his mug and Isaac refilled it. "What do you plan to do with your half?"

"I'll head south too, but not to Kentucky," the banker said. "Maybe Louisiana would be a good place. I hear that money can be made as if it grew on trees down there."

Both men laughed quietly, the rum having eased the tension.

"I came by to tell you that two more prizes are expected within the week. Do you know about them?" Garv asked.

"Yes I do. They were taken just off shore from New York.

One of them has a considerable amount of gold aboard. I understand it was pay for the British troops."

"How much?" Garv asked quickly.

"Don't know for sure, but it might be as much as twenty thousand. Nice little bit to add to our, ah, retirement fund," Isaac chuckled gleefully.

"The longer we wait the bigger it will get," Garv said, joining in the laughter. "But if we wait too long something could happen to it. I'll let you know when we'll leave."

***

Eventually, Alexis discovered that Jon had not been wounded on the first voyage of the Retribution, and she believed that Garv had only tried to warn her and ease her worry on that evening long ago.

Mrs. Sloan softened her attitude toward Garv, but still had reservations about his character. He could be entertaining and witty, and make Alexis forget for a few moments about her longing for Jon. But, he drank wine and rum too freely, and she questioned his character.

Garv and Alexis rode in a hired carriage to the cottage, after an evening at the Paget's home. A delightful dinner and dancing to the music of a string quartet.

Garv dismissed the carriage, and they walked to the edge of the terrace. The harbor lay before them, glistening in the moonlight. A dozen ships rode at anchor, their lights reflecting off of the water. He stood close to Alexis.

"A beautiful end to a beautiful evening," he whispered.

Alexis laughed. "All of that champagne has turned you into a romantic," she said.

"Maybe so," he said. "I'll be going back to Kentucky soon."

"I'll miss you Garv."

"I plan to build an estate larger than any in England. It will be magnificent. Tobacco and cotton. There will always be a need for tobacco and cotton. I'll build a manor house and buy enough slaves to run the whole estate. You could be part of it you know."

Alexis had consumed more than a few glasses of wine herself, and it took a while for her to understand Garv's words.

"What do you mean?"

Garv's arm slid around her waist and pulled her against him.

"I didn't think you would be so coy, Alexis. I'm offering you my name. The Kendrick name is a noble one. With the wealth we will have and with our beauty, you would be the queen of the territory."

She tried to gently push him away, but he held her fast.

"Garv, please. I don't want to live anywhere but here."

"How can you refuse me? I can offer you wealth. We'll establish a new branch of the Kendrick family. We'll rule over hundreds of square miles. Tenants will look up to us as Lord and Lady."

She pushed hard against him, and he released her.

"I thought you would jump at the chance. It's Jon isn't it. You can't be in love with him."

He turned away and began pacing around the terrace,

waving his arm.

"I know what happened the last time he was in port. He hardly even came here to see you."

"Yes he did," she said loudly. "Many times."

"He's been gone for more than a year now. If he loved you, he would never stay away so long. I would never leave you like that."

His speech became loud and slurred. He reached for Alexis, but she twisted away easily avoiding him.

"He's nobody. I can offer you a family name with meaning and history. He's only a colonial," he said, in a whining voice.

His loud voice had awakened Grace and Mrs. Sloan and Grace began to cry.

The cottage door flew open, and Mrs. Sloan stood in the doorway.

Garv stopped suddenly, swaying slightly. He stared at Mrs. Sloan silently. Then he said stiffly, "Please forgive me. I have apparently been misled by your . . . actions."

"What actions?" Alexis said angrily. "It would be best if you left now."

Garv made an attempt to take her hand again, and Alexis moved away.

"I said leave, dammit!" Alexis shouted.

The venom in Alexis' voice startled Garv. He turned and retreated down the path toward the harbor.

***

The midmorning sun filled the bank with bright cheerful

light. The teller had arranged his cash drawer, and the bookkeeper had just started sharpening his pens and filling his ink pots. Isaac Miller walked to the front door to unlock it and officially begin the business day.

He had scarcely removed his key from the lock when the door flew open and Garvin Kendall Kendrick strode into the room.

"In your office," he said peremptorily.

Isaac Miller followed him into the office. When the door closed, Garv began speaking in a low, intense voice. "Next Tuesday night. That's the time we'll do it. You be with a group of friends so no one will guess you had a part in it. The gold will be too heavy for me to carry, and I won't have time to load a pack horse. You start carrying gold to your house a bar or two at a time. We don't want anyone to notice you carrying a bag that's too heavy."

"I'll blow up the safe and make it look like a robbery. Then I'll meet you and take my half. If you think you can take more than your share, remember I spent two years in the Kentucky wilderness. I can hunt you down anytime I want to. If you want to come with me, I'll guide you to New Orleans. We can both live like kings there."

"I thought you wanted to build an empire in Kentucky."

"My plans have changed. Kentucky will have to wait."

"Are you sure no one will see you breaking into the bank?"

"I'll see to it that the town will be too busy to notice."

***

Garv had originally planned to settle in Kentucky and his

plans had included Alexis. Isaac wanted the high life of New Orleans and now Garv agreed to guide him there, planning to return to Kentucky eventually. Large land holdings would raise his status with his family back in England. And he still hadn't given up with Alexis. When she saw what wealth, real wealth, could do for a man or a woman, she would forget about Jon.

Even though Jon had rented storage space in one of the Paget's warehouses to hold his captured goods, a portion of his wealth had been converted to gold and held in Miller's bank. Garv smiled when he thought about Jon's coming losses. Alexis might not be so taken by him then. He would be just a poor sailor and a colonial at that.

***

Late Tuesday night, Garv, dressed in his buckskins and with his pistols, knife, and tomahawk in his belt, stood quietly in a grove of trees near the bank building. He looked up the hill and saw the lights burning in Miller's house, only about two hundred yards away. Isaac had told Garv that he had invited three friends to dinner and to play whist. He would have his alibi, but Garv wished that Isaac and his friends had met at some place farther away.

Garv turned and looked toward the harbor. A faint, red glow appeared against the black, starless sky. The Paget warehouse fire had started, just as he had planned and paid for. He smiled to himself. Revenge would be sweet.

Garv mounted his horse and rode slowly toward the bank building, now dark and deserted. At the back of the bank, he broke a window as quietly as he could. The night watchman sat with his head rolled back in drunken slumber. Miller had left a bottle of rum in a conspicuous spot, knowing that the old man could not resist. Garv pulled him to the window and lowered the limp form to the ground. No need to make this a murder as well as a robbery. His horse nickered softly as Garv dragged the old man to the edge of the timber.

The glow from the fire grew brighter, and Garv chuckled with satisfaction. No one from town would even notice the blast at the bank.

Miller should have taken his friends somewhere else, farther away, he thought again. The fuse would give him time to get away, and then he could circle back to Miller's house and collect the gold. Doing it this way, there wasn't any chance of being caught at the bank.

Garv took the package of gunpowder Isaac prepared from his saddle bag and carried it back inside the bank. He set the charge as Isaac had instructed him and strung the fuse out the window. He took a shielded lantern from his saddle, opened the shutter and held the fuse in the flame. Just as soon as the fuse began to sputter, he picked up the reins and led the horse toward the trees. Long before he reached them, a loud explosion threw him to his knees. His horse reared and tried to break away from him. As he calmed his horse, he saw figures running from the Miller house toward the stables.

Garv leaped into his saddle and rode toward the trees. He crashed through the timber without slowing. Three of the four pursuers, who had mounted before the echo of the blast died away, began riding after him, heedless of their own safety. Their mounts had apparently been left saddled while they played whist.

Garv broke out of the woods into an open field, riding as fast as his horse would carry him.

His experience in Kentucky gave him a small advantage. He led the three men into heavy brush and timber. Tying the reins to his saddle, he jumped to the ground and hid behind a fallen tree. His horse galloped on. The riders went by him following the riderless horse. He began running through the timber, back along the path they had taken, then left the trail and headed into dense forest. He ran for an hour and then hid in the thick branches of an oak tree. The sky had begun to grow light when he heard the three horsemen searching for him.

"We ain't gonna find him here. If he got this far, we'll never catch him. We'll have to wait 'til full daylight," one of the men said.

"If we don't catch him, it'll go hard on us."

"Yep, it will. Isaac will be mad as hell. We'd best keep lookin' even if it is too dark to see anything."

The searchers wandered off into the heavy brush.

***

The dim light of early morning barely allowed Garv to see his way through the forest. The three riders had moved away from him, and he moved as silently as an Indian. He returned to the edge of the forest around Miller's house and watched silently. He could see the bank building. Nearly a dozen men had gathered around it, talking and waving their arms.

"Sheriff, what are you waiting for?" an elderly man shouted. "You should be going after them devils. We all had good money in the bank."

"Where do you want me to go you old fool? We need someone to track them. I'm waiting for Jacy. He's the best tracker in the territory."

"He ain't nothin' but a damn Indian drunk," the man shouted back.

Jacy, who had been approaching from the timber, heard the remark. He had crossed Garv's trail, but he led the sheriff's party away in another direction.

***

Isaac Miller walked back to his house after the crowd had left. In his study he poured himself a generous glass of rum and sat before the fireplace smiling to himself.

"Are you happy with yourself?" Garv said from the shadows.

Miller froze with his glass halfway to his lips. Then he continued his motion and took a large gulp.

"Garv," he said in a voice filled with delight. "You made it after all. I worried about you."

"And I worried about you Isaac, or rather I worried about what you did with the gold."

"It's all right here Garv, just waiting for you. I'll show you."

Isaac Miller walked to the door of a closet under the

stairway. "It's in there. Go ahead, see for yourself."

As Garv bent over to turn the knob, Isaac reached for a heavy vase. He raised it over his head, but before he could bring it down, Garv drove his knife into Isaac's chest. Isaac fell to the floor, blood pumping from his wound. He groaned and reached out for Garv, but then fell back, motionless. The bleeding became a trickle. Isaac Miller would never spend any of the money he had stolen.

"I should have told you that I heard your men talking about how you planned this thing. Having the horses saddled and ready so they could catch me easier, and making that fuse too short for me to get to the trees. Now I'll take all of the gold."

***

Garv rode away from Isaac Miller's house leading two horses. One carried the gold in saddle bags, and the other horse saddled, ready for another rider.

Garv, his mind filled with fury at the banker's scheming, cursed him and all the rebels. The loss of his land in Kentucky, the scorn heaped on him by that colonial woman, that common banker trying to steal his gold, all played on his mind. Worst of all, that arrogant rebel pirate who had tricked him in that underhanded way and taken his ship, as well as his arm and his career. His mounting fury focused on Jon. The man who had taken it all from him. Now he could strike back with a vengeance. He would take his woman.

The trail to Louisiana would be hard. He would hire men to help him after he had gotten away from Boston. Once there, he could get another ship and arm it as a privateer. But now he would take the one thing that Jon loved above all else. Alexis would go with him. She would try to resist, but the gold and his plans would make her accept him. She would be rich beyond her wildest dreams.

Garv rode to the cottage where Alexis lived. He dismounted and knocked on the door. No one answered. He knocked again, much louder. After a long pause, Alexis opened the door a crack. Garv forced the door open and saw her wearing her night gown and light robe, an extra ordinarily beautiful sight.

"Come with me Alexis," he said rapidly. "I have enough gold to buy anything you want. We'll go to Louisiana. You'll be the Queen of New Orleans. Nothing will be too good for you. Quickly now, there's no time to lose."

He took hold of her wrist and pulled her out of the house.

He's insane, Alexis thought. She struggled desperately as he dragged her toward the horses. She dared not scream. If Mrs. Sloan woke up and tried to stop him, he would surely kill her Alexis thought.

"I have to pack some clothes," Alexis said trying to pull away.

"No you don't. We'll get some on the way."

He dragged her to the edge of the lawn.

"Look," he said exultantly. "See how the warehouse burns. Jon won't have anything when he returns. I have all the gold he had in the bank, and I had Paget's warehouse burned. He'll be penniless. Now you see that your only hope is to come with me."

As he exulted, he relaxed his grip on her wrist. She twisted free and ran. The chopping block at the back of the house always had an axe next to it. She flew around the back of the house with Garv close behind her. She couldn't see the axe, instead she picked up a piece of heavy oak firewood. She turned and swung blindly.

Garv staggered backward and collapsed, blood running from his nose and split scalp. He struggled to his feet and took a step toward her. She drew back the heavy oak billet to swing again. Garv, half blinded by the blood running into his eyes, couldn't see well enough to avoid the blow. He awkwardly drew back. Alexis altered her swing and struck his extended leg. The shin bone broke with a crack and Garv screamed. He fell to the ground and moaned in agony. Mrs. Sloan opened the cottage door as Alexis staggered around the corner.

"Quick," Alexis gasped. "Get Grace and come with me. It's Garv. He's gone crazy."

They ran down the hill to the nearest house and pounded on the door.

Their neighbor sent his son for help and then took his musket from its place over the fireplace. He loaded it and cautiously walked back to the cottage. He found traces of blood but no body and no horses.

Chapter Thirty-Six

Retribution ran before a north-easterly wind, both main and foresail over the starboard rail. Gypsy followed, half a mile off her lee quarter. From the port side of Retribution's quarter deck, Jon watched a large merchant ship, almost dead ahead and less than four miles away. Jon smiled and waved, hoping that someone on the merchantman would be watching. Through his own glass Jon saw two officers in idle conversation, apparently totally unaware of their danger. While he watched, the officers suddenly looked aloft, and then began shouting orders. Figures appeared on deck and climbed the rigging. The ship began turning downwind and royals appeared above her topsails. In a matter of a few minutes, the square rigged merchant ship was running with the wind on her larboard quarter.

"We'll lose her soon I fear," Scotty said to Jon.

"I agree, but it won't hurt to follow her as long as we can. She's running hard. If the wind freshens something might carry away and then we'll have her."

Scotty nodded and then walked forward. Jon heard him roaring orders to the crew to rig a down haul on the main boom and watch the trim on the fore staysail.

Gypsy slowly ran past them, her greater size and spread of sail working to her advantage when running down wind.

As the day wore on, the wind increased and both schooners were moving at great speed and rolling in the heavy swell. Gypsy could still be seen ahead, but the prize had dropped below the horizon.

Jon paced the tiny quarter deck wondering if the strain on the sails and rigging might result in damage to his ship. He raised his glass and looked at Gypsy again. Rob stood at the taff rail, waving vigorously, and pointing ahead. Signal flags were now flying from Gypsy's main mast. The simple code they had arranged between themselves told Jon, "Engaging an enemy".

The sun had settled low in the west when Retribution reached Gypsy and her prize. The prize appeared to have lost her foremast, and both ships were firing as rapidly as they could. Jon sailed a course that would have passed the British ship downwind of both the prize and Gypsy. At the last instant he shouted, "Helm hard alee. Starboard guns fire as you bear."

Retribution sailed rapidly across the stern of the prize. As the guns fired one by one, each ball traveling the length of the deck causing terrible casualties and heavy damage and taking only one shot from a stern chaser. Before Jon could bring his ship about, the relatively clumsy merchant ship started to turn to bring her larboard side guns to bear on Retribution. When she turned she exposed her stern to Rob's guns, and received another horrible raking, this one from Gypsy. Her captain raised both arms above his head and shouted his surrender.

Neither privateer had sustained anything other than minor damage. The American crews raised a jury mast on the prize and knotted and spliced the damaged rigging. Prisoners were moved to the two privateers and a prize crew was put aboard the British ship. The three ships sailed for the harbor at Balboa on the Spanish coast, where Mr. Paget had an arrangement with an agent.

Chapter Thirty-Seven

"Monsieur, Monsieur, wake up please."

Scotty's eyes flew open and he pulled himself erect in his chair. He cursed himself for falling asleep when he should be watching over Jon lying in the bed.

"I have come to take away the bandages."

Scotty recognized the voice of Doctor Cuvier.

A falling spar had crushed Jon's hand during a battle with a British ship. His wound had become infected and refused to heal. When he lapsed into delirium Scotty took command of the <u>Retribution</u> and sailed directly to Brest, the nearest French port. There he found Doctor Cuvier, a noted, if unconventional, physician.

"He must be moved to a quiet room. It is essential for his recovery," the doctor had stated when he first saw Jon on board the <u>Retribution</u>.

Scotty rented a small cottage. The doctor insisted that the walls and floors be scoured until they met his approval. The doctor's own daughter, Marie, had washed the bed linen and the clothing that Jon now wore. When the doctor judged the house to be acceptable, he allowed Scotty to have Jon carried in. Doctor Cuvier visited twice a day.

Scotty sat by Jon's bed whenever he could be away from the <u>Retribution</u>. Repairs of the damage from several battles called for the presence of an officer at all times. Gil Harper, a competent and able ship's officer could be relied on to oversee the work, but details needed to be discussed before decisions could be made.

Jon had drifted in and out of consciousness for two more days and the infection became steadily worse.

***

"We must care for his wound, and hope," the doctor said. "Now please assist me while I remove the bandage. Hold his arm as still as you can."

Doctor Cuvier began to unwrap the bandage from Jon's left hand. Dried blood made the cloth adhere to his skin, and Jon cried out in pain. He tried to pull away from the doctor, but Scotty held his arm fast. The doctor looked at the bandage and sniffed it carefully. He looked at Scotty and shook his head.

"I know that you want to do the best for your Captain. There is no choice now. Gangrene has set in. I must amputate his hand."

"There's no choice?" Scotty asked.

"His hand is so badly smashed that it would never be useful

to him. I have seen many such wounds. Some of them healed and gave the patient a degree of function. None of them had been as badly crushed as this. Now, gangrene has set in and will spread. His whole arm, if not his life, will be lost. We have no choice."

The doctor walked to the door. "Marie," he called to his daughter, "put a poker in the fire. We must amputate Captain Weaver's hand."

The doctor laid out his set of instruments on a bedside table. Scotty tied Jon to the bed frame, and then held his left forearm as tightly as he could.

Doctor Cuvier picked up a large knife and quickly cut into Jon's arm, well above the infected hand. Scotty held the arm as still as possible. He closed his eyes while Jon struggled, even in his unconscious state. Scotty had seen many horrible wounds on board ship and had never felt the least squeamish, but bile rose in his throat when he heard the rasp of the bone saw, and then the thud as Jon's hand fell into the basin that Marie held.

"Hold this wad of cloth in place," Cuvier commanded.

Scotty held the cloth over the end of Jon's arm, watching as blood began to soak through.

"Tighter," the doctor said.

After taking the basin out of the room, Marie returned carrying a red hot fireplace poker.

"Good. Thank you Marie. Now Mr. Lachlan, let me hold the bandage while you hold his arm as still as possible." The doctor removed the bandage and quickly applied the red hot metal to the wound. Jon screamed and struggled.

The wound stopped bleeding, and the physician sewed a flap of skin over the end of Jon's arm.

"There," he said with some pride. "The stump will heal, and he will have no continuing pain. I personally have treated several seamen who had lost an arm or a leg. They recovered and became completely capable of working aboard a ship. In a few days you can take him back aboard."

"You must expect him to feel depressed and saddened at the loss of his hand. Most men who lose a limb do. Be patient and careful. From what you tell me, he is a strong man who is driven by his desire to punish the English. He will recover in a month or two without any assistance."

Jon's recovery came more slowly than Scotty had expected. He didn't sleep well and sometimes spent the entire night restlessly turning in his bed, or sitting propped up by pillows staring out of the window.

Marie stopped by whenever she could find the time from her housekeeping and nursing other patients for her father. Her dark eyes and nearly black hair, her friendly relaxed demeanor, so different from women in Boston. Jon now looked forward to her visits, her cheerful talk and laughter raised his spirits every time she visited.

Jon finally agreed to be moved to his ship. He rarely left his cabin however. He disliked the looks he imagined the crew gave him. Sometimes he thought they pitied him and sometimes he believed they doubted his ability to actively take command of the ship. He stayed in his cabin as much as possible and waited for the ship to be ready. His mental state alternated between black depression and short bursts of manic energy.

"If we're to meet <u>Gypsy</u>, we need to sail soon, Jon," Scotty told him one day.

Jon scowled and turned away without answering. He went below to his cabin.

The elation of the privateering venture had left him. He didn't dwell on the events that took place while at sea. Instead his thoughts turned back to the days on shore in Boston.

"I didn't realize how much hope I still had," Jon thought. "She disliked me even when I was a whole man . . . ."

"She could marry anyone she wanted . . . ."

"There ain't many women that are as beautiful . . . ."

"Now she'll never . . . ."

The ship swung at anchor, fully armed and loaded with provisions, waiting for her owner and captain to give the orders to sail.

***

Doctor Cuvier came aboard ship at Scotty's request to check Jon's progress. Upon examining the arm he found no infection and surprisingly little tenderness in the injured area. However, Jon remained quiet and morose.

"His wound is healing well. I don't know of any reason for you to stay in port any longer Mr. Lachlan. However, he is not the energetic man you described to me before the operation. Is there something that might be troubling him?" he asked. "Perhaps something bothering him from his past. Anything that might seem small to you, but important to him?"

Before entering the harbor at Brest, the Retribution had been at sea for a year with occasional short stops at various ports. Scotty wasn't aware of Alexis' anger, only that Jon and Alexis seemed less interested in each other when the ship sailed from Boston. Nothing had occurred at sea that could cause Jon's mental state.

"Perhaps he needs to get away from the ship. If he went ashore and walked around the city, the change of scene might help him," the doctor said. "Tell him I ordered it if he doesn't want to listen to you."

Jon did resist the order, but Scotty persisted. He reluctantly agreed to take a short walk each day. Scotty picked Colin O'Neil to accompany Jon in case he wandered into the wrong street.

When he finally ventured out, Jon wore a coat in spite of the warm weather. The pain had stopped days ago, but he held his left arm in a sling. He adjusted his coat to cover the arm so that passers by wouldn't notice his missing hand.

The walks through the city in bright summer sunlight did improve Jon's outlook. However, he couldn't bring himself to give the order to sail.

He walked for hours with his eyes on the pavement ahead of him. Only occasionally, did he raise his head to look at the city parks and buildings.

***

"Captain Weaver," Marie called from across the street. "It's good to see you again."

"It's a pleasure to see you again too," Jon replied. He smiled at her. Her dark hair and quick open smile reminded him of Alexis. "I don't believe I ever thanked you for your care after my operation."

Memories of his operation and his recovery flooded back into his mind. She had cared for him during his lowest point. Her cheerful disposition and her skill as a nurse had helped Jon tremendously.

Jon attempted to remove his hat with his missing hand. He mumbled an embarrassed apology for his clumsiness.

"Don't apologize Captain Weaver. There is no shame in being wounded in battle."

She walked along side Jon for several blocks. Colin discretely let them precede him by half a block.

"Do you walk often, Captain Weaver?" Marie asked.

"Yes, I do. Colin comes with me so that I won't be beaten and robbed if I wander into the wrong neighborhood."

"I live down this street. You and your man come and have a cup of coffee. I think he looks tired," she added tactfully.

The house appeared quite ordinary from the street. When they went inside, Jon saw that the entire house consisted of one room, a small one at that, with sleeping areas divided off by curtains.

"Papa, I have brought home our Captain Weaver. We are going to have coffee. Would you like a cup too?"

"No, not now. I have already had some."

Marie glanced at him.

"Yes, earlier today," he said lamely.

Jon enjoyed the coffee. Marie and Jon talked easily while Colin and the doctor said only an occasional word.

Jon found it easy to converse with Marie even though they had very little in common.

"Sir," Colin said hesitantly. "Mr. Lachlan expects us back soon. He worries like an old . . . ." He stopped and swallowed. "I mean he might want us back, sir."

Jon glanced through the only window and saw that the sun had moved well to the west. Time had passed more rapidly than he had thought.

***

Jon returned to the ship to be greeted by Scotty's questions about a sailing date.

"I stopped by Doctor Cuvier's home to have some coffee with him and his daughter," Jon told him. Then lying only a little bit, "The good doctor suggested it would be wise to remain in port for another week."

"Damn," Scotty said under his breath. Then aloud, "I understood you to say you wanted to sail as soon as ever possible."

"If I said that, then I've changed my mind."

The edge in Jon's voice silenced Scotty's protests.

***

Jon and Colin left the ship the next morning. They stopped to buy coffee, rolls, a few eggs, some sugar, and even a live chicken. They walked on to Doctor Cuvier's home. There they found that breakfast had already been eaten, and the doctor had left for the day.

Marie saw the coffee and rolls and immediately began to grind the beans in the Doctor's mortar and pestle.

"We do not often get coffee this fresh," she said. She inhaled the aroma deeply.

Colin sat in a chair against the wall. He listened to Jon and Marie, but nothing they said appeared the least bit interesting to him. When Doctor Cuvier returned from seeing his patients, Jon and Marie were still sitting at the table talking.

Marie jumped to her feet and took his medical kit from him.

"Did you stop at the hospital father?"

"Yes," he said crossly. "It is filthy. No matter what I say, they won't even wash their hands between operations. My success with operations is far better than any of them. Still they say I have an unhealthy preoccupation with cleaning my hands and my instruments. Some of them say it disturbs their patients. Today the hospital director told me I could not treat any more patients there."

"Is that so bad?" Jon asked. "You treated me in a rented house."

"Most people cannot afford that, Jon. You are lucky. You are wealthy enough to afford to rent a house and have it scrubbed clean. Also, you came to me, not one of those filthy ones who think they are physicians."

"Have a cup of coffee father," Marie said. "It will make you feel better."

"We must not waste coffee my dear. It is too expensive."

"Colin," Jon said. "We should return to the ship. Doctor Cuvier, I know you are disturbed. Perhaps a short walk might relieve some of your cares. You could make a tour of our ship if you like."

Doctor Cuvier grunted and shook his head.

"Earlier in our voyage one of our crew died after being wounded in much the same way as I had. Our surgeon's mate amputated the hand, but the seaman died when infection set in."

Jon said nothing more, but he saw a hint of interest in the Doctor's eyes.

"Marie? Would you like to see our ship too?"

"Yes, I would like nothing better."

***

While the doctor had been on the ship twice before, he had never been below decks, and Marie hadn't been aboard at all. She had seen ships in the port for many years, and the complexity of the rigging always fascinated her. And then she saw the guns. Ugly, squat things designed only for killing. They repelled her, even though she understood the necessity for them.

As they walked along the deck, she surprised Jon by not only asking questions, but by paying close attention to the answers. Her questions showed a depth of perception that many men lacked.

"You have a quick mind to understand so well, Marie," Jon said. He could not help but be reminded of the intelligence and skill possessed by Alexis. For a moment a pained look crossed his face.

***

Jon suggested they go below decks, so the doctor could see their facilities for caring for sick and wounded.

"Don't be too surprised at what you see, Doctor," Jon said. "We don't have a surgeon on board, just one young man. We refer to him as a surgeon's mate, but he is only a former butcher's apprentice."

After inspecting the tiny area set aside for medical care, the doctor began his familiar lament.

"The conditions here are better than most hospitals, but still not acceptable. The floor is clean but should be cleaner. Also, if you have more than five or six men who are sick or wounded, you would be hard pressed to get them all into this small area. If you moved this wall a few feet and hung some curtains over there, you would have a more adequate facility."

"We may not be able to move that bulkhead," Jon replied. "Perhaps there is a more suitable and larger space on board." When he noticed the doctor's blank look, he went on. "'Bulkhead' is what we call a wall on board a ship, and if you say 'floor' to a sailor, he might not understand. We call them 'decks'."

The doctor looked at Jon blankly, but nodded his head.

"We need a physician, not merely a surgeon. If we could tempt you to join us, you would be paid as an officer and share in our prize money."

Doctor Cuvier nodded. "It could be interesting, but who would care for Marie?"

A strong female voice interrupted. "Marie can take care of herself."

"It would be difficult for you my dear," Cuvier said. "It could be many months before I could send you any money. How would you live?"

"You wouldn't need to worry about that if I sailed with you."

"Oh no dear, it would be too dangerous. Captain Weaver would never allow it."

But Captain Weaver welcomed the idea.

"Below decks there are places that are well protected from gunfire. Marie would be quite safe with us, even in a battle."

Jon had forgotten his feelings about Alexis sailing on his ship. Her situation differed from that of Marie, he told himself. Marie wouldn't try to join the battle. She would stay below in safety. Besides, she had no real future in France if her father sailed with Jon.

"You could both sail with us. We plan to spend a month or two looking for prizes and then return to Boston, in Main Territory."

In response to blank looks from both of them he explained, "Boston is our home port in America."

"I've never thought of leaving France, Captain Weaver."

"I have," Marie broke in. "I would prefer to be as far away from this war with England as I can be. I have seen too many young men leave home and never return, all for nothing. Just for a madman's political ambitions."

"Be careful what you say, even on this ship someone might overhear. And remember there is also war in America," said her father.

"Our war with England goes on and on. The American war will end before ours I believe," she replied.

"We are fighting to keep our freedom, not to conquer others. But France has been a good friend to us," Jon said. "I won't criticize her."

"Your offer is attractive Captain Weaver. If I can't work with the hospital, it will be difficult to keep working at all," Doctor Cuvier said. "Perhaps Marie and I should talk this over tonight."

At sunup the next day Doctor Cuvier and his daughter arrived at the pier with a few meager belongings. A boat sent in by Scotty brought them to the Retribution. The doctor's medical kit and his instruments made up the largest part of their dunnage. One average-size bag carried clothing for both of them.

"Will the rest of your baggage be coming later?" Scotty asked.

Marie flushed slightly. "No this is all we will bring aboard," she said severely.

Scotty, taken aback by her reaction to his innocent question, stammered a red faced apology.

Marie touched his arm. "I am sorry I spoke so severely Monsieur, I am afraid I embarrassed you. But you see, a physician does not grow wealthy in Brest. Especially, when he insists on treating people who cannot pay at all."

The Retribution had been ready for weeks, and sailed that same day.

***

Dr. Cuvier had the sick bay moved forward under the forecastle and then supervised stowage of his medical supplies. The space below the forecastle gave better access to the heads, an important convenience for sick men. The nearby cook stove would keep the space warmer than other parts of the ship in the winter chill. He planned to ask for more skylights that could open for ventilation during hot weather.

Marie and Dr. Cuvier shared a small space under the quarterdeck. Two beds, a desk of sorts, one chair, and canvas curtains to give some small amount of privacy.

Jon's arm had healed and no longer caused pain if he accidentally bumped it against something. However, he hadn't recovered his old self confidence. On occasion, he tried to use his missing left hand and suffered embarrassment when he realized what he had done. An occasional spilled glass of wine disturbed him greatly. When the ship rolled, he sometimes tried to hold onto the shrouds with his left hand, resulting in an undignified fall.

"Jon," Marie said to him one day, "You must get used to using your left arm. The carpenter could make you a device to hold a sort of hook onto the end of your arm. Then you could use your left arm much more effectively."

He refused to follow her advice, preferring to try to hide his arm under his coat.

***

They set course toward the planned rendezvous with Gypsy. When they met, Jon and Rob exchanged information. Earlier, Rob had spoken to the captain of a small French sloop and learned that a convoy of British ships had been sighted en route to Gibraltar.

"There's still time to catch them," Rob told Jon. "We'll have to chase them for a few days, but we can get them before they reach Portugal."

The two ships headed toward the expected route of the convoy and patrolled the area. They sailed as far apart as they could without losing sight of each other in order to see a wider strip of ocean.

At mid morning on the eighth day, a cry of "Signals from Gypsy" came from Dermot O'Neil in Retribution's maintop. Scotty ran up the rigging with a telescope and read the signal flags flying from the Gypsy's rigging. He called them to Jon, who decoded the message using the simple private code he and Rob had prepared. The message confirmed that an armed British ship had been sighted and gave the distance and her course. Jon brought the Retribution up to close hauled and set a course that would keep the Gypsy between Retribution and the British ship. If the British didn't have a good man in the top, they might not see the Retribution until after they engaged Gypsy. As they neared the warship, the sails of the convoy appeared on the horizon.

"Mr. Lachlan," Jon shouted. "Load with chain shot. We'll try to cripple that escort ship."

"Do you think there might be another warship convoying these ships?" Gil asked.

"It's possible," Jon said with a slight, and he hoped inaudible, tremor in his voice. "We'll deal with that when we come to it."

The enemy ship, with its sixteen guns, would have given a single privateer a brisk fight, but the two American ships working together silenced her. Her sails hung in shreds and several guns lay dismounted. Casualties littered her deck.

Jon and Rob left the crippled British escort ship to pursue the convoy. The British merchant ships had scattered hoping to elude the two privateers. They sailed for the closest ship, a large lightly armed merchantman. Jon ranged along side the British ship and fired at her gunports. Rob crossed her stern and threatened to rake her. The British ship struck her colors immediately. Rob broke away from the action and sailed after the scattered convoy.

Jon held the Retribution hove to while a prize crew went aboard the captured ship.

When all had been secured on the prize ship, Jon sailed after a second merchantman. It surrendered without a fight when faced with armament superior to her own. A prize crew went aboard and set a course for Balboa.

Rob had caught and engaged another armed merchant ship that stubbornly refused to surrender.

Jon sailed his ship across the merchantman's stern and raked her. He came about and prepared to rake her again. The British captain saw Jon's intent and struck his colors. Rob rushed his prize crew aboard her.

The lookout on the Retribution shouted, "She's under way again Captain." He pointed aft and Jon saw the British warship already hastily repaired and trying to tack upwind toward them.

The relatively clumsy square-rigged ship could not sail close enough to the wind to reach the two schooners. But the prizes, also square rigged and even slower than their escort, would be recaptured if the two schooners could not stop her.

Jon and Rob sailed their ships downwind toward the British ship. "Grape shot," Jon shouted to Scotty. "Load it on top of the balls."

Jon sailed toward the ship on a course to pass larboard side to larboard side. At the last moment he shouted, "Helm alee. Fire as you bear."

The Retribution turned and crossed the bow of the British ship, her guns firing at a deliberate pace. At the same time the Gypsy ran down along the larboard side, firing broadside into her hull. Both privateers came about and ranged up along opposite sides of their quarry. Broadside after broadside, gunfire smashed into the hull of the enemy ship.

Jon stood on the quarterdeck hanging onto the rigging with his right hand. A loud crash and a blast of gun smoke lifted him off of his feet and rolled him across the deck. He regained his footing awkwardly, still dizzy. He saw that the blast had come from a British six-pounder not more than ten feet away. Luckily the shot, most likely aimed at the mizzen mast, had missed him by five feet or more. The muzzle blast alone had knocked him down violently. As the British gun crew started to reload, Jon got to his knees, pulled his pistol from his belt, and calmly shot the gunner. Before the linstock could be recovered, musket fire from Retribution's top scattered the gun crew.

Jon leaned back to look at the main top.

The face of Dermot O'Neil peered down at him, smiling with delight as he rammed home another charge in his musket.

The damaged British ship could not answer the fire of the two privateers. She had been hulled again and again. Five of her twelve guns had been silenced. Her captain lay motionless on the deck. The First Lieutenant struck her colors.

Rob sent a prize crew aboard her. The <u>Gypsy</u>'s First Mate, Axel Hanson, led the prize crew. He inspected the hold of the captured ship and found water flooding in from started seams and shot holes. When he returned to the deck, he noted that the ship had already settled enough to make the railing on the British ship below the level of the deck of the <u>Retribution</u>.

"We'll have to abandon her," he called to Rob.

Without waiting for an answer, he set the prize crew to work carrying wounded British sailors back aboard the <u>Gypsy</u> and the <u>Retribution</u>.

The two privateers and their prizes set a course for the port city of Balboa on the northern coast of Spain, near the French border.

***

"Pass the word for Chips," Jon bellowed.

"Only six inches of water in the well sir," the ships carpenter reported. "Looks like we didn't get hit much at all. There's some damage on deck, but they never hit any of the spars."

"If we meet another enemy ship, will we be ready to fight?"

"Oh yes sir. I'll see to it."

***

The fighting had ended an hour ago and Jon suddenly realized that he had not visited the sick and wounded.

Dr. Cuvier, working over a patient, didn't respond to Jon's presence. The surgeon's mate couldn't be found. Instead, Marie worked as her father's helper. Jon watched her hold a semiconscious man still while her father probed the man's wound. When she finished, she washed the blood off of her hands and left to bring more clean water from the galley.

In the gloom of the sick bay, with men moaning and sometimes screaming, Marie's calm presence seemed ethereal. Jon stared at her, fascinated. She saw him as she held a dipper of water to a wounded man's mouth. When the sailor had enough to drink, she spoke to Jon.

"Jon?" she said. "Are you hurt?"

"No, I came down to see the wounded. I didn't expect to see you here. A young woman should not be in a place like this."

"These men need help. What does my age and gender have to do with helping here. Father can't do everything. That butcher's apprentice you had for a surgeon's mate is worse than useless. He won't even keep himself clean. Father won't let him into the sick bay."

"I'm glad that you are here to help with the wounded. After the guns stop firing, you won't be in any danger. Just stay in the hold until then, and you will be as safe as in your own home."

Marie smiled and nodded.

"Yes, Captain Weaver."

She had come up to the sick bay to help with the wounded as soon as she heard the cannon fire, but knew it would be pointless to argue.

***

The wounds varied from minor cuts and scrapes to serious life-threatening injuries. Jon walked through the sick bay, pausing to say a word of encouragement now and again. He saw both Colin and Dermot O'Neil there. Colin suffered a deep splinter wound in his thigh that could have caused the loss of the leg if he had been treated by the usual ship's surgeon. Dermot sat on the deck next to Colin's cot. Jon thought of his earlier misgivings about the two Irishmen, Colin in particular. He patted Dermot's shoulder as he walked by.

"Take care of him, Dermot. We need men like him."

Dermot looked up a Jon and nodded wordlessly.

***

The prizes reached Balboa where Mr. Paget's agent took charge of them. He had the captured ships and their cargoes evaluated and put up for sale. Both privateers had signed on a few new hands from the crew of the British escort ship. Men who had been pressed into the British Navy. Most of them Americans, and all of them eager to get aboard an American ship.

While on shore in Balboa, Rob, Jon, Dr. Cuvier, and Marie dined ashore as often as possible. The cooks on the two ships prepared good healthy food, but even the best cooks couldn't perform miracles with the limited stores. One evening Rob was seen in company with a local woman and didn't appear at the tavern they had chosen. The three friends dined without him, the good doctor mumbling to himself about various diseases that Rob might be exposed to, shaking his head sadly. Marie whispered crossly to him and Jon sat silent, his face turning hot and red. The good doctor finished his meal and left to return to the ship.

The conversation between Jon and Marie had become somewhat stilted until they each consumed two glasses of wine and were able to talk more easily.

"I apologize for my father," Marie said.

"You don't have to apologize, least of all to me." Jon said emphatically. "He is a good man and saved my life as well as several others on board Retribution."

As they walked back to the ship Marie took hold of Jon's left arm and pressed it against her. Jon covered her hand with his right hand. Marie laid her head against his shoulder.

The next day Jon and Rob conferred and agreed that they should return to America. The two ships had captured seventeen prizes, some of them very rich, during the eighteen months they patrolled the eastern Atlantic. The officers could expect to be comfortably well off as long as they lived, and even the lowliest seaman would have more than he could ever have expected to earn in a lifetime as a merchant sailor.

Mr. Paget, as owner of Gypsy would receive one-fourth of the value of all of the ships and cargos that Jon and Rob had captured. As owners of the Retribution, Jon and Alexis would also receive one-fourth of the value of the captured ships and cargoes, to be shared equally between them.

As Captain, Jon would get a full eight shares of the remainder of Retribution's half of the value of the captured ships and cargoes. Gil and Scotty each earned four shares. Dr. Cuvier would be given four shares, but only of the prizes taken since he came aboard. After much discussion, Marie received one-half of a seaman's share of the last three prizes because of her continuing work in the sick bay.

The two ships sailed southwest to find the trade winds that would take them home in a few weeks. Instead of the trades, they found a dead calm, interrupted by puffs of wind from unpredictable directions. The ocean swell made the ship roll relentlessly, even with Retribution's fore and aft rigged sails sheeted in hard. Jon finally ordered the schooner's sails lowered and furled. The constant rolling had begun to cause damage to the gear.

It became routine for Dr. Cuvier, Marie and either Gil or Scotty to dine with Jon in his cabin. The Doctor and Marie made excellent guests. Their stories about life in France and some of the doctor's more interesting patients held the rapt attention of the three officers. Jon, Scotty and Gil had embarrassingly little skill at small talk, but Marie and her father effortlessly kept up the conversation.

***

Often times, Jon and Marie sat at the Captain's table alone. Gil or Scotty would have left to take over the next watch, and Dr. Cuvier would prefer to be with his books or his patients.

On one such evening, Marie asked, "How is your arm by

now Jon." She moved to a chair closer to him.

"It's fine," Jon replied sliding the remains of his left arm under the table.

"Let me see it. Are there any tender spots or any discoloration? My father says that you haven't complained at all. I would feel better if you did complain a little, then he would look at it more often."

"I hate the looks of it," Jon said vehemently. "I don't want to show it any more than I have to."

"Don't be ridiculous," she said sharply. "Here, let me see how it looks."

She examined the arm carefully. It gave him little or no pain when she pressed against the end of the stump. A healthy color showed that no infection had set in.

"It looks healthy, Jon. Have you had a hook made for it."

"I doubt that anyone on board knows how it would be done. I think I would just as soon tuck my sleeve in and keep it out of the way."

"I think you had better have the ship's carpenter make one for you. I can tell him how to do it. My father has taken a wounded arm or hand many times. I've seen how his patients recover. If you don't get a hook made, you might never again be an active man. You know that you wouldn't have fallen from that cannon blast if you had been holding onto the shrouds with a hook instead of your hand."

"Now I must go before the entire ship begins to gossip."

They both rose from their chairs. A sudden lurch as a

larger wave hit the ship, and Marie lost her balance. Jon reached for her with his left arm, and held her from falling. She moved against him, his left arm holding her.

She smiled into his eyes. "See, your arm is not entirely useless." Then she quickly kissed him on his cheek and left the cabin.

Jon stood staring at the closed door and then at the end of his left arm. Then he walked to the door and opened it.

"Pass the word for 'Chips'."

Chapter Thirty-Eight

Chips, as ships carpenters had been called for as long as anyone knew, had made several hooks or wooden legs in his lifetime. On a fighting ship, injuries to arms and legs occurred frequently.

The finished product looked hideous to Jon. Marie encouraged him to use his left arm as much as possible. He still couldn't lose his disgust at the sight of the cumbersome, awkward hook.

As Jon grew more skillful with his hook, he lost much of his dislike for it. He learned to climb the shrouds to the maintop with only a bit more effort than before. His skill with the arm increased, and Marie tactfully made suggestions and worked with him whenever he needed encouragement. She watched proudly as Jon became more skillful. She also discussed improvements with the ship's carpenter. He made a new arm with a much better appearance, less bulky, and with a smaller hook made of polished steel. The carpenter had added a clever arrangement that held the hook firmly, but allowed it to be removed and replaced with another device, for example, a specially made seaman's knife or even a dinner fork. With Marie's encouragement, Jon became more skillful as time went by.

The trade winds returned at last, and the two schooners sailed briskly toward the Caribbean. Every day brought beautiful sunrises and sunsets and new surprises for Marie. Dolphins riding the bow wave almost close enough to touch, a dozen flying fish on the deck one morning, and always the delightful steady trade winds carrying them westward.

Jon walked the deck with Marie when weather permitted. When they were on deck together, the crew left them discreetly alone, often exchanging knowing smiles among themselves. In Jon's cabin, where they were so often left alone after the evening meal, they talked even more.

"You know the captain quite well now I believe," Dr. Cuvier said to his daughter one morning.

Marie turned away, her face feeling hot and flushed.

"Don't worry my dear. I am sure he is an honorable man. I merely wish to know how he is progressing. His mental attitude still worries me. How do you think he will adapt to life on shore?"

"He seems to be recovering now, father," she said looking at the deck as she spoke.

"Yes, he is much more at ease with his hook. And I might add, much more pleasant to be with. He seems quite content." He smiled at Marie as she again lowered her gaze to the deck at her feet.

"But I'm not so certain how his mind will react when he steps ashore in Boston. Much will depend on how his family and friends treat him."

"He has no family, father," Marie said.

"Then I hope he has good friends."

Jon did have good friends both on board his ship and on shore in Boston. At times he thought of Alexis, but she now seemed to be part of another life. A pleasant part of that life, not so important a part now.

***

The Caribbean proved to be a fruitful cruising ground. Before a week had passed, Jon and Rob encountered a convoy escorted by one small British warship. The cargo vessels scattered, while their escort courageously sailed to intercept the two privateers. As the guns roared and splinters flew, Jon paced back and forth on the quarterdeck, tense and nervous. His strong will power kept his voice calm as he directed the helmsmen and shouted orders to the crew. The British ship fought bravely even though she was outgunned. After a short battle, she sat dead in the water, dismasted, battered and sinking. The two schooners sailed after the cargo ships, taking three of them.

After the battle, Jon realized that his knowledge and skill had allowed him to perform as well as he ever had before his loss. The missing hand made no difference at all on board his ship. It made no difference to anyone in his crew, and no difference at all to Marie.

Rob and Jon sailed together for four more weeks and took three more small prizes. With his confidence restored, Jon grew more bold. Twice he recklessly brought the <u>Retribution</u> along side a larger armed merchant ship and captured her by boarding. Each time he led the boarders waving a cutlass in his right hand and his hook replaced by a knife on his left. With each battle, Jon grew more outgoing and the conversations at his table became more enjoyable. Scotty and Gil no longer excused themselves at the first opportunity, and Marie smiled more often.

Jon and Rob set captured sailors ashore when their ships became too crowded. The freed sailors spread stories throughout the Caribbean of the American ship captained by a one-armed madman. Jon had begun to enjoy life again.

***

After a particularly hard fight with a large well armed merchant ship, Rob brought the <u>Gypsy</u> within hail of the <u>Retribution</u>.

As Rob's crew lowered a boat, Rob began to bellow through his speaking horn.

"Heave to, Jon. I want to talk to you."

Jon ordered the topsails backed and waited for Rob to arrive.

In the privacy of Jon's cabin Rob said, "My crew thinks we have enough. A seaman's share will make life comfortable for a good long time. We've been at sea for more'n a year now. They're tired of it."

Jon nodded. He knew many of his crew also wanted to get back to their families. As their prize money mounted up, many of the crew lost their desire to fight. This year at sea had been hard and dangerous, and they had seen too many men, friends and neighbors from back home killed or maimed.

"I know, Rob. We'll all be well off with our prize money," Jon said resignedly.

He dreaded returning to Boston. On board a ship he was the equal of any man, but ashore he would be a cripple. How would his friends react. Todd and his father. Would they pity him? Would the hook repel Mrs. Sloan and Alexis?

"Think about the damage we've done to the British, Rob. That's more important than money."

"We've done our share of damage. I intend to head north. If your crew is anything like mine, they're tired of being at sea. It's time for both of us to head north."

Jon reluctantly joined Gypsy and sailed Retribution toward Boston. The two ships escorting their latest prize.

***

As the Retribution sailed nearer to Boston, Jon became silent and irritable.

"Mind your course," he snapped as he walked by the helmsman. Dermot O'Neil had held the Retribution on the proper course for the last two hours. He accepted the rebuke. He knew Captain Weaver dreaded going ashore in Boston.

The dinners in Jon's cabin had ended shortly after they had started north. Jon's silent gloominess did not make him pleasant company.

He once more had trouble sleeping and when he did, he dreamed of both Alexis and Marie. Although he had known Marie for only a few months, he had developed a growing attraction to her. Sometimes he thought that she might feel something stronger than just the sympathy a nurse would give to any patient. Her smile seemed to grow brighter when she saw him, and he liked her and enjoyed her presence. At least she wouldn't avoid him because of his hook.

Jon invited Marie and her father to his cabin for dinner that night. After the meal Jon and his guests talked about trifles for several minutes, then Dr. Cuvier excused himself. The conversation lagged, Jon mumbled uncertainly. Then he rose to his feet and took Marie's hand.

"Marie, I'm not a good hand at words. You know that there is a woman in Boston that I have loved for many years." Marie lowered her gaze and turned away, her vision clouded by tears. "But now," Jon continued hurriedly, "I find I don't really need to return to her. You have become more important to me than anyone else on . . . ."

His words stopped as Marie flung herself at him kissing, clinging to him, and crying.

When Jon asked Dr. Cuvier for Marie's hand, the good doctor laughed with delight. "So you've finally realized you love her, eh? You are probably the last man on the ship to know that." He laughed again. "Of course, Jon. Of course. I am delighted."

Jon stood on the deck of the <u>Retribution</u> as they entered the harbor at Boston, standing stiff and erect with his left arm, hook and all, against his side. He shouted orders in a loud, clear voice and the crew instantly obeyed. The anchor dropped as the ship turned into the wind and came to a stop. With her sails furled, the flooding tide pushed her back until the anchor's flukes dug into the bottom and the cable came taut.

Several boats left the pier and headed toward the Retribution. Mr. Paget and Todd came aboard from the first boat to reach them. They greeted Jon with great affection.

Dr. Cuvier and Marie came on deck and joined the three men. Jon made the introductions and Marie moved to Jon's side and held his arm. Jon covered her hand with his and the conversation continued.

In the back of his mind, Jon heard the order given to rig a bosun's chair. He trusted both Scotty and Gil completely and thought no more about it.

Suddenly, a young child attacked Jon, nearly knocking him down. She wrapped her arms around his waist.

"Mr. Jon, Mr. Jon, it's me, Grace. I missed you."

Jon laughed in delight. Kneeling on one knee he said, "Why Grace I'm so glad to see you too. My how you've grown."

"Are you going to stay home now? Miss Alexis would like that. They brought us aboard in a chair like a swing. It was great fun. Are you going to live here with us?"

The excited child noticed Jon's left arm for the first time.

"What happened to your hand?" she cried.

Jon's face reddened, but he smiled and said, "Well,

sometimes things don't go as we would like, Grace," Jon started to explain his loss. Grace didn't listen, considering the details to be unimportant compared to his return to her and Miss Alexis. She took him by his right arm and began to pull him across the deck.

"Miss Alexis wants to see you so much."

He saw Mrs. Sloan and Alexis approaching.

Alexis saw the attractive woman standing at Jon's side, and she knew that Mrs. Sloan had been right. Jon had found someone else. Her smile faded as she lowered her gaze, fumbling for a handkerchief in her purse. Her eyes grew misty and she turned away to hide her tears.

As Marie watched, a sudden animosity toward the woman called Alexis grew within her. The silly fool should never have let him go to sea without her.

Mrs. Sloan frowned and shook her head. She had told Alexis what might happen. Now, sadly it had.

Chapter Thirty-Nine

The small church had become intolerably hot and still the wedding ceremony dragged on. Jon guessed that the temperature had reached nearly one hundred degrees. He could hear Gil, sitting in the second row, muttering to his wife, who replied with angry muttering of her own, telling him to be quiet and watch the ceremony.

Rob Clay sat stiffly in his seat as befitted a hard bitten, seafaring man.

Scotty, standing next to Jon, grew paler by the minute. His misery stemming from the rum and wine he had imbibed in so liberally the night before. He desperately wanted to sit down. He closed his eyes and promised himself he would never drink again.

The entire Paget family including cousins, aunts, and uncles, filled the second row. Todd sat with perspiration running down his face, seeing nothing but Alexis sitting across the aisle.

Mrs. Sloan, Alexis and Grace sat beside Rob. Grace watched with rapt attention during the whole ceremony, oblivious to the stifling heat and the drops of perspiration running down her face.

The church had filled to capacity and late comers stood two deep behind the last pews.

When at last the final words had been spoken, the newly married couple turned to walk up the aisle.

The size of the crowd startled Jon. People he had never seen before had come to the ceremony to see the famous Captain Jon Weaver and his bride. Crowded as it was, Jon couldn't see many of his crew. In fact, he saw only two of the Retribution's crew, and they left before Jon and Marie were half way to the door.

Jon had invited his crew to the wedding. They knew that the church wouldn't hold one fourth of them, and apparently no one wanted to come only to stand in the back for the ceremony. Still, he thought, a few of them could have made the effort to walk up the hill and say congratulations.

Disappointed and slightly bitter he mumbled to himself, "I thought at least a good number would have been here."

As they stepped through the door, blinking from the bright sunshine, they heard a great cheer.

Retribution's crew lined both sides of the road. The O'Neil brothers assisted Jon and Marie into an overly decorated white carriage that stood before the church doors. The newlyweds rode through the town along streets lined with cheering seamen. Jon waved to the sailors with his good hand, and Marie held his other arm firmly, as if she thought he might still get away.

As they drove at a stately pace, many of the seamen ran beside them through the streets. Now Jon could see that the _Gypsy_'s crew had joined the throng.

***

The driver took a long circuitous route through the town, and finally reached the little house they would live in until their new home could be built.

Mrs. Sloan and Grace, waited at the door. Alexis had excused herself and retired to her room.

Scotty sat in the living room, elbows on his knees, holding his head in his hands.

Rob Clay entered from the back door wiping perspiration from his face. He had just carried four kegs of rum from the delivery wagon, around the house, to the back yard.

After much handshaking and congratulations, Jon found a wooden box and stood on it to address the crowd.

"First, I want to thank everybody for coming and making this wedding day even more joyful."

Marie stepped up on the box with him. "This has been a wonderful surprise to us, one we will never forget. And we love you all," she shouted.

Both crews broke into rousing cheers.

When the cheering died down, Jon said, "In some mysterious way four kegs of rum have appeared in the back of the house. Captain Clay swears he knows nothing about them. I know no one will listen to a toast after the rum is passed out, so I'll say it now."

"Here's to the two best crews that ever sailed out of New England, and New England sailors are the best in the world."

"With the best Captains too," came a shout from Colin O'Neil.

The cheering lasted until the first sailors appeared from behind the house carrying mugs of rum. From then on, most of the men concentrated on drinking and not on the newly married couple.

The rum flowed freely. Jon and Marie circulated through the crowd of crew members and friends. As time passed, the sailors became louder and rowdier. Before the fights started, Jon's bosun began moving them back to their ships.

As the last men left, the voice of <u>Retribution</u>'s bosun drifted back from the path.

"You best not step out of line with that lady, Captain. Ain't a man in your crew don't love her as much as you do."

Laughter died away as the sailors walked down the hill toward the harbor. Jon leaned close to Marie and said, "You'll never have to worry about that."

Chapter Forty

The <u>Retribution</u> swung at anchor in the harbor for a week, repaired, provisioned and ready for sea. The crew had grown restless. They waited for Jon to set a departure date.

Both Jon and Rob, as well as their crews, had lost part of their fortunes in the bank robbery and the warehouse fire, although the fire hadn't been as complete as Garv had hoped. An even larger part of the prize money had not reached Boston yet when Garv left with the gold. His officers and crew had swiftly prepared Jon's ship for sea, but Jon's zeal for privateering had faded since his marriage, in spite of his losses.

Scotty and Gil had overseen all the shipboard work. Occasionally, Jon came aboard to inspect the work and give directions.

Rob sailed as soon as possible for the Caribbean in hopes of regaining some of his loss.

Still Jon's ship sat idle in the harbor.

He delayed his departure, reluctant to leave Marie. Even though he loved Marie, Jon worried that Alexis might still be in danger from Garv. When Todd first told Jon of Garv's attempt to abduct Alexis, Jon swore to find Garv and take revenge. His common sense told him that it would be useless. Garv had left more than two months before <u>Retribution</u> had reached Boston.

Every day Jon and Marie drove their carriage to the site of their new home. The workmen had finished the foundation and now the framing had begun. For the first time, they saw how the house would appear when finished. They walked around the site, and then sat on a low, stone wall.

The joy of their married life made them even more aware that Jon would leave shortly. The thought of leaving became almost unbearable to Jon as their time together grew shorter. But his crew had worked hard to prepare for another cruise, and Jon knew he must not disappoint them.

"I suppose you'll have to leave soon," Marie said to him.

After a long silence, Jon said, "Yes, I will."

"I heard that you are losing crew to other Privateers."

"Nothing to worry about," Jon replied. "When we sail, they'll be more than enough men eager to sail with us."

"Will they be as good as the men you have now?"

Jon didn't reply.

"I don't want you to go to sea without the best crew you can get."

Jon smiled and nodded. No one had ever cared so much about his well being before.

"O Lord, it's hard to feel good about sailing again."

"But you must Jon. Even in peace time sailors have to leave their wives and families."

"All sailors ain't married to a woman like you."

She leaned closer and kissed his cheek.

***

They didn't talk about Jon's departure any more as he drove the buggy back into town. Instead of driving up the hill to the cottage, he drove to the pier. Scotty saw them from the ship and sent a boat in. Jon climbed aboard the ship, using his hook as easily as other men used their hands. Marie, handicapped by her voluminous skirts, suffered the humiliation of being swung aboard in a bosun's chair.

Jon made a cursory inspection of the ship and then addressed Scotty.

"Do you think she's ready, Mr. Lachlan."

"Yes sir, I do," Scotty replied promptly.

"Then we'll sail on the morning tide."

"Gil, how many men do you need to fill out the crew?"

"Only three men have left, Captain. I can get one of them back. The other two ain't any loss, and there are plenty of replacements around the docks."

"We want experienced seamen. No green hands. If you find an extra gunner or two, take them. I'll be ashore until six o'clock tomorrow morning."

Marie took his arm as they walked to the rail.

Gil and Scotty looked at each other and smiled with relief.

Their captain had taken command again.

***

"I'd like to go with you Jon, but I know it's impossible," Marie said as Jon drove the carriage back toward the cottage.

"A captain who would take his wife on a cruising privateer would be the most irresponsible man alive," Jon said firmly.

"Well," she said stiffly, "I didn't get hurt when I sailed with you."

"Yes, and I thank God for that every day."

"I won't ever try to stow away again." she said, secretly smiling to herself.

Chapter Forty-One

The <u>Retribution</u> sailed straight east and then south, easily out distancing two small British ships attempting to blockade the port. Jon had arranged with Rob to meet near Nevis, a tiny island in the Caribbean.

After three days of sailing back and forth east of Nevis, the lookout shouted, "Sail ho."

"Where away?" Jon shouted.

"Port beam. Can't see nothin' but her topsails. Might be a brig."

"Mr. Lachlan, set a course to intercept that ship."

"Yes, sir"

"Lookout, can you recognize her yet," Jon shouted.

"No, sir. She's heading dead for us."

"Is she square-rigged?"

"Yes, sir. Can't tell if she's a brig or a ship."

"Mr. Lachlan, clear for action."

"Aye, sir," Scotty said. Then began shouting orders to the crew.

Jon stood on the quarterdeck watching the stranger as it drew nearer.

"On deck. She's a Privateer. A good-sized one, maybe twenty guns. I just saw her run 'em out."

A twenty-gun ship with a well-trained crew would make short work of <u>Retribution</u>.

"Gil, set a course to clear the southern tip of Nevis. Keep us close to the island. We'll come up a point until we get out of the lee of Nevis. Then we can harden up to close hauled. Keep to the west side of the passage. With any luck, we can run away from her." As Gil carried out Jon's orders, Jon watched the strange ship through his glass. A flaw in the wind made her yaw and Jon could see her gunports. Eleven of them on the larboard side. Twenty two guns at least. More than that if she had bow and stern chasers.

"A British privateer, not truly a ship by British standards," Jon said to Scotty and Gil. "She doesn't have the style of the Navy."

Running down wind toward the <u>Retribution</u> the British had Jon's ship trapped as surely as a fly on a window pane.

"Take her in closer to the island, Gil," Jon said calmly. There's plenty of water there.

As the <u>Retribution</u> turned to put the island between them and the British ship, a cry, "Another sail!" came from the lookout, even though the ship he saw had all sails furled.

Before Jon could ask "Where away," he saw the schooner

riding at anchor near the shore.

"It's Gypsy Captain. I can even see Captain Clay on the quarterdeck."

"Gil," Jon shouted, "Bring us within hail of Gypsy."

When they came within hail, Jon shouted, "A British Privateer will be coming around the point within a few minutes. She's got at least twenty-two guns, probably six-pounders. Between us, we can take her."

"Hold on, Jon, I've got news for you. The war is over."

"What?"

Jon couldn't understand those simple words. He had grown up in a country at war. The words didn't make sense to him.

"The war's over. We boarded a British merchant ship last week, and she carried some newspapers from London. The war has been over for near two months."

Jon stood at the rail, too surprised to respond. Then he shook his head and shouted back to Rob, "I doubt that Privateer knows about it. She might come around that point ready to blow us out of the water."

"Come closer and anchor Jon, bow and stern. Put spring lines on your cables. Then we can both keep broadside to her. Don't fire unless they fire first."

Retribution's anchor dropped and she sailed on with one topsail driving her.

When Jon judged that Retribution had let out enough cable, he ordered the topsails furled and dropped a second anchor. The bosun rigged spring lines from the anchor cables to tackle on deck.

Hauling on these lines would turn the ship in any direction.

Both schooners cleared for action, and both flew white flags at the mizzen top. Rob had a boat lowered, ready to be rowed to the British ship.

The anchoring had taken several minutes. The British brig came into sight and turned away when she saw the two ships. After a moment of confusion on their quarterdeck, she hove to. Rob's First mate, Watt Taylor, dropped into the jolly boat bobbing along side of Gypsy, and the boat crew began pulling for the British ship. Jon saw Watt scramble up on to the deck and unfold a newspaper.

The captain of the privateer looked at the paper's headlines and then at the two schooners. He shouted orders, and a white ensign blossomed at her mizzen peak. Then she quickly turned toward the two privateers. She closed with the two schooners leaving the nearly swamped jolly boat in her wake, the boat crew splashing in the water.

"Damn careless of him. The news must have put him off a bit. Her master wants to talk to us it appears," Jon said to Scotty.

Scotty looked nervously at the approaching ship and then ran down the ladder from the quarterdeck to the main deck. He walked rapidly along the deck, speaking to each gun crew.

Jon watched the approaching privateer and the men on her quarterdeck. A sudden flurry of motion and Jon saw Watt Taylor running to the rail, waving his arms and shouting. Then the crack of a pistol shot. Watt Taylor fell over the side and sank out of sight. The stranger's white flag came down and the Jolly Roger ran up in its place.

Before Jon could issue an order, Retribution's guns roared in a well-aimed, rippling broadside. The first ball smashed the wheel, killing the helmsman. The following shots dismounted three of the pirate's guns and shattered her bulwarks sending splinters flying. The pirate veered as she fired a ragged poorly aimed broadside of grape shot that went low, striking the hull.

On Gypsy's quarterdeck, Rob had begun shouting orders before the pirate's guns had finished firing. Rob's men hauled on the spring line to bring Gypsy's guns to bear. Before either the Pirate or the Retribution could fire again, Gypsy's broadside crashed out. The pirate ship staggered. Her crew frantically rigged steering tackle, and she bore away. Their treachery had not achieved the surprise she hoped for, thanks to Scotty's caution. As the pirate picked up speed, Jon saw splashes of water near the swamped jolly boat. They were firing at the seamen in the water.

Before either schooner could raise anchor and give chase, the pirate brig had turned, flying before the wind, well beyond the ability of either schooner to overtake her. As Jon watched through his glass, he made out a figure on the quarterdeck awkwardly leaning against the rail. If the ship had been closer, he would have seen a man loading a pistol with one hand while holding it fixed between his hip and the rail. He loaded his pistol in this manner because he didn't have a left arm.

***

Jon walked the deck of the Retribution as she and Gypsy sailed north. He walked with his head down looking only at the planks in the deck. The cold wind, overcast skies, and constant drizzle chilled him through his heavy jacket. Occasionally, he sighed deeply. Privateering had ended. The only life he had known since he turned fifteen. He already missed the thrill of the chase. The wonderful satisfaction of using all of his skill to bring the <u>Retribution</u> close to an enemy ship where his guns could bring her to bay. The intoxicating smell of gunpowder, the shouting and confusion of a battle. His ability to block the fear and confusion from his mind, while giving commands to his crew, expecting and receiving instant obedience. Leading his crew onto the deck of an enemy ship, knowing that they followed him without question, had filled him with almost indecent pride.

He remembered his first fight on the deck of the <u>Mary P.</u> and how he had leaped aboard the British privateer to cut down her colors. Then the memory of Alexis firing at the two British crewmen left on the deck of the schooner. He smiled at the memory. She is a regular hellion he thought. He would always remember her fondly, but now Marie centered his life. Marie would be waiting for him. He wouldn't need to sail away from her again. If shipping became his occupation, she might even sail with him.

Dr. Cuvier now practiced medicine in Boston, and Mrs. Sloan and little Grace were there. The Pagets too.

For the first time since that bloody day in the Mohawk Valley, Jon had a family and a circle of close friends. A reason to return to Boston. He had had shipmates for years. Good solid dependable men, who he liked and admired, and whose company he enjoyed, but they weren't family.

Now he had a beautiful wife and a place in a community.

He raised his head to look at the gray overcast sky. A strong cold wind drove Retribution's lee scuppers under during gusts. Cold Atlantic spray struck his face and that of Dermot O'Neil at the helm. Crew men crouched at the weather rail seeking shelter from the bitter cold wind.

"It's a fair wind for home," Jon shouted to Scotty who had just come on deck as the watch changed. "Altogether a beautiful day." Then he threw his head back and actually laughed.

Scotty, Dermot, and the crewmen within hearing, looked blankly at him and at each other. Jon didn't notice.

***

Retribution and Gypsy sailed together into Boston Harbor. Residents of Boston gathered along the shore to cheer the returning heroes, but Jon wasn't interested in the adulation or even thanks from the crowd.

From the top, Dermot shouted, "On deck. There's a carriage coming down the hill, going like fury. Looks like Miss Marie, I mean Mrs. Weaver." He gulped, hoping Captain Weaver would forgive his overly familiar words.

Captain Weaver didn't notice. He shouted, "Mister Lachlan, sway out the jolly boat. I'll be going ashore."

As he stepped ashore from the boat, he saw the carriage careen around a corner and start down the pier.

Jon started running toward the carriage as the driver pulled the wild-eyed horses to a stop. They had not settled down, still prancing, jerking the carriage about when Marie stood, preparing to jump to the ground. Two arms circled her waist from behind and held her from falling.

Jon laughed at the sight. When he reached the side of the carriage, he held out his arms and lifted her to the ground. She clung to him with all of her strength. He held her against him, thrilled and totally amazed that this woman actually loved him.

He dimly noticed that someone else had left the carriage. Todd Paget handed Alexis down and the two stood smiling, Alexis holding Todd's arm closely.

Another carriage drew up, somewhat more sedately. Mrs. Sloan and Grace stepped down and joined the circle of friends. Then Dr. Cuvier joined the crowd, Henry August and Mr. Paget arrived. All of them smiling and shouting congratulations on his safe return.

The war had ended, and Jon Weaver, once a homeless orphan boy, had at last found his home.

Willett, Dick.
Privateer :

F
WILL

420777

	DATE DUE	

Jack M. Barrack Hebrew Academy Library
272 S. Bryn Mawr Avenue
Bryn Mawr, PA 19010

55701188R00210

Made in the USA
Lexington, KY
30 September 2016